Erik's REFUGE

NYSSA KATHRYN

An NW Partners Book
Cover by Deranged Doctor Design
Developmentally and Copy Edited by Kelli Collins
Line Edited by Jessica Snyder
Proofread by Amanda Cuff and Jen Katemi
Cover Photography by Andrey Bahia at Wander Book Club

❀ Created with Vellum

The choice is simple…surrender or perish.

In the blink of an eye, he became her everything. Her hero. Her savior. Her whole world. Hannah and Erik are finally building the future she's longed for…but it doesn't include a family. Erik's already felt the pain of losing a child before he even experienced the joy of holding them in his arms. It's not something he'll risk again.

So when Hannah begins to notice symptoms, and a test confirms her suspicions, her happy reality comes to a screeching halt. Forced to pivot, she can only pray Erik is willing to do the same.

Found at his most broken, put back together piece by piece by the strongest, most incredible woman he's ever met, Erik considers himself as whole as he's going to get. He's found the light at the end of the long, dark, desolate tunnel that had been his life for so long, and emerged on the other side a new man, capable of giving Hannah the future she deserves.

Until she tells him her secret.

For the woman he loves, Erik will struggle to heal his one remaining wound. A feat made more difficult when an old enemy resurfaces…determined to tear Erik's whole world asunder once again.

ACKNOWLEDGMENTS

Thank you to everyone who helped me finish this trilogy in the way it deserved.

Savannah, thank you for checking over everything to do with Hannah's Type 1 Diabetes. It was so important for me to be accurate and authentic, and you helped me achieve that.

Kelli, thank you for being the first eyes on this manuscript and filling any and all plot holes.

Jessica, thank you for making sure my sentences read in the most efficient way..

To my proofreaders, Amanda and Jen, thank you for being that last line of defense. You give me confidence to release my book baby into the world.

To every member of my ARC team, thank you. I so appreciate the time it takes to not only read but also review my work. I read every one of your reviews, and they are everything.

Thank you to my readers. If you picked up this book, you are the reason the next gets written.

Thank you to my beautiful husband, Will, for steering this ship, and making sure I have the capacity to do what I do. You are the most beautiful husband and father anyone could ask for.

And, finally, thank you to my daughter, Sophia. My work takes time away from us, but I hope that in watching me do what I love and support our family, you can see how powerful women can be.

PROLOGUE

They haven't realized yet. That it isn't the great love of their life who'll piece them back together. It isn't the perfect family or the great support system. It isn't even the bank balance or the job. It's themselves. Only themselves. And the day they realize that will be the day they understand just how powerful they are.

CHAPTER 1

*V*oices pricked at Hannah Jacobs's skull. Deep voices, one familiar.

Erik.

She wanted to open her eyes and tug him toward her. To grab him with both hands…have him hold her. But she couldn't. It felt like her eyes were glued shut. Either that, or her lids were so heavy they refused to work.

So instead, she focused on his words, trying to force her foggy head to piece them together into sentences that made sense. But he sounded like he was at the other end of a long tunnel, his voice muffled and far away.

God, what was wrong with her? It kind of felt like when she had a hypo and her blood glucose levels went too low, but worse…so much worse.

She tried to lift her arm, then her finger, but neither worked.

Other sounds came into focus. A high-pitched beeping. The click of shoes against vinyl tile. And what was that smell? Disinfectant combined with cleaning products?

A hospital. She was in a hospital. Why?

Panic sped up the beats of her heart, pumping her blood faster.

Footsteps closed in on her, and for a moment, hope seized her chest that Erik would pull her out of whatever darkness she'd found herself in. Warmth covered her hand from one side of her body, while an unfamiliar voice sounded from the other.

She tried to separate her lips and talk. To ask Erik what was going on. But too soon, the fog in her head thickened, tugging her mind and body deeper into the darkness and silencing the world around her.

* * *

HANNAH WASN'T sure how much time had passed—maybe minutes, maybe hours—but she continued to come in and out of consciousness for what felt like days. To flicker between awake and asleep, her body betraying her with how immovable it remained.

It was the slight tightening of something around her hand that finally pulled her back to reality again. The touch was subtle but so familiar that she forced herself to focus on it. To allow it to keep her here and conscious, instead of getting pulled back into the dark.

She tried to move her hand, expecting to be met with resistance…only this time, her pinky twitched.

Hope caught her breath. She tried again, this time moving her other fingers as well.

She was doing it. She could move. Was she finally coming out of whatever fog had been holding her hostage?

After a small scrunch of her eyelids, she slowly attempted to peel them open. The light hit her so hard that she immediately snapped them closed again, tears pricking at her eyes.

Three heartbeats—that's how long she waited before trying

again. The light still hurt, but she refused to let it force her eyes closed.

Flickers of pain pinged at her skull. She focused on the plain white ceiling. The lights. Then turned her head to the machines around her.

She *was* in a hospital. Slowly, she turned her head the other way. Her lips separated, whisps of air tugging into her chest in little pants.

Erik.

He was asleep, his back rising and falling in slow succession as he sat on a chair, his upper body hunched over the bed. Her gaze trailed to his fingers, curled around her right hand. Even as he slept, his hold on her was tight, as if he feared someone would try to pry them apart.

Deep, dark circles shadowed his eyes. He looked tired. He never looked tired. No matter how little he slept, he always gave the impression he was ready to take on the world.

Her fingers itched to reach across and trace the shadows. Wipe them away. How long had she been here? How long had *he* been here?

Careful of the drip, she lifted her left hand and ran her fingers through his hair. That simple touch made awareness zing down her arm and hit her hard.

Suddenly, his eyes flashed open, and he shot into a sitting position. The second his gaze collided with hers, it darkened, the hazel turning almost black.

"You're awake." His deep, raspy voice wrapped around her, cocooning her in his familiar safety.

"I'm awake," she whispered, her ribs aching at the two words. And not just her ribs. Her head. Her knee. "Why am I here?"

His brows slashed together. "You don't remember?"

She furrowed her brows, trying to tug back her last memory. "We were fighting. I left to drop something at work, but then…nothing."

Pain laced the depths of his eyes. "Yeah, Angel. We fought. I shouldn't have let you leave like that, but I did."

Why shouldn't he have let her leave? She'd been upset, but she'd driven upset before. "Did I crash my car?"

"Someone hit you from behind and drove off." Rage carved his words into soft growls. "You hit a tree. You have a bruised knee and ribs, and a concussion. But it could have been worse."

No wonder she felt like hell. "Who found me and got me to the hospital?"

"Someone drove past and saw you. They stopped and called the police. The only thing is, you were lying outside the car and doctors don't think you could have done that yourself."

She frowned. "So…the person who hit me took me out of the car, then left?"

"Maybe." The muscles in Erik's cheek clenched. "Maybe it was Moreno and he saw the car coming, so he left you on the side of the road."

That still didn't make sense to her. Wouldn't it have been just as quick and easy to slip her into his car?

"I was hoping you'd know when you woke up," Erik finished.

High beams flashed in her mind. The roar of an engine. And the fear…God, she almost felt it again.

She shook her head, pain immediately zipping through her skull. "It's all a blur… I'm sorry."

"Don't be. You're here and you're alive."

"So you think this was Moreno?"

"Yes. Police said there have been incidences of tailgating in the last few months by teenagers, but with Moreno still out there…"

It would be stupid not to think it was him. Panic started to well in her belly. And uncertainty and fear.

"Hey. It's gonna be okay," Erik whispered. "I'll protect you."

She looked up, not sure what he saw in her eyes, but it couldn't be good based on his next words.

His frown deepened. "I'll get Andi."

"Andi?"

"She's been doing some shifts in the hospital and has been looking after you a bit. She's on now."

She frowned when something pricked at the back of her mind…their last fight. The baby.

Oh, God, the baby!

"Did Andi or any of the other doctors say anything else about my health?"

"You have some bruising. They've also been keeping a close eye on your blood sugars and making sure they stay in range."

She studied his face. He didn't know. *How* didn't he know? Was their baby okay? Was the pregnancy healthy?

"Erik—"

The knock on the door cut off her words, and a second later his sister walked in. Andi wasn't dressed in her usual jeans and T-shirt. Today she wore a crisp white coat, and there wasn't even a hint of a smile on her face.

"Hannah, you're awake." Her voice was gentle as she stopped beside the bed. "How do you feel?"

"A bit sore. My knee, ribs, and head hurt."

Erik's fingers tightened around her hand.

Andi nodded. "Can you give me your pain on a scale of one to ten?"

"Maybe a six?"

"I'll up your pain medication." She made a note on her board. "Can you remember how you got here?"

"No, but Erik told me someone hit me while I was driving."

"It's okay that you don't remember. In fact, it can be normal after a head injury. Usually, the memory comes back."

Usually?

Andi looked across the bed to Erik. "I need to speak to Hannah alone."

His eyes narrowed. "No. I'm staying."

Andi straightened, not seeming intimated by her older brother at all. "No. You're not. Go. Get a coffee. I need to have a private talk with my patient and you need to look after yourself."

He opened his mouth, but Hannah stopped him with a graze of her thumb across the back of his hand. "Erik…please. I'll be okay."

The muscles in his forearms flexed as if preparing for a fight, but he rose. "I'll be back soon."

"Coffee *and* food," Andi said firmly.

When he glared at his sister, she just glared right back.

They waited until the door closed behind him before Andi stepped closer, gaze shifting between Hannah's eyes.

"You know," Hannah said quietly.

"You're eight weeks pregnant."

"Is the baby…" Tears gathered in her eyes. God, she couldn't even finish the sentence.

Andi touched her hand. "The baby is absolutely fine. Your pregnancy is healthy and on track."

The air shuddered out of her, and she closed her eyes. Thank God.

She pressed a hand to her belly, as if wanting to protect her child with her touch.

"He doesn't know," Andi stated.

Hannah's eyes flashed open, the tears still threatening to fall. It hadn't been a question, but still, she shook her head. "Are you going to tell him?"

"No. That's not my place, Hannah. You tell him when you're ready, okay? It doesn't have to be now, when you're both recovering from this. It can be a later time, when you and Erik are feeling stronger and more equipped to deal with the news."

Stronger…because Erik would need to be strong to find out he was going to be a father. The news would hit him hard. He'd told her more than once that he didn't *want* to be a father. That he couldn't. And now he wouldn't have a choice.

"I'm scared." The honest words flew from her lips.

Empathy flashed in the other woman's eyes. "For now, focus on getting better."

She nodded. One thing at a time.

"Now," Andi continued, "I can see you've already spoken to our endocrinologist who specializes in pregnancy. She's been in a couple of times to check on you. She's not here right now, but when she arrives, I'll let you know."

"Thank you."

There was a small pause. "Are you okay?"

The question sounded more like one a friend would ask than a doctor. "You said tell him when I feel ready…but what if that day never comes? He doesn't want kids."

Sadness flashed over Andi's face. It came and went so quickly, Hannah almost missed it. She knew exactly what Erik had lost and what that loss had done to him. "We rarely know what we want or need until it arrives. I believe it'll be okay because he loves you."

He did…but things felt like they'd be far from okay.

* * *

ERIK HUNTER STEPPED into the hospital cafeteria. He could barely breathe. His chest felt too tight, his muscles a second away from snapping.

But Hannah was awake. Breathing. *That* was what he needed to focus on.

He ran his hands through his hair, fucking hating the tremble in his fingers. The call from Andi to tell him Hannah was in the hospital had almost sent him to his knees. It had blackened his world to the extent the drive to the hospital was a blur. And the second he'd seen her lying in that bed, it had taken everything inside him to not be sick. The bile had crawled up his throat, choking him.

He stopped in front of the small coffee shop. He'd barely slept or eaten in twenty-four hours and needed the caffeine.

His fault.

The words were on repeat in his damn head. His fault for not locating and killing Moreno. His fault for letting her leave his home last night.

He ordered his coffee before moving to the end of the counter, forcing air to move in and out of his lungs. He needed to pull himself together. He needed to be okay for her.

In his pocket, his phone vibrated with a text.

Chandler: Any change?

Erik: She's awake.

The phone rang immediately.

"Is she okay?" Chandler asked before Erik could get a word in.

"Yes. In a bit of pain, but that's it. Andi's with her right now."

"Thank God."

Erik could think of a lot fucking stronger things to say. "Are you still keeping an eye on nearby car repair shops to maybe find the car that hit her?"

"As much as I can. I've hacked into some systems. Nothing so far to match the accident. It's not a surprise, though. He probably either disposed of the car or got a private mechanic to fix it without a paper trail."

Probably. That asshole.

"You gonna tell her about Nico?" Chandler asked.

Erik's jaw clenched. "Yes. I don't want any secrets between us. But I don't know when. I don't want to drop a bomb on her while she's recovering from this."

Chandler had found her stepbrother. The guy had created an entirely new identity. Instead of Nicholas Spalder, he now went by Nixon Stone. It was smart, keeping to the same initials and a similar first name. He'd even started his own successful business out of Chicago, finding missing persons. People hired him from all over the country, and he had a whole damn staff of employees working for him.

Except right now, the person missing was Nico, and Erik and Chandler couldn't find him. "You located him yet?"

"No. His office says he's taken time off from work, and I can't find where he's gone. He's not in his Chicago apartment. There are no plane or train tickets in his name. But I'll keep looking."

Goddammit. "What about Moreno?"

"Nothing. He fucking disappeared."

Erik closed his eyes, fury pulling at his limbs. Chandler was the best damn tech guy Erik had ever known, yet two men were evading even him.

His friend sighed. "I'll keep looking into both of them."

"I know you will. Thanks."

"And Erik…look after yourself."

Despite everything, his lips twitched. "You sound like my sister."

"Good. More people looking out for you."

He shook his head before hanging up. He was about to shove his phone into his pocket when it rang again, every muscle in his body freezing at the name on the screen.

Jake Moore…

What the hell was *he* doing calling? Erik hadn't spoken to Jake in years. Not since their final mission. The man had been like a brother. A member of his team in the Marines. And he'd been there on that final mission, when everything had gone to shit and they'd lost half their team and almost lost their own lives as well.

But Jake hadn't been just a teammate. He'd also been cousins with the newest team member…the guy who'd broken rank and fired early, giving away their location.

For a moment, Erik didn't move, just watched as the phone continued to ring in his hand.

When it finally stopped, his hand dropped.

He hadn't spoken to *any* of the guys on his team since he'd gotten out. He hadn't been able to. How did you talk to a team when you'd been their leader, responsible for their lives, and you'd let half of them die?

Acid coated his gut, and he shoved the phone into his pocket. He wasn't sure why Jake was calling him, but he couldn't deal with that right now. His focus needed to be on Hannah. On making sure she healed and remained safe.

He was just picking up his coffee when something prickled at the back of his neck. He stopped, his gaze discreetly moving around the room.

What the fuck was that? It felt like someone was watching him.

The fury in him coiled, threatening to overflow. He needed to get back to Hannah, and he needed to get back to her now.

CHAPTER 2

*E*rik's knuckles whitened on the wheel. "I still think this is too soon."

Way too fucking soon. The woman had only gotten out of the hospital two days ago, for Christ's sake. She should be at home, resting.

Hannah smoothed fingers over his arm. "We're just leaving the house for a coffee. I'll be okay. It's not like I'm about to run a marathon."

"You can barely walk—"

"I can walk fine. I've just got a bit of a limp." The pad of her thumb caressed his skin. "Erik, I was in the hospital, lying in a bed, for close to a week. Then yesterday, I spent the entire day resting. I need to get out before I lose my mind."

He knew that. Hell, he'd feel exactly the same. But fuck, it didn't make it easier. All he wanted to do was keep her home where he had a good security system and she was protected.

The police still thought it was teenagers who'd hit her, despite the tailgating culprits being adamant they didn't do it and no evidence found on their cars.

Erik knew better. It was Moreno. It had to be. He just didn't know why the asshole had left the scene. Because the other car had scared him away?

He had too many unanswered questions. Questions that had been on replay in his head for days.

"Erik…" Hannah's eyes held concern. "Are you okay?"

He could have laughed. She was asking *him* if he was okay? "Yeah, Angel. I'm okay." It was a damn lie. He pulled into the parking lot beside Black Bean. "Quick in and out."

"The second I finish my lavender oat latte, we can leave, but not a second sooner. I've been dreaming about Rita's lattes."

"I made you a latte yesterday."

"And it was wonderful…but it wasn't Rita's."

For the first time in days, his mouth stretched into a smile. "I feel like I should be offended."

She cupped his cheek. "Don't be. Rita spends all day, every day perfecting her coffees. Hers *should* be the best."

He shook his head as he climbed out of his Corvette and went around to her side. As soon as she stood, he curved an arm around her waist. He hadn't been able to stop touching her since she'd woken up. Hell, even when she'd been unconscious in that hospital bed, his hand had always been on her, as if he needed to reassure himself that she was still alive and breathing.

As she limped across the parking lot, it took everything in him not to stop and lift her in his arms. They were damn lucky nothing was broken.

"You know, I can almost hear you growling in your head," she said.

This time he actually chuckled as they pushed into Black Bean. The place was busy, which was normal for a Friday morning. He didn't like it. He wove through the tables to the counter. The second Rita's gaze fell on Hannah, she lowered the empty mug in her hand and rounded the counter.

"Can I hug you?" Rita asked.

Hannah's features softened. "Of course you can."

The older woman pulled Hannah into an embrace, and he reluctantly let her go. Word about Hannah's car crash had gotten around town damn quickly, but in a small town like Redwood, that wasn't a surprise.

"Norman and I were so worried about you." Rita pulled back. "Are you okay?"

"Yes. Erik and my medical team have taken great care of me. Thank you for the basket of treats you sent to the hospital. I ate them way too quickly."

"You're welcome, dear. We're just glad you're okay." Rita moved back around the counter. "Now, what can I get you two? The usuals?"

Erik dipped his head. "Yes, please. Double shot for me."

"I'm dying for my lavender oat latte," Hannah groaned.

"Done." Rita turned to the machine.

He was just helping Hannah onto a stool when voices sounded from a nearby table.

"Shit, Charlie—watch out."

"Fuck, Charlie, no."

But it was too late. The crack of his gun sounded—the enemy knew they were here.

Erik froze, trying to pull himself out of the abrupt memory. Then there was the bang of a chair hitting the floor.

The men in the compound whipped out guns. Erik and his team fired, but there were only fourteen of them and what felt like hundreds of the enemy.

Erik cursed and rolled as bullets pelted all around him, the world exploding in a sea of gunfire.

"Erik?"

He flinched when a warm touch on his arm pulled him out of his memories. He scanned the table of guys who'd triggered the waking nightmare. Half had their backs to him.

He glanced at Hannah to see concern etching her face.

"Where'd you go?" she asked quietly.

He opened and closed his mouth, his breathing rate too damn fast. "Nowhere."

Disappointment laced her features, but this wasn't the place to reveal his deepest, darkest memories. He hadn't had a flashback in… God, it had been years. Had the calls from Jake triggered it? The man had called him three more times since the hospital.

He forced his expression to ease. "How's your knee?"

"My knee's fine. Erik—"

"And your ribs?"

She tilted her head. "My ribs are fine, and so is my head."

He lowered his mouth so his lips hovered over hers. "And the rest of you is perfect." He kissed her, the softness of her lips seeping into him. Calming him. Wiping out any remnants of the flashback into his past.

When he lifted his head, her eyes were hazed. "I can see what you're doing, buddy."

"Kissing you?"

"Distracting me."

"Is it working?" Hell, *he* was distracted, how could she not be?

"You know it is."

His phone rang, and he tensed, almost expecting it to be Jake again. Hannah felt it, because she was back to looking at him inquisitively. He tugged his phone out to see Chandler's name on the screen.

He shifted his attention back to Hannah. "I'm just going to step outside and take this."

"Okay, but don't take too long or I'm buying a bagel."

"Get the bagel." One more kiss and he moved across the café. "Hey, Chandler."

"Hunter, how's Hannah?"

"Good." His gaze moved over the street. "We're out of the house for the first time since the accident. At Black Bean."

"How'd she twist your arm into that?"

Yeah, Chandler knew him well enough to know he'd have kept her home for a damn month if he could have. Longer. "She looked at me with her gorgeous blue eyes and I caved."

Chandler laughed. "Uh, yes, I see how that could be effective."

"What are you doing?"

"Actually, I'm calling because I have a lead on a possible location for Moreno."

Erik's muscles tightened. "Where?"

"I saw him on CCTV footage in a bar in Seattle. He had a drink and left. That's all. It almost looked like he was waiting for someone. I was thinking, if you don't want to leave Hannah, I might ask Rachel to go down there and talk to the owner."

Erik ran his fingers through his hair. "That's a good idea. I'd come, but—"

"You need to stay with her. I know. Rachel doesn't need anyone to go with her. She can take care of herself."

If anyone could, it was her.

His gaze moved inside the café, his muscles going tight when he saw a man talking to Hannah. He had his back to Erik, and he stood too damn close to her. "I've got to go, Chandler. Talk later."

He'd just hung up when the guy beside Hannah turned so Erik could see his face. His world slowed, every muscle in his body icing…

Charlie.

* * *

Hannah watched Erik outside the café as he spoke on the phone, curiosity still thrumming through her veins. What had just happened? One second he'd been here with her, and the next he'd gone somewhere else entirely. Where, exactly, she wasn't sure.

What had instigated the change?

Her phone vibrated from her pocket, and she saw a text from her best friend.

Brigid: When am I seeing you? I need daily visits to remind myself you're okay.

Hannah: I could come over Sunday? Girls' afternoon?

Brigid: Is that gonna be okay with Mr. Protector?

Hannah: He'll insist on driving me and checking your security, but I'm sure he'll be fine

Brigid: Done. If you're up for a drink, I'll supply the sangria, you supply the laughs.

Her belly clenched at the mention of alcohol. She hadn't told Brigid yet—or Erik. There'd been so many moments she'd tried to tell Erik, but he'd been so on edge since her accident, and it just never felt like the right time. But then, was there ever a right time to tell a man he was going to be a father when he'd explicitly told her on multiple occasions that he *couldn't*?

Oh, Jesus. She just needed to do it. Tear off the Band-Aid.

She turned back to the counter as Rita set the two coffees in front of her. "Here you go, honey. I'll get started on that bagel. Let me know if you need anything else."

"Thank you."

Hannah sipped her coffee. Oh, man, it was good. She'd missed Rita's lattes. How the woman made them light-years better than any other shop, Hannah had no idea, but she was an addict.

She was just setting the mug on the counter when someone came to stand beside her. At first, she thought it was Erik. He was the same height and breadth.

"Is everything—" Her words faltered…not Erik. A tall, dark-haired stranger. "Sorry. I thought you were someone else. You look a bit similar."

"So he's dashingly gorgeous, too?"

Her brows rose. She wasn't sure how to respond. "He is to me."

"He sounds like a lucky man."

Okay, this was feeling far too much like flirting. "I'm the lucky one. Excuse me."

She turned back to her coffee, wrapping her fingers around the mug.

"So, this mystery man have a name?"

Hannah opened her mouth, but before any words could make it out, Erik's voice cut in.

"What the fuck are you doing here, Charlie?"

Hannah spun around to see a very hard, very angry-looking Erik standing close, his eyes locked on the guy beside her.

"Hunter?" The guy sounded shocked.

"Answer the damn question," Erik growled.

"I'm in town to sell my grandmother's house."

The muscles in Erik's forearms tensed.

"You, um, know each other?" Hannah asked quietly. The question sounded stupid to her own ears. Of course they knew each other.

There was a beat of silence before Erik responded. "Charlie was on my team for my last mission."

She frowned. Then shouldn't they be friends? Weren't military teammates like family?

Charlie cleared his throat. "I was just leaving. Guess I'll see you around town."

The only evidence of Erik hearing Charlie's words was the slight clenching of his jaw.

Charlie's gaze flicked to Hannah. He dipped his head before stepping away.

For a moment, Erik didn't move. In fact, it almost looked like his mind was somewhere else completely.

She touched his arm. "Erik." His gaze flashed to her. "Are you okay?"

The frown remained etched on his brow as he shook his head. "Not really."

Well, at least he hadn't lied this time.

He stepped to the counter beside her. She waited for the door to close behind Charlie and his friends before turning to study Erik. "What aren't you telling me?"

He wrapped his fingers around his coffee, the muscles in his forearm flexing. "He was the new guy on the team during that last mission."

Something hard and uncomfortable coiled in her belly. "Wait…that means he was the guy who—"

"Broke rank and got half the team killed. Yeah."

CHAPTER 3

$\mathcal{E}$rik's fist slammed into the bag.

Every muscle in his body hurt. Every limb was on fire. But he kept going. It was only eleven, but Hannah was already upstairs in bed. He wouldn't be asleep for hours.

The bag flew back at the force of his hit.

The world was alight with gunfire, the sounds exploding through the night, deafening everything else.

Erik hit the bag harder, memories swirling with reality, creating a deadly concoction.

He rose from his hiding spot behind a wall and fired at the enemy. Three kill shots for three separate men, all between the eyes. He'd just dropped back down when he saw Joey collapse a few feet away.

The world stopped, colors darkening until everything was almost black.

Joey's eyes were open, the wound in his forehead bleeding out.

Gone. Joey, a man who was like a brother, family...was gone.

Erik growled and hit the bag again and again.

Charlie Moore was in town. A man Erik had counted on never seeing again. But he should have known there was a possibility, shouldn't he? He knew Jake and Charlie had a grandmother close by. Was that why Jake was trying to get through to him? He knew his cousin was close and wanted to warn Erik?

Fuck, he didn't want to deal with this right now. He had to focus on finding Moreno. He didn't need the flashbacks or the living, breathing reminder in the form of Charlie of the lives that had been lost that day.

When his phone rang, he finally stopped his fists and pulled off his gloves before lifting it to see Rachel's name on the screen. "You find anything in Seattle?"

"Nothing." Frustration laced her voice. "The bartender didn't know shit. Just said the guy was waiting for someone who didn't show. He had a drink, stared at his phone a lot, and left."

"Shit."

"Oh, I have a lot stronger words. I'm driving back now."

"Thanks for chasing down the lead."

"We're both in this, Erik. I never leave a case unfinished, and I won't be starting now. Moreno slipped out of our grasp, but *I will* find and end him."

He was damn grateful to have the woman on his side. "I wish I could be more help. I'm sure it was Moreno who ran Hannah off the road, and I want to end the fucker for it."

"Regardless of who finds him, we will. And in the meantime, we'll keep Hannah protected. But you need to stop blaming yourself."

He frowned. "How do you know I'm blaming myself?"

"Because I've known you too damn long, and I can hear the self-deprecation in your voice." There was a small pause. "Is that all it is, or is something else wrong?"

How the hell did she do that just by hearing his voice? "Charlie's in town."

"No fucking way...Charlie, as in the idiot who didn't listen to orders on that mission?"

"Yeah."

"What the hell is he doing in Redwood?"

"His and Jake's grandmother owned a house here. They're selling it."

"And you saw him?"

Erik ground his back teeth at the memory of how close the man had stood to Hannah. "Yeah. He was in Black Bean."

"Does that mean Jake's in town?"

"Don't know. He's called me a few times."

"What did he say?"

"Nothing. I didn't answer."

There was a short pause. "Why not?"

His hand fisted, but he remained silent.

"What happened all those years ago wasn't your fault," Rachel said quietly.

"I was the leader."

"*Still* not your fault. You did everything right. It was all on Charlie. Which is exactly why you made sure the command knew what happened and he was removed from duty."

"I knew he wasn't a team player before we left."

"Yeah, and at best you could have requested the commander take him off the mission, but he probably wouldn't have. It wasn't your choice who went and who didn't."

She was right, but fuck, it was hard to accept. "I've got to go, Rach. I'll talk later."

He hung up before she could respond and scrubbed a hand over his face. When he moved up the stairs, he didn't go straight to his bedroom, instead stepping into the guest bathroom down the hall, not wanting to wake Hannah.

She'd been tired since getting out of the hospital. Going to bed early, sleeping late. On Monday, she would return to work. If it was up to him, she'd remain home until they found Moreno. But that wasn't his decision.

He turned on the water and stepped under the stream, the heat burning his skin.

When he'd first gotten out of the Marine Corps, he'd lost so much. Half his team. Vicky. Their unborn child. He'd honestly questioned whether they were losses he could even survive. The pain had eaten at him to the point that he'd expected his world to implode.

Somehow, he'd learned to numb it all…until Hannah. She'd saved him. Allowed him to feel without pain. To see without darkness.

He had to protect her from Moreno…the alternative wasn't an option.

He stepped out of the shower and dried off, then headed down the hall to the bedroom. The second his gaze found her, curled on her side on the edge of the bed, he felt her everywhere. In his skin. His chest. His damn heart.

God, she was beautiful, in so many damn ways.

He dropped the towel and pulled on briefs before sliding into bed. Immediately, he wrapped his body around her, tugging her into his chest. Her soft moan wove its way inside him, slowing his heart, allowing the air to flow in and out of his lungs with a bit more ease.

But even though he held his entire world in his arms, he didn't sleep. Instead, he listened to her soft breaths, reminding himself that she was safe and alive. And allowing that knowledge to warm every crevice inside him that had long been cold.

* * *

SOMETHING PRICKED at Hannah's sleep. A sound. Like a deep rumble, almost a growl. It vibrated against her back, shifting her from asleep to awake.

Slowly, she flickered her eyes open to see the moonlight slipping through a crack in the curtains, casting a dim glow throughout the room.

Another growl sounded, this time louder. Another vibration against her back.

Slowly, she rolled over. Erik's arms still encased her, but now she could see his face. His brows were tugged together, and every so often there was a small flinch of his muscles.

He was having a nightmare.

She lifted her hand to touch him but hesitated. The last time she'd woken him from a bad dream, he'd mistaken her for the enemy and rolled them both to the floor. His fingers had wrapped around her throat, and for a split second, she actually thought he might hurt her.

Unease trickled down her spine.

She wet her lips, her voice barely a whisper. "Erik…"

Nothing. No flicker of movement. No flutter of eyelids. Her hands ached to touch him. Offer him some comfort. She barely stopped herself.

The next growl was louder. More pained. And the look on his face… God, it was sheer torture.

She needed to wake him. This time, she didn't hesitate. She cupped his cheek and leaned forward so her forehead was touching his. "You're safe, Erik. Come back to me."

There was a small pause in the movement of his chest. A silencing of his heavy breaths.

She grazed her thumb back and forth across his cheek and repeated the words again and again. Telling him he was safe. Asking him to come back to her.

When his eyes scrunched, she stilled. Then, slowly, his eyes opened and his gaze collided with hers.

The air whooshed from her chest. "You're awake."

His fingers tightened on her hips. "Are you—"

"You didn't hurt me. I'm okay. You were having a nightmare. You sounded like you were in pain." She swallowed, studying him through the darkness. "What were you dreaming about?"

A part of her wondered if he'd keep it to himself. Try to shield her from whatever pain was disrupting his world.

Instead, the frown between his eyes deepened. "My last mission as a Marine."

"Because you saw Charlie today?"

He nodded slowly.

Today had been an awful reminder of his past. A past he wasn't fully healed from and probably never would be. "Will you tell me about your team?"

He was so quiet for so many beats, she thought he'd refused. Then, finally, he spoke.

"We were a team of fourteen. We lost seven good men that day—Theo, Julian, Fletcher, Alex, Thax, Jarrad, and Joey. They all added different things to the team. Some of them were jokers. Others more serious. Joey used to do this thing when the mood was low where he'd sing. Sometimes under his breath. Sometimes so damn loudly you'd block your ears."

"Was he good?"

"He was fucking terrible."

Hannah smiled.

"But he lifted the mood."

She almost thought she saw a hint of tears in his eyes, but then he blinked it away. She ran a forefinger over his hairline. "So Heaven gained seven angels that day?"

"It was a damn good day for them."

"What about the men who survived?"

"Me, Jake, Maverick, Austin, Will, Tanner...and Charlie. Everyone except for Charlie had done dozens of missions together before. We always knew death was a real possibility. Yet, when it came, none of us were ready."

"I don't think you can ever be ready to lose people you love." She traced the lines beside his eyes with her gaze. "Did you know Charlie's grandmother owned a home here in Redwood?"

The pain turned into anger. "Yeah. Charlie and Jake are cousins. Jake had mentioned it a few times. I just never let myself consider the possibility of that leading Charlie here to Redwood."

"Have you spoken to any of the guys since?"

"No. We lost contact."

Another loss he'd had to endure.

Erik's fingers tightened on her hip. "Jake, one of the guys on my team…he called. I didn't answer."

She nodded.

His brows slashed together. "Aren't you going to tell me that I should have taken his call?"

"No. That's your choice. Only *you* know who you can handle in your life."

His eyes darkened. "How did I get so lucky with you?"

She lifted a shoulder. "I'm the angel you didn't know you needed."

"Oh, I knew I needed you. I just didn't know how to find you."

She touched her forehead to his again. "Thank you."

"For what?"

"For being honest with me about your pain." Because it *was* pain. A deeply ingrained pain that had scarred him. And talking about it couldn't be easy.

"You're my person."

Those words…they did something to her. "And you're mine. Forever."

She lay her head on his chest and listened to the thumps of his heart beneath her ear. Thumps that beat right into her own chest.

CHAPTER 4

*H*annah knocked on Brigid's door. She didn't need to look at Erik to know he was scanning the hall of the fourth floor. He was anxious, and she didn't blame him. But at the same time, she desperately needed to chat with her best friend.

She pressed a hand to his chest. "I'll be okay. You had new security installed on her place and you won't be far."

He glanced down at her, looking like he was a stone's throw away from scooping her up and making a run for it.

The door flew open, and Brigid gasped before pulling her into a gentle hug. When she pulled back, she met Hannah's gaze. "Was that okay? Did I hurt you?"

Hannah shook her head. "My ribs are still just a bit tender, but that didn't hurt at all. In fact, I'll probably need more hugs throughout the night."

"Done."

Hannah glanced to Erik. "I'll see you in a couple hours."

"I'm going to check the apartment." He stepped inside and moved through each room. When he returned, he was calmer…

slightly. He lowered his head and kissed her, then looked at Brigid. "Doors locked and alarmed at all times."

Brigid's voice softened. "Of course."

Once Hannah was inside, she almost felt bare without Erik. He hadn't left her side since she'd woken in the hospital.

"How's the knee and head?" Brigid asked as she typed in the alarm code.

"I'm still getting a few headaches, and my knee's a bit sore, but I'm okay. The true test will be when I return to work tomorrow and don't have Erik forcing me to rest every hour."

Brigid moved into the kitchen. "I'm so glad you have him to keep you safe. Everything you've been through in the last few months…it's more than anyone should have to endure in a lifetime."

There was an odd tone to Brigid's voice. Guilt?

Hannah slid onto a stool at the kitchen island, watching her friend closely. "How are you doing after everything with James?"

There was a small tensing of Brigid's muscles before she opened a cabinet and pulled out two glasses. "Honestly? I feel like an idiot, and I still kind of hate myself for what I did. I don't know if that will change anytime soon."

Hannah leaned forward and touched her friend's hand. "Hey, you made a mistake by bailing him out of jail, but his actions when he *did* get out were solely on him."

"He hurt you. He could only do that because I gave him access to you. You're my best friend. God, I bailed him out after he tried to *kill* you. I was stupid and selfish and—"

"*Hurting*. Brigid, you were heartbroken. We don't always think properly when we're in pain."

Tears gathered in Brigid's eyes. "I wasn't thinking at all. And I still don't know why you forgave me."

"Because you're my best friend and I love you. Because you need me right now more than any other time."

"I *do* need you. It's only because of you and Henry that I'm even slightly okay. Oh, and Leo too. That guy is a one in a million. I hope he and Henry never break up."

"He's beautiful. Do you know he baked me lasagna while I was in the hospital? Lasagna!"

"Was it good?"

"I licked the container clean. It was the best I've ever eaten." Hell, she was salivating just thinking about it.

Brigid laughed. "Well, I don't have lasagna, but I do have a pizza in the oven, and if you're up for a drink I have a big jug of sangria."

Crap. "Brigid—"

"But, if you're not, that's okay. I also have soda and juice and mineral water." She took the array of drinks out of the fridge.

"I can't drink alcohol tonight, Brig."

"Because of your head injury. Of course. We have a ton of other options."

"Not just because of my head injury."

Brigid laughed. "What, are you pregnant?"

At Hannah's silence, Brigid's gaze flew up. It took several long seconds for realization to widen her eyes. The jug of sangria hit the counter with a hard thud. "You're pregnant?"

"Yeah."

Brigid screamed and ran around the counter, then pulled Hannah into her chest so quickly, Hannah released another *umph* at the impact.

"Oh my God, I'm sorry!" Brigid pulled away. "I'm just...I'm in shock!"

"Well, that would make two of us."

"How far along are you?"

"About two months."

If possible, Brigid's eyes widened further. "Are you shitting me? Why didn't you tell me the second the stick turned pink?"

"Actually...that's what I came here to tell you the night I found you unconscious on the floor and James waiting with a gun."

Some of the light left Brigid's eyes. "Another reason to hate the bastard. How do you feel? And, Jesus, what did Erik say?"

"I feel okay. Nauseous. And my blood sugars have been all over the place, but my endocrinologist said that's normal." She fiddled with the charm on her bracelet. "And Erik...doesn't know yet."

Brigid's brows slashed together. "He doesn't know? Why haven't you told him?"

"So many reasons."

"Okay...start with the first." She pulled up a stool in front of Hannah.

"I keep trying to tell him and I just...freeze up. He's been so worried about me since I got out of the hospital. He blames himself for the crash, thinks he shouldn't have let me leave after we had a fight. And now he's dealing with some other stuff from his military days. I just keep waiting for the time to feel right, but it never does, and when I go to say it, fear just takes the words out of my mouth."

"Oh, Han..."

Hannah ran her finger over the angel charm. "Plus...he doesn't want kids."

"Men say that all the time. Then they find out the love of their life is pregnant and everything changes."

She shook her head, tears gathering in her eyes. "No. He *really* doesn't want kids. You know how I told you he was married, and his wife was killed?"

Brigid nodded, sadness seeping into her eyes.

"Well...Vicky was six months pregnant."

The air whipped loudly into Brigid's chest on a huge gasp. "Jesus Christ!"

"Yep. And Erik blames himself for that too. Now he's scared to ever have that kind of responsibility again, in case..."

"In case he loses another child and feels that kind of pain all over again?"

"Yep. I need to tell him. I just don't know how to get the courage. I don't think he'll leave me when he finds out, but what if he resents me?"

Brigid frowned. "Making a baby is a two-person endeavor."

"I know, but what if he starts to regret...us?"

Brigid's eyes softened. "Hannah. You really don't see it, do you?"

"See what?"

"You are that man's entire world. When he looks at you, it's like he stops seeing everything and everyone else." Brigid tucked a lock of hair behind Hannah's ear. "I'm not saying the news won't hit him hard, because it will. Maybe you'll go backward in your relationship a few steps, and he'll have to figure out how to heal that broken part of himself. But he'll return to you. He'll *always* return to you."

Tears pressed at Hannah's eyes. "You sound so certain."

"I am."

This time, Hannah leaned forward and wrapped her arms around her best friend. This was why she'd come here. Why she'd needed Brigid today. Because she'd needed someone to tell her it would all be okay.

The sudden banging on the door had Hannah and Brigid jumping apart.

Hannah shot her gaze toward the door. "Are you expecting anyone?"

"No."

Hannah opened her mouth to say they should call Erik, when shouted words came from the other side of the closed door. "Open up, Brig!"

The air rushed from Hannah's chest...Henry.

Brigid rushed to the door.

The second it was open, Henry walked into the apartment like he owned it. "Oh, thank God—you're here too, Hannah. Saves us a trip."

She cocked her head. "What are you talking about?"

"We're going to Tatum's."

Brigid closed the door. "Why exactly are we going to Tatum's?"

"Because Leo and I had a fight, and I need alcohol and loud music."

Hannah opened her mouth to tell Henry she shouldn't leave the apartment, but he really looked like he needed his friends. She'd call Erik.

* * *

"WE'RE HERE to join them, right, not to drag Hannah home?" Rachel asked as they climbed out of his Corvette.

The muscles in Erik's arms tensed. He'd been at home doing research with Rachel when he'd gotten the text from Hannah, saying they were headed to Tatum's.

A part of him didn't want to be pissed off. She needed a break from everything. But she'd just gotten out of the hospital, for fuck's sake, and Moreno was still out there.

"Erik?" Rachel shoved his shoulder as they moved to the entrance of the hotel bar.

"We're here to check in and make sure she's okay."

"Hm. Maybe tell that to your face, because right now it's giving off all kinds of I'm-gonna-kill-someone vibes."

They stepped into the bar, and his gaze raced around the packed room. The second he saw her, he sucked in his first full breath since the message. She was on the dance floor with Henry and Brigid, swaying to the music. Her head was back, hair down, and the smile on her face was so fucking radiant, it almost took him to his knees.

When she laughed at something Henry said, it was like the rest of the world just disappeared.

"Okay, I can see she's safe and you're already in your Hannahtrance mode." Rachel patted his shoulder. "I'll go get us some drinks."

Erik weaved through the throng of people, his eyes never leaving her. The second he was behind her, he slipped his arms around her waist. She gasped, but before she could say anything, he lowered his mouth to her ear. "It's me, Angel."

She turned in his arms, her gaze shifting between his eyes. "Are you mad at me?"

"I'm not happy to be here." But, fuck, it was hard to be mad at the woman.

"I'm sorry. Henry just needed to get out, and he's been such a good friend to me that I didn't want to say no."

"It's okay. You're safe, and I'm here now."

She leaned her head against his chest, and it was like every fear and anxiety just drained away. How the hell she did that with a single touch, he had no damn clue. "Why did Henry need to go to a bar?"

"He's fighting with Leo."

"I thought they never fought."

Hannah laughed, and the sound hit him right in the chest. "Leo didn't invite him home with him for a family event this weekend."

"Uh-oh."

"Exactly."

He cupped her cheek. "You feeling okay, mixing alcohol with the pain meds?"

A strange look crossed her face, but it came and went so quickly he couldn't place it. "I'm not drinking. How was your work with Rachel?"

Erik lifted his head to see Rachel standing at one of the tables, beer in hand. A guy Erik didn't recognize was beside her, probably hitting on her. She got that a lot.

Hannah followed his gaze. "Ah. She came with you." Yet again, something strange crossed Hannah's features.

"Hey. You aren't still worried about her and me, are you?" He'd thought by now, Hannah would know that he was utterly chained to her.

"She's beautiful. And such a badass. You two share a bond that you and I will never have."

"She's a friend. A good friend. Like a sister."

Hannah raised a brow. "A sister?"

"Yes. The only woman I see as more than that is you. It will only ever be you."

Her features softened. "I love it when you say that."

"Then I'll say it again and again."

Hannah wet her lips. "Brigid said something similar today. She said we'd always return to each other."

"Always." He said it as the vow it was, because nothing and no one was tearing him away from this woman.

She swallowed, seeming to want to say more.

"What is it, Angel?"

"When we get home, there's something we need to talk about."

He wasn't sure why, but his gut knotted. "You can talk to me about anything, anytime."

"I know. But when I tell you this, I want it to be just you and me. No roomful of people. No music."

That didn't ease the tension inside him. But he didn't show it. Instead, he forced his features to relax. "Okay."

*H*annah had smiled more in the last hour than she had in the last week. Brigid and Henry were currently arguing over who could sing the loudest. Rachel was pretending she wasn't amused, but Hannah saw the twitch of her lips. And Erik hadn't stopped touching her all night.

She could almost forget what she planned to do what they got home...almost.

She leaned into Erik's side. Immediately, he dropped his head and kissed her temple. "Getting tired?"

"Yeah, we should go soon." Even if the idea did fill her with a bit of terror. "I'll just go to the bathroom first."

"I'll come with you," Brigid said, voice far louder than it needed to be. The woman had had a few too many drinks.

She linked her arm through Hannah's and they moved across the room.

Brigid leaned heavily into her side as they walked. "Do you think I'll find my Erik Hunter one day?"

"You'll find your person, Brigid. I am absolutely certain of it."

"Soon?"

"Probably sooner than you think." They stepped into the bathroom. "But in the meantime, being a single pringle isn't terrible, is it?"

"Mm, you make me want Pringles."

Hannah laughed.

When she stepped out of the cubicle to wash her hands, her gaze went to her reflection, shifting down to her belly. In a few months, she'd be showing. Even if by some miracle, Erik said he was okay with the news when she told him, would that change when he saw the bump?

"Hey." Her head shot around to see her best friend standing beside her. "You okay?"

"I'm going to tell him when we get home."

Brigid stepped closer, any signs of drunkenness fading. "Remember, he loves you. It'll be okay."

She nodded quickly. Maybe too quickly.

"If you want," Brigid started as they pushed out of the bathroom, "tomorrow I can come over with some of my special cookies. Find out how it went."

Hannah laughed. Brigid was the worst baker she'd ever met, and everyone, including Brigid herself, knew it. "I don't really feel like being poisoned on my first day back at work."

"Hey. I have never poisoned you. Have all my batches turned out perfect? No. But they don't taste terrible."

Yeah, but they didn't taste great, either.

They were heading back toward the table when someone in the crowd caught Hannah's attention. It was only the back of a guy, but the sight stopped her in her tracks, causing her throat to close and her heart to pound.

"What is it?"

Brigid's words competed with the buzzing between her ears. "I'll be right back."

She wasn't sure if her friend heard her, but she didn't wait to find out. Her feet almost moved of their own volition, quick steps, her eyes never leaving the back of the guy's jacket.

A part of her brain knew what she was doing was crazy, that the man she saw couldn't possibly be who she thought it was. But the other part of her, the irrational, emotional side, couldn't stop until she saw the man's face.

She moved faster, her shoulders slamming into strangers as she walked, her hip catching the edge of a table. She muttered apologies but never once took her eyes off the man.

He slipped outside and she didn't think, just followed. Fell through the doors, then stopped dead.

He was gone.

Cool air brushed her face, and with it, common sense.

God, what was she doing? Of *course* it wasn't Nico.

Nico was gone. He'd died in a fire. She'd attended his funeral.

Her heart thumped. Nico was *long* gone.

She sucked in a deep breath and turned, almost colliding with a large chest. A hand shot out, fingers wrapping around her arm to steady her. She frowned when she recognized the man.

"Charlie…"

"Hey. I was just heading in and saw you standing alone out here. Are you okay?"

Okay? She'd just followed a ghost out of a bar. Surely that made her just a little bit insane. "I'm fine."

"Are you sure? Your face is white."

She opened her mouth, but another voice boomed before she could respond.

"Hey!"

Charlie's fingers dropped and he stepped back.

Then Erik was between them, angry gaze cutting into the other man. "Why the fuck are you touching her?"

"Erik, it's okay." She grabbed Erik's arm to pull his attention away from his ex-teammate, but he didn't so much as glance at her.

"I was just checking that she was okay," Charlie said calmly.

"Really? And that required touching?"

"Erik. Stop." Hannah's voice was firmer this time. Louder. "I smacked into him and he steadied me. That's all."

The door to the bar opened and Rachel stepped out, followed closely by Brigid and Henry.

Erik stepped forward so his face was mere inches from Charlie's.

This time, Rachel grabbed his arm. "Hunter...step back."

Charlie's gaze never strayed from Erik's. The beat of silence that passed was so thick and tense, Hannah almost wanted to retreat herself.

Finally, Erik turned toward Hannah. "You ready to go?"

She nodded, her gaze shifting to Charlie, then back to Erik.

Without a word to Charlie or their friends, Erik led her across the parking lot.

* * *

CHARLIE HAD SHOWN UP *AGAIN*. Not only that, but this time, he'd touched Hannah.

Erik worked hard to keep the anger in check, even though it threatened to spill out into the world around him. They were almost home, and there'd been silence the entire drive.

A warm hand touched his arm. "Erik...are you okay?"

"I can't look at that guy without feeling angry." And he certainly couldn't look at the guy touching Hannah.

Her fingers curved around his thigh. "He didn't seem to have any bad intentions."

Erik slipped his hand over hers, and he squeezed. "Why'd you go out there?"

He felt her muscles tense, and the sound of her inhale was sharp.

"When Brigid came back alone, I was worried," Erik continued when she remained silent. "I just caught the back of your head as you stepped outside."

"I thought I saw someone I knew."

"Who?"

She bit her bottom lip. "Nico."

Erik almost slammed his foot on the damn brake. "You saw Nico?"

"I *thought* I saw Nico. I know it sounds crazy. Nico's gone. I just…my brain convinced me for a moment that it was him."

He pulled into the garage. This time *he* was silent for several beats, trying to process her words.

"Erik?"

"He's alive."

Her gaze shot across to him. "*What?*"

"You know that Chandler's been looking into his death since we found out he was recorded as dying in a fire, rather than by the bullet I put in his chest."

Hannah nodded slowly.

"The night you got into the crash, Chandler called to tell me he'd found Nico. He's been living in Chicago under a new identity and running his own business, finding missing persons."

Hannah's mouth opened and closed, tears gathering in her eyes. "No…he…he was confirmed dead. I went to his funeral!"

"No one identified the body. He probably staged it so people would *think* he was dead. He's alive, Angel. But we just don't know where he is right now. He's taken leave from his work."

When a tear fell down her cheek, he swiped it with the pad of his thumb.

"Why wouldn't he tell me?" she whispered. "Why would he let me believe he's dead?"

"I don't know. But when we find him—because we will—we'll find out." He cupped the back of her neck. "I wanted to tell you sooner, but with everything going on, I decided to wait."

So many emotions moved over her features. "So…it could have actually been him tonight."

Erik's muscles tensed. He hated the idea of another unknown

factor being at play. Yes, Hannah thought Nico was a good man, but everything Erik had read on him contradicted that. "It's possible."

"But I don't understand. If he wanted me to think he's dead, why would he risk coming to Redwood?"

There were so many possible reasons. But the one that Erik kept returning to…maybe he was reconnecting with Moreno and the trafficking organization. He wouldn't be sharing that thought with Hannah though…not tonight.

"I don't know, Angel, but like I said, we'll find out."

She nodded slowly.

He climbed out of the car, then helped her from her seat. With a hand on the small of her back, he walked with her through the house and upstairs.

When they stepped inside the bedroom, she slipped off her shoes and headed toward the bathroom.

"Are you okay?" His voice cut through the silence.

Her gaze flashed toward him. "I don't know. Just…thinking, I guess. I might have a shower and go to bed."

Before she could step into the bathroom, he slipped his fingers around her wrist and tugged her against him. "Hey. Weren't you going to tell me something?"

Her eyes widened, and for a split second, he almost thought he saw fear. "Yeah. But tonight's already been a lot, and I'm honestly exhausted. Can we talk tomorrow after work, maybe?"

"Are you sure? It seemed pretty important."

"It is, which is why I think we should wait. I need to be in the right headspace." She looked like she was going to walk away again, but she stopped and cupped his cheek. "I love you, Erik. And my love for you is not temporary or fragile. I will *always* love you."

"I know, Angel. I'll always love you too."

Her eyes softened, and she reached up and tugged his head down. The touch of her lips against his stirred something deep inside his chest. It made him want her. Need her with an intensity that almost scared him. Neither feeling was anything new.

He turned them, pressing her to the wall as he reached for the hem of her shirt and tugged it over her head. Hannah groaned, in turn reaching for his shirt and helping him tug it off before undoing her jeans. When her bra, the last piece of her clothing, fell to the floor, he lifted her up and pinned her to the wall with his body.

Her fingers slid through his hair, her hips grinding against him.

Fuck, she was everything. His calm in the storm. His peace when there was nothing but chaos in his world.

He cupped one breast, finding the nipple and grazing it with the pad of his thumb.

Hannah writhed, pulling at the strands of his hair.

He tugged his mouth from hers and dipped his head, capturing one pebbled nipple between his lips and sucking.

The cry from Hannah was fucking magic.

He slipped a hand between her thighs and swiped a finger across her clit. She whimpered, and he did it again, wanting more. When he touched a finger to her entrance, it was to find her soaking. So damn ready for him.

He slid inside, his thumb continuing to work her clit.

Her hips pushed against him, her fingers pulling and tugging. "Erik…now."

With no fucking patience, he shoved down his jeans and positioned himself at her entrance. He didn't push in right away, instead teasing the back of her ear with his lips while rocking just the tip of his cock inside her. "You're so damn beautiful, Angel."

"*You're* beautiful, Erik. Every piece of you." Then, she tightened her legs and sank, forcing him inside her.

His breath stopped, his lungs not fucking working.

Her lips touched his ear. "You and me…forever." She rocked her hips, and he groaned.

"Forever."

He pulled out and thrust back into her soft body while her fingers tangled in his hair, her moan the most delicious fucking sound he'd ever heard.

He rocked into her again and again, every thrust annihilating, making the fire inside him burn hotter until the world faded to nothing but the two of them.

He continued to move, to cup her breast and play with her as he tasted her flesh.

When her body started to tense, he rolled her nipple between his thumb and forefinger. She pulled her mouth from his, threw back her head, and screamed his name. Broke so violently, he felt as if he was all that kept her together.

He continued to thrust. To watch the woman fall apart in his arms.

When his own body started to tense, it was too soon. He wanted this moment to drag on. To live inside her just a little bit longer. But he couldn't—he shattered with her. Split into so many pieces, he wasn't sure he'd ever be put back together. He kept rocking until he had nothing left. Until she had every part— the whole, the cracked, and the broken.

CHAPTER 6

The warm water hit Erik's shoulders. He was up early, but then that wasn't new—he was always up early. There was a new gym in town called Hendrix, so he'd called his old friend Ryker to come to Redwood and check it out with him. Ryker ran his own boxing club in Lindeman, and he was damn good in the ring.

Rachel was coming over to trail Hannah to work to make sure she remained safe.

He tipped his head back, flickers of last night running through his head. Of having Hannah. Holding her.

He should feel good about them. Hell, he should be over the goddamn moon at everything they'd shared the previous night. But despite the declaration of love and what they'd shared, he couldn't shake their last argument before she'd driven away from his house all those weeks ago.

She wanted kids…and he didn't.

They'd never resolved that argument. Fuck, how could they? He couldn't be a father.

He turned off the shower and stepped out, then grabbed a towel and wrapped it around his body.

In the bedroom, he didn't go straight to the drawers, instead taking a moment to watch her sleep. The slow rise and fall of her chest. The sigh from her lips.

His phone vibrated from the bedside table.

Ryker: Running a bit late. Blakely's forcing me to eat her pancakes. See you soon.

Erik: I can't imagine there's much force being used. Just throwing on clothes. See you when you get there.

He shoved his phone into his pocket and opened the top drawer. Before grabbing any clothes, he reached to the back and wrapped his fingers around a small black jewelry box.

He tugged it out and opened it, the diamond shining back at him. A couple weeks ago he'd been so sure about asking her. He'd pictured the slim band sliding over her finger perfectly.

But how could he just ignore her want for a child? How could he trap her into a marriage like that?

He snapped the box closed and pushed it to the back of his drawer. He had no idea what to do. He was too much of a selfish bastard to end their relationship. Even the thought made a wild pain course through his limbs like he'd never felt before.

He'd just finished pulling on clothes when Hannah's phone vibrated. She didn't even stir. If it was a call, he'd leave it, but it could be her glucose monitor.

Quietly, he crossed the room and lifted her phone. Not her glucose monitor. He frowned at the text from his sister, the words flashing on the locked screen.

Andi: Hey. Dr. Sarah, your pregnancy endocrinologist, had a lunchtime cancellation pop up today if you want to take it?

Erik's entire body locked, darkness closing in around him.

Pregnancy endocrinologist?

No.

No. It had to be wrong. Hannah wasn't pregnant.

His breaths became fast and shallow, his gaze rising to Hannah as her eyes started to open. The corners of her lips were just tugging up at the sight of him when they suddenly stopped. He wasn't sure what she saw on his face, but it had some of the color leaching from her own.

"What's wrong?" she asked, voice barely a whisper.

He handed her the phone, so fucking aware of the tremble in his limbs but unable to stop it. "What is this?"

For a moment, she just looked at the phone like she didn't want to take it. Then, slowly, she slipped it from his fingers. The remaining color drained from her face.

And then he knew. It felt like a million rocks on his chest. Yet, still, he asked…

"Hannah, are you…pregnant?" He could barely release the last word from his throat.

It took longer than it should have for her to look up, and when she did, he saw everything. The fear. The desperation. And the answer to his question.

Pregnant. She was *pregnant.*

He stumbled back.

She slid her feet over the side of the bed, covering herself with the sheet. "Erik—"

"How long?" He wasn't sure if he was asking how long she'd known she was pregnant or how far along she was. Maybe both.

"I'm eight weeks pregnant. And I've known for about two weeks."

His gaze lowered to her stomach, hidden by the sheet. A baby. She was carrying a baby.

Their baby.

Suddenly, his mind flashed back to Vicky's stomach. To the way it had steadily swelled with his child. The kicks he'd felt. The heartbeats he'd listened to at the appointments.

Then he'd lost them both…and his world had crumbled.

"I know you're scared," Hannah whispered, tears glistening in her eyes. "You don't think you can do this. But this can be a good thing. We can *choose* to turn it into a good thing. To turn your scars into something beautiful."

"No, Hannah, this is different. I can't…" Can't what? Heal this wound? Become the man she needed him to be?

He ran his fingers through his hair, a million emotions paralyzing him. Annihilating every bit of calm in his life. He felt like the ground was disappearing beneath his feet and he was falling, lost in one terrifying fraction of a second.

"You can." Hope shone in her expression. "Erik, you are so much stronger than you think you are. You have the power to heal. We *all* have the power to heal."

His gaze slipped back up to her blue eyes. "You've always seen more in me than anyone else. But this time…this time, you're wrong. I am incapable of being what this child needs me to be."

A protector. That's what their child would need. Exactly what he'd been unable to give to his last.

The thought set a trail of new wounds inside him, burning and destroying everything in their path.

Hannah's brows pulled together as a tear slipped down her cheek. "So where does that leave us?"

He had no fucking clue…because he couldn't lose Hannah. But he also couldn't be a father.

But you will be.

The whispered voice in his head tugged him in so many directions, he almost fell to his knees. The darkness started to close in around him again, this time accompanied by a loud buzzing in his ears.

"Erik—"

"I need to go."

He turned before she could see the depth of his destruction. He jogged down the stairs quickly, like he was being chased. It was only when he was behind the wheel, the car dark around him, that he felt the full weight of what he'd just learned. It sat so heavy on his chest that it felt unbearable. Immovable.

A baby. They were having a *baby*.

He closed his eyes and leaned his head back.

"They're gone, honey. Vicky and the baby are gone."

His mother's words whispered in his head. Words he'd remember forever. Words that tormented him. Destroyed him. And now he was at risk of history repeating itself.

⚓ ⚓ ⚓

HANNAH SAT in her car for so long that the minutes beat into each other. She'd hoped the tremble in her fingers would recede or her heartbeat would slow.

It didn't.

He knew. Erik knew she was pregnant. And the moment had been every bit as bad as she'd known it would be. Hell, it had been worse. The fear in his eyes was like nothing she'd ever seen before. All she'd wanted to do was promise him that it would be okay. That *they'd* be okay. And she'd tried...but honestly, she wasn't sure what their future held. It was up to Erik to fight for them, heal himself, but he could only do that if he was willing.

She set a hand on her belly. The only thing she knew for certain was, no matter what, she'd love and protect this child with everything in her.

With a deep inhale, she climbed from her car, spotting Rachel's truck not far down the road. She'd seen the woman trailing behind her on the way to the office. She wasn't surprised. Moreno was still on the loose, and even though Erik wasn't happy, he'd want her to be safe.

As she walked to the door, she checked her phone for what had to be the hundredth time that morning. She'd called Erik twice and sent him a message. She just wanted confirmation that he was okay.

But no...nothing.

She pushed into the building. When she passed Leo's office,

he looked up, a gentle smile spreading across his face. "Hey. You're back. How are you doing?"

She tried for a smile but was sure it came out all kinds of wrong. "I'm good. I still have a few bruises but pretty much back to normal. Thank you for showing a couple of my homes while I was gone."

"You know I have your back, Hannah."

She swallowed. "Everything okay with you and Henry?"

Leo sighed and tapped his pen on his desk. "I asked him to come in today so we can talk about it. Me not inviting him home wasn't personal. My parents just…they struggle to accept that part of my life sometimes. And I guess the coward part of me succumbs to the ease of not flaunting it in their faces."

"Henry likes to be flaunted."

"I know. And he deserves to be."

"Tell him that."

Leo nodded slowly. "I will. Thanks, Han."

Reuben stopped beside her in the hall. "Hannah! It's good to see you back. How are you doing?"

"Okay."

"That's good, but I don't want you to push it. Just do a half day today."

She frowned. "Oh, no, it's okay, I can—"

"I insist. Leave at lunch and rest. The work will still be here tomorrow."

She gave him a small smile. God, she was lucky to have him as her boss. "Okay, thank you."

Rueben nodded. "Do you need anything from us?"

"No, I'm okay." She touched Reuben's arm. "Thank you for being so understanding."

"Of course, Hannah."

She moved to her office and didn't take her first full breath until she sat behind her desk.

As her laptop loaded, she lifted her phone to send a text.

Hannah: Have you seen Erik this morning?

Andi: No, but he mentioned he was trying the new gym in town. Is everything okay?

Hannah: He knows.

Three dots popped up, then disappeared.

Hannah: If you happen to see or hear from him, can you check that he's okay for me?

Andi: Of course. Are you okay?

Hannah: Not really. But I knew it would be hard.

Knowing something and being ready for it, though, were two different things.

She turned to her screen and tried to concentrate as she worked, but when a knock sounded at her door an hour later, she realized she'd barely done a thing.

"Come in."

The door opened and Henry stepped in, a grin on his face. "Hey. Just wanted to let you know I've already forgiven Leo. We're going for coffee before I get back to work. Want one?"

The idea of putting anything in her stomach made her feel sick. Hell, even her cereal had been hard to get down this morning. Or maybe that was just the lingering pregnancy nausea. "No, thank you."

He watched her for a beat too long before stepping farther into the room and closing the door behind him. "What's wrong?"

"Nothing." God, she was an awful liar. Especially when it came to lying to one of her best friends.

Henry crossed the room. The second he lowered in front of her, he took her hands. "Hey, it's me. I can tell you're not okay. What's going on?"

She blinked back tears, no part of her wanting to cry again. She'd already shed so many tears. She took one deep breath before whispering, "I'm pregnant."

Henry didn't react at all. There were no raised brows. No

flinch or questioning look or congratulations. "Okay. And why is that making you upset? You'll make a wonderful mother."

Despite everything, Henry's words made warmth filter through her chest. "I told Erik this morning."

"And he wasn't happy?"

She laughed, but there was no humor behind it. "He's told me on multiple occasions that he *cannot* be a father. That no part of him is capable of having a child."

"He's scared."

She sniffed. "A paralyzing, immovable kind of fear."

"Han…no fear's immovable. That man was terrified to let the world touch him for years. He's getting better. But he's still got a ways to go."

"What if he can't get there?"

A tear dropped to her cheek, and Henry wiped it away. "What if he does? He loves you, and he loves to do that whole 'I'm going to tear down the world to protect you' thing. I have no doubt he'd feel that way about his child too."

She swallowed.

"But if he doesn't…*I'll* step in. I'll be whatever you and this baby need me to be, and so will Brigid." He gently brushed some hair behind her ear. "Because we're your family. We've been your family since the day you arrived in Redwood. And family looks after each other. We'll look after you *and* your child."

Emotions warred in her chest. Love. Gratitude. Relief. Brigid and Henry had proved that family could be created. They'd made sure she'd never been without.

She tugged him into a hug. His arms engulfed her, holding her as she cried. And for the first time that morning, she felt like everything might just be okay.

CHAPTER 7

*E*rik hadn't waited for Ryker. He'd seen the bag and just started pounding, beating the shit out of it like the bag was a demon inside him. The nightmare that ran through his head again and again, taunting him.

He tried to quiet his mind, but he couldn't. The words repeated again and again.

Pregnant. Hannah was pregnant with their child.

Every part of him rebelled against the idea. Against the very thought of having a child to protect.

The responsibility weighted him to the ground, threatening to tumble him to the floor and crush his bones.

The door to the gym opened, but he didn't look up. The space was split into machines on one half and boxing bags and a ring on the other. He'd filled out the forms and come straight over here. He'd barely paid attention to the guy at the desk, taking out his mitts and pulling them on, blocking out the world with his earbuds.

He felt Ryker before he saw him. His friend dropped his bag a few feet away. "Hey."

"Hey." Erik's voice didn't even sound like his own. It was deep and guttural, a perfect mirror of the fucking storm of emotions in his chest.

"This place looks cool," Ryker said as he pulled on his gloves. "I asked the guy at the counter if he was the owner, but he said he wasn't. The owner's not in today."

Erik didn't respond, just hit the bag harder, sending it back with force.

There was a beat of silence before Ryker asked, "What's going on, Erik?"

Again, he said nothing, instead putting his entire focus on making the bag fly. On exerting everything he had.

"Don't want to talk about it? Fine. Spar with me."

Finally, Erik paused and glanced at Ryker. "No."

Ryker raised his fists. "Yes."

"I'm not in a good headspace right now."

"I can see that. Exactly why you need to hit me."

When Erik remained still, Ryker stepped forward and jabbed. Erik blocked the hit, but another immediately came toward him, and he slipped to the side this time.

"Is it Hannah?" Ryker asked.

Erik's muscles tensed at the mention of her name. The memory of the tears that had rolled down her cheeks when he'd left her. He'd hurt her by not being able to give her what she needed, and he fucking hated himself for that.

"It is," Ryker answered for him, jabbing again before serving a cross punch.

Erik blocked both, then threw the first of his own. The punch caught Ryker in the side.

His friend didn't even flinch. "Felt good, didn't it?"

Erik jabbed again, but Ryker dodged it before countering.

Eight years ago, boxing had saved him. But right now, it was doing nothing to ease his anxiety. He was falling and there was nothing to grab on to. No one to pull him back.

"Tell me, Erik."

Two more jabs, and the two simple words fell from his mouth with the impact of explosives detonating around him. "Hannah's pregnant."

Ryker stopped, his body turning to stone, his face showing every emotion Erik was trying to hide. He'd once shared with his friend what had happened to Vicky and his unborn child, so Ryker knew just what this did to him.

"How far along is she?" Ryker finally asked.

Erik's chest heaved, but he couldn't suck in a single full breath. "Eight weeks."

"And she told you this today?"

Erik pulled off his gloves and threw them to the floor, running his fingers through his hair. "Yeah. She told me today."

"What did you do?"

"I let every fear, every nightmare in my head, come alive. Then I ran like the fucking coward I am. I ran so far and fast, I'm not even sure how much of myself I took with me." A lot of him had probably been left behind. The good part. The part that had healed since meeting Hannah.

Ryker frowned but remained silent, like he was waiting for more words.

And sure enough, they fell out of Erik, each as heavy as the last. "After Vicky and our baby were killed, it felt like there was this dagger inside me…constantly twisting and turning. Gutting me. I could barely get out of bed. The only thing that helped was promising myself that I would *never* allow that to happen again. That I would never feel that again, because I would never be responsible for another woman and child. I broke the first vow by falling for Hannah…and now she's pregnant."

And he was right back where he had been eight years ago. That familiar darkness started to hedge his vision, threatening to blacken his entire fucking existence.

Ryker pulled off his own gloves, his gaze on his hands. "Did I tell you that I started seeing a therapist?"

Erik frowned. Ryker and the three members of his team had almost died on their last mission. Not only that, but when he'd gotten home, he'd found out that people he'd cared about over there had been killed because of him.

Erik shook his head. "You didn't."

"I was struggling," Ryker said slowly. "People I loved were killed because of me, and even after the people responsible were gone, I still felt the anger. I needed to be better for Blakely. So I got help."

"And did it help?"

Ryker's attention shifted to something over Erik's shoulder, but he was almost certain his friend wasn't looking at anything in particular. He was in his head, in the past.

"He was good. And a lot of what he said helped. But there was one thing in particular that struck hard." His gaze shifted back to Erik. "And I'm gonna tell you the same thing, in the hope that it will help you too."

Erik's hands fisted but he remained silent, almost certain no therapist's psychobabble could help.

"In order to heal, you need to let go of the person you became to get through the war." Ryker stepped closer. "Let him go. He was the person you became to survive losing your wife and child. And you *did* survive. But he can't come with you on this next journey."

Something inside Erik's chest shifted. He *had* become someone else to survive his losses. Hell, he wouldn't even recognize the man he'd been prior to Vicky's death. He'd built walls. Defenses. Set boundaries. Could he let all that go?

Ryker stepped forward and gripped his shoulder. "Did you hear me? You made it, Erik. You fucking did it. But now, you need to let him go. You need to *live* in the new world you're creating with Hannah."

* * *

Henry: I could bring pizza.

Brigid: I could bring cereal.

Henry: Ew...cereal and pizza?

Brigid: Or...cereal on pizza? Hannah's dream?

Hannah: Um, no, not Hannah's dream. And no thank you. I'm going for a walk.

Henry: Boo. Where are you walking?

Hannah: Just behind my house. Erik and I have been walking the same trail every lunchtime.

Although, today, it was just her.

Brigid: That's no fun. You should at least be walking with your best friends. With food. Come here and we can walk with snacks.

Hannah: I'm okay. But I appreciate your help. I appreciate the cereal on pizza suggestion less.

Hannah dropped her cell to the bed and tugged on her sneakers. She was unbelievably grateful in Rueben telling her to just work a half day. She and Erik had made a habit of walking this same trail each afternoon just to make sure she got out of the house and moving, and today she needed the fresh air and movement more than any other day.

Somehow, she'd managed to convince Rachel she was fine at home. Although, the woman wasn't aware she'd be going for a walk.

Erik still hadn't called or texted. Emotions continued to stir in her belly. Fear. Sadness. Uncertainty. She kept telling herself to give him time, but what if, after giving him space, his answer was still that he couldn't do it?

Before stepping outside, she tapped her watch. A bit high, but not too bad.

Her pump beeped at her, alerting her that it was almost out of insulin. She wouldn't be gone long, so she'd change it when she got home.

Leaving her phone in the bedroom, she headed downstairs. A

part of her was desperate to run and exhaust her body, but her knee wasn't good enough for that.

Outside, her feet sank into the wet dirt as she crossed from Erik's yard to her own. Putting her earbuds in, she walked as fast as her knee allowed, trying to clear her mind. She was just entering the trees in the woods behind her house when bright lights flashed through her head.

Headlights.

She stopped and blinked. What was that? A memory?

Bits and pieces had started coming back to her. Snippets of that night. But she didn't want snippets. She wanted every little detail. Had she felt fear before the crash? Had she seen the person who'd carried her out of the vehicle?

She took a deep breath, speeding up her steps.

She stopped at the fallen trees blocking the path. She frowned. Had that fallen in a recent windstorm? She wouldn't be surprised. There was a lot of wind at night around here.

Rather than risk hurting her knee, she moved off-trail. There were more fallen trees on the way, and only really one path option as she walked.

She was a couple minutes in when something sounded behind her. It was loud enough that she heard it over the music in her ears.

Once again, she stopped, pulling one bud out and turning her head. There was nothing. Well, nothing that she could see. Had it been an animal? The branches cracking in the wind?

A drop of water hit her forehead, and she looked up to see the sky was gray. It would rain soon.

Another five minutes and she'd turn around.

She walked deeper into the woods but decided to keep one earbud out.

When a popping noise sounded from behind her, followed by a small burst of dirt near her feet, she stopped, glancing behind her. What the hell was that?

Slowly, she lifted her gaze, something hard and uncomfortable coiling in her belly.

When she saw nothing again, she started moving, this time at a slow jog.

At the next popping noise and spray of dirt, she flinched and stumbled back. Was that...a *gunshot*? Was someone shooting at her? The sound wasn't loud, so...a silencer on a pistol?

Her heart started to pound, and she looked up in time to see a flicker of movement behind a tree. She stumbled back another step.

There—a figure. Wearing all black.

They were too far away for Hannah to see a face, but they were there.

This time, she didn't think—she just turned and ran.

At the sound of pounding feet behind her, her heart sped up, fear causing the beats to stumble over one another.

When her foot hit a tree root, pain shot through her right leg, almost sending her to her knees. She barely caught herself. She wanted to look back to see who was chasing her, but that would slow her down.

She followed the only clear path in front of her, the air in her lungs straining and the throbbing of her knee intensifying.

The pounding feet grew closer.

They were going to catch her. Oh, God! Would they shoot? She tapped her watch, about to click on Erik's name, when she suddenly skidded to a halt at the surprising sight of a hole in the ground. It was wide and deep. So deep that if she'd fallen, she wasn't sure she'd be able to get back out.

What the hell? It almost looked like a grave! Who had dug this?

A pop and burst of dust. She gasped and spun, then losing her footing, she fell right into the hole.

CHAPTER 8

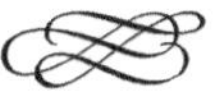

$\mathcal{E}$rik pulled his Corvette into the garage. It was late. Definitely later than he should be. He'd taken the day to try to get his head together.

He loved Hannah. Fuck, he loved her so much, and he *wanted* to be everything she needed him to be. He just wasn't sure he was capable of it.

A part of him knew that he'd do anything for her. Scale any mountain. Fight any battle. Hell, he'd tear off his own skin before leaving her. That made him *want* to be okay for her. Need to be okay.

He leaned his head back against the headrest. He'd taken a first step today. After speaking to Ryker, he'd booked his first appointment with the same therapist. It was a Skype session, and it was in a week. He wasn't sure if it would help. He felt like he was in a dark tunnel with no way of getting out, but for her, he had to try.

He climbed out of the car and moved into the house. It was quiet, but that wasn't a surprise. Hannah had been going to bed early lately. Because of the pregnancy?

Shit, how was her diabetes handling the pregnancy? He hadn't even considered that.

He climbed the stairs and went straight into the bedroom, needing to see her. Touch her. Apologize for this morning.

He stopped in the doorway, his skin chilling. The bed was empty.

He moved to the closed bathroom door and opened it to find it empty as well.

What the fuck? Had she gone back to her place? Her G70 was in the garage, and her old Honda had been totaled after the crash. She had to be somewhere close.

He was about to leave when something on the bedside table caught his attention. Her phone.

She wouldn't have left without it.

He checked every room upstairs. When he found them all empty, he rushed downstairs and did the same thing.

Fuck. She wasn't here.

He stepped outside and crossed the distance from his house to hers. He didn't knock on her front door, instead using his key. The house was dark and cold, and that alone made the dread churn in his gut. Because if she was here, she would have turned the heat on. Hell, she usually made *his* house feel like a sauna.

The second he stepped into her bedroom, his stomach dropped.

Another empty fucking room.

Was she at a friend's house? Had they picked her up? She often saw Henry at work, since he dropped by to visit Leo. And today had been her first day back…

He pulled his phone from his pocket.

Henry answered on the second ring. "Erik?"

"Have you seen Hannah?"

There was a moment of pause. "Not since this morning at her office."

Goddammit. "Did she tell you she was going anywhere after work?"

"She only worked a half day. She texted around lunchtime that she was going for a walk in the woods behind the house."

Erik's eyes shot to the wooded area visible through her bedroom window, his heart pounding hard in his chest. They usually walked the track together. Had she gone alone and something happened to her?

"And that was the last you heard from her?"

"Yeah. Brigid and I were messaging most of the afternoon, but Hannah never responded. We assumed either you got home and she was busy, or she was working."

Erik started toward the woods, acid filling his gut, nearly choking him. "Henry. Call the paramedics."

"Is something wrong?"

"Yes. Send them to Hannah's house."

He ran, his feet pounding the wet earth, rain pelting his shoulders. He hoped he was wrong about her still being out here. Or worse, had she been taken from these woods? Fuck. He begged and prayed to be wrong, but her car was at home. Her phone was on the bedside table. And no one had heard from her since lunch. It was too big of a coincidence.

Had she fallen into the water? Why the hell hadn't he started her swimming lessons long before now? He kept telling himself it was important, but they never got around to it.

The air whipped across his face, branches scratching at his skin.

Why the hell hadn't he come home earlier? Why hadn't he been here for her?

He ran down the trail, his gaze continually moving around the woods. It was dark, but thanks to the moon casting a bright glow over the area, he could see almost everything.

When he came to a fallen tree on the trail, he stopped. She

wouldn't have climbed over that, not with her knee the way it was.

Something in his gut told him she'd kept going, though. He turned into the woods. There were no other trails, but there was a clear path. It was the only way she could have gone.

The river wasn't far, the fast-moving water loud. His heart contracted at the possibility that Hannah had somehow fallen in.

Suddenly, his gaze caught on something. A blackness deeper than the dark of the woods.

Was that a fucking *hole* in the ground? It was big and clearly man-made.

Fear swirled through his veins as he changed direction, heading toward it.

The second he reached the edge, his world careened to a stop, a paralyzing fear unlike anything he'd felt before almost dropping him to the ground.

Hannah…

She lay on her side in the dirt, body completely still.

Was she breathing?

Forcing his frozen muscles to move, he jumped in, immediately crouching beside her. "Hannah? Angel, can you hear me?"

She didn't move. He felt for a pulse, and the air rushed out of him. It was there. Faint, but there.

He lifted her watch, tapping on the screen to see her Dexcom reading of eight hundred and ten.

Shit, shit, shit! It was higher than he'd ever seen it. Too high.

A mix of fury and fear and devastation swirled inside him, creating a deadly concoction. Gently, he slipped his hands beneath her back and legs and lifted her. Because she was so light, it was easy to hoist her up and out of her hole. He set her on the ground before pulling himself out.

Again, he lifted her, trying to shield her body from the rain as he ran. Her skin was like ice, her face paler than a ghost. He forced his body to move fast, praying that his mistake to come home late wasn't a fatal one.

* * *

ERIK PACED THE WAITING ROOM. It was the middle of the night, but he couldn't sit still. Andi had been on, and the second her gaze had fallen on Hannah, he'd known it was as bad as he'd thought.

He ran his fingers through his hair, wondering how the hell he was supposed to just stand here and wait for another second. He needed an update! He needed reassurance, someone to promise him she'd be okay.

But no one had done that. Probably because *they* didn't even know yet.

Fuck.

He turned at the sound of the door opening, and his father stepped in, immediately crossing the room toward him.

"What are you doing here?" he asked, the pain so distinct in his voice that there was no missing it.

"Andi called. Said you needed someone. Your mother wanted to come too, but I held her off."

Erik's gaze shifted to the hall. "It's bad, Dad. It's really bad. She was outside, in the cold for hours. Her diabetes… She was too high."

"Let's sit down, son."

"I can't."

"You can. You need to sit down before you *fall* down."

He *felt* like he was going to fall down. Crumple to the damn floor. With fisted hands, he forced his feet to move and lowered to the seat.

"How did this happen?" his dad asked.

Erik dropped his head into his hands. "I don't know. I found her in a dug-out hole in the woods behind her house. She was so still, Dad. For a second, I thought—"

The words caught in his throat. Hell, he could barely think it without a cascade of pain.

Yet again, his father gripped his shoulder. "But she had a pulse."

It wasn't a question. "She had a pulse." Erik ran his fingers through his hair again, almost pulling the strands from the roots. "I left her upset this morning. I just…walked out."

"Why?"

"She's pregnant." For some reason, it felt easier to release the words than previously. Maybe because almost losing her made everything else pale by comparison.

The change in his father was subtle. A quick intake of breath. A weighty moment of pause. Erik expected more questions. Maybe about how far along she was or how Erik was doing with the information.

Instead, his father's voice softened when he said, "You'll make a wonderful father."

Erik frowned and looked up.

"That's what you're worried about, isn't it?" his dad asked quietly.

"Today's confirmation of why I *can't* be in this position. I didn't protect them! I can never seem to protect the people I love."

"You found Hannah, you brought her here, and she has a pulse. You did everything right, son."

"I should have been there earlier."

"But you were there before it was too late. Because of you, she's getting the help she needs and has a fighting chance. And when she pulls through, when *they* pull through, you will be everything she and that child need you to be."

Emotion clogged Erik's throat. Hannah and Ryker had told

him similar things already today, yet having the words come from his father, the man who'd raised him…it hit differently.

"I want to," he whispered. "I want to be the man they need."

"And that's the difference between a man who heals and a man who doesn't—he wants it more than he fears it."

And God knew he'd let fear dictate his life for too long. "This morning, I would have said that wasn't possible. Now…after seeing her lying there, thinking for a split second that I'd lost her…I'll do *anything* if she just returns to me."

"That's love, son." His father wrapped an arm around his shoulders. "Your mother and I are so proud of you. You've overcome so much in your life. And you're still here. Still open to living and loving. That's strength. *You* are strength." Tears gathered in his dad's eyes.

Erik pulled his dad close. Immediately, his father's arms wrapped around him.

For the first time that evening, Erik thought he might be okay.

He wasn't sure how long they sat in the waiting room. He told his dad a number of times he could go, but the man remained. Erik was grateful. So fucking grateful. Because his father's calming presence was the only thing to keep his mind from imagining the worst.

Finally, after what felt like hours, Andi stepped into the room.

He rose and rushed toward her. "Is she okay?"

"Yes."

The air whooshed from his chest, and he felt his father's hand on his back.

"Her insulin pump was out, and she went into diabetic ketoacidosis. We've finally managed to reverse the ketosis and correct acidosis. We've also had her on fluids and have been monitoring her electrolytes, glucose, and osmolality."

"Is the baby—"

"Baby's fine," she confirmed quickly.

Erik's knees almost folded under the weight of the relief. They were both okay. "Can I see her?"

Andi's eyes softened. "Of course. She's not awake yet, but she's in room seven just down the hall."

Erik nodded and spared one more glance at his sister and father. "Thank you. Both of you."

His father squeezed his arm before Erik rushed down the hall. But he'd barely stepped into the room when his feet ground to a halt.

She looked so small in the hospital bed. There were so many tubes attached to her body. Too many.

Slowly, he forced himself to cross the space between them. When he reached her side, he was afraid to touch her. Memories of being in this same place less than two weeks ago came back to him. Tormenting him.

Gently, he reached down and lifted her hand. Then he lowered into the chair beside the bed and dropped his elbows to the mattress, his eyes on Hannah. Forever on Hannah.

"Come back to me, Angel. I need you."

CHAPTER 9

Hannah's feet pounded the earth, air soaring in and out of her lungs. Someone was chasing her. She didn't know who or why, but they weren't friendly.

She twisted around a bush, barely stifling a cry when a branch whipped across her face, cutting into her skin. She'd just rounded a tree when the ground beneath her feet gave way.

A scream so loud it deafened the world around her released from her lungs, and she scrunched her eyes, waiting for the pain of hitting the ground. It never came.

When she opened her eyes, it was to find her hands on the steering wheel of her Honda, the vehicle moving at a high speed.

Her breath caught at the sight of high beams behind her. They were closing in fast.

Fear wrapped its icy fingers around her throat as she pressed her foot to the gas. The lights blinded her as they closed the distance. She tried to force her old car to move faster, but instead of the distance growing, it was shrinking.

Oh God...

Bile crawled up her throat as she swung her rearview mirror away.

Come on, come on, come on. She had to gain some distance!

The car hit her bumper. She screamed and fought the wheel, barely remaining on the road.

But she didn't have time to breathe a sigh of relief because barely a few seconds later, they sped up and hit her a second time, harder. Desperately, she tried to get back on track, but she couldn't. The car spun and hit a tree.

Pain shot through her limbs, a low buzz starting between her ears.

She tried to move. To open her eyes and get out. But everything hurt too much. Her knee. Her ribs. And her head... God, her head hurt.

The world was just starting to darken when a noise sounded beside her. Then arms slipped around her back, lifting her from the seat. She expected pain, but all she felt was comfort. Because there, pressed against her side, was a warm chest.

For a moment, she thought it was Erik. The body was strong and big like his...but there was something different.

She tried to open her eyes. She needed to see who was carrying her. Whose chest she was pressed against. But it was like her eyelids were glued shut.

She started to shift her body, forcing her limbs to move and her body to wake. There was something familiar about him.

Her movements became more aggressive, the desperation to know who it was clawing at her.

Her heart was pounding in her chest when she felt warmth on her cheek. Then a voice in her ear.

"Angel...you're safe."

That was all it took for her heart to slow, her breathing to go back to normal, and a semblance of peace to re-enter her limbs.

She attempted to open her eyes, and this time, she wasn't met with resistance. Erik sat on a chair beside the bed. He was leaning forward and cupping her cheek.

"You're awake," he whispered, the relief in his voice so distinct that she felt it.

"I'm awake." She swallowed. "You're here."

"Of course I'm here. There is nowhere else I'd be than by your side."

Suddenly, her hand shot to her stomach. "Is—"

"Our baby's okay, Angel."

The air rushed from her lungs, leaving her dizzy.

His gaze shifted between her eyes. "Do you remember what happened?"

She frowned, the first part of her dream coming back to her. It hadn't been a dream though, had it? "I went for a walk. There was a fallen tree, so I went off track. I heard something..." She closed her eyes, trying to pull back the memory. "I heard something behind me. A noise. Popping."

There was a small narrowing of his eyes.

"I walked faster," she continued, the monitor beeping quicker as her pulse picked up its pace. "I heard another sound, and it took me a moment to realize they were bullets striking near my feet. But not loud. Silenced bullets. When I turned around, I saw movement. Someone dressed all in black. So I started to run. I kept running until I found..."

"A hole," Erik said before she could.

Her eyes shot to him, widening. "Yes. And when I tried to turn, I think...I think I lost my footing and fell. I couldn't get out and had run out of insulin..."

Jesus Christ...someone had *hunted* her. Shot at her.

She wasn't sure if she made a noise or Erik just saw the fear on her face, but he leaned closer, the pad of his thumb swiping her cheek. "We're going to get him. You *will* be safe."

"It's just never-ending," she whispered, a desolation she couldn't stop dripping into her voice. "It feels like the second one person is arrested or killed, someone else sets their sights on me!"

Anger narrowed his eyes. "I know. But we've fought off every other enemy and come out stronger on the other side. I *swear* to you that I will protect you again. And Moreno will pay for this."

The way he said it made her want to believe him. And he had

saved her before…too many times to count now. But this felt entirely different. Maybe because she was pregnant, and it wasn't just her life they needed to protect anymore.

"I didn't find you until the evening," Erik said softly, pain weaving through his words. "I'm so sorry. I should have come home earlier. I should have been there for you. If I'd just come home to you while it was light—"

"Erik…stop," She couldn't handle the anguish that bled out of him. "This isn't your fault. I should have stayed inside. I just…I needed some fresh air."

"And you should be able to get fresh air without being targeted. I promise you, I will do a better job of protecting you."

Her brows flickered. "How are you feeling about the baby?"

There was a small hesitation before he spoke, and man, that hesitation hurt. But then he slipped his fingers through hers.

"I still feel this paralyzing fear about the prospect of having a child. But for you, for *us*, I would face *any* fear. Tear myself apart no matter the pain, to be the man you need me to be." He leaned closer. "You're my whole world. You'll always be my world. And I will do everything I can to be okay for you and the baby."

Tears she couldn't stop misted her eyes. "Erik…thank you. I've been so scared to tell you. I thought I'd lose you."

He leaned his head forward, gently touching her own. "You will never lose me. Not if we live a thousand years and make a thousand mistakes. You are *mine*. You will always be mine. And I will always be yours."

* * *

THE DAY WAS a mix of doctors and nurses coming in and out of Hannah's room. They wanted her to stay in the hospital for a few nights to monitor both her diabetes and the concussion.

Erik would stay here with her for as long as they needed. She was alive and awake, and that was something he would never take for granted. But the entire day, he had to force himself to remain calm, when that was the last fucking thing he felt. He didn't want Hannah seeing the depth of his anger. The way it pulsed through him like poison moving through his blood.

Someone had gotten to her. Hurt her. *Again.*

Moreno. It had to be. The event was fuel on the fire of Erik's fury. He was going to find this asshole, and he was going to murder him.

The police would be arriving soon to interview Hannah, but if Chandler couldn't find this asshole, he doubted the police stood a chance. He'd watched his video surveillance, just in case, but there'd been no one there, probably because the asshole was smart enough to not go anywhere near the house.

Hannah's eyes were closed when a knock came at the door.

She opened her eyes. "Come in."

Two officers stepped into the room. "Hi, Miss Jacobs?"

"Yes."

"I'm Officer Paddick, and this is Officer Stark. We're here about the incident at your residence."

Hannah patiently told the police everything she'd already told Erik. Hearing it a second time was like a kick in the gut. All he wanted to do was get up. Go. Find the asshole. Find out why she was being targeted.

When she was finished, Officer Paddick nodded. "We're still searching for Miles Moreno, after your attempted kidnapping by James Paley. We haven't been able to locate him."

Erik ground his teeth together. He'd expected that, but hearing it didn't make it any fucking easier.

"We also found the last of the kids who've been tailgating locals."

Hannah straightened. "And?"

"It wasn't any of them. They all have alibis, and none of their vehicles have evidence of being involved in a rear-end collision."

Erik pulled out his phone as the officers continued to speak, sending a text to Chandler.

Erik: Have you found him yet?

Chandler: No...I'm sorry. Everything okay?

Erik: Someone almost killed Hannah yesterday. I'm guessing we know who. When we have a location, I'm going. And I'm going to murder the fucker.

CHAPTER 10

"I can't find either of them," Chandler said quietly over the phone the next afternoon. "It's like both Moreno and Nico just up and disappeared."

Erik cursed, his gaze shooting up and down the hospital hall-way, then into Hannah's room. Henry and Brigid were by her bed, and the three of them were deep in conversation. Still, she glanced up at him, her brows flickering when she caught his eye.

He forced his features to soften and gave her a small smile before she turned back to her friends.

"Hannah thinks she saw Nico at the bar the other night," Erik said, voice lowered.

"What the *fuck*? So he's in Redwood?"

"Don't know." Erik scrubbed a hand over his face. "I keep coming back to the same thing. Moreno's missing. Nico's missing. They have a connection in that they were both part of the same human trafficking organization. What if..."

"They're working together," Chandler finished for him. "Do you really think Nico would do any of this to his former foster sister? You said she thinks of him as a brother."

"I have no fucking idea who he is or what he's capable of. But I'm not ruling anything out."

"Okay, well, I'll keep working on it. But, hell, Nico's the fucking owner of a successful company now. He has money and resources. If anyone can move around without being traced, it's him."

Erik's hands fisted. "You're better than he is. You've always been the best, Chandler."

At the sound of footsteps, Erik turned to see Rachel heading down the hall toward him, two coffees in hand. She'd been there all morning. She'd gone so far as to bring both him and Hannah breakfast from Black Bean so they didn't have to eat hospital food yet again.

"I have to go, Chandler. I appreciate you putting so much time into this."

"Anything for you. You know that."

He'd just hung up when Rachel stopped beside him and handed him a to-go cup.

He slipped it from her fingers. "Thanks. Did you get it from the cafeteria?"

"Abso-fucking-lutely not. You think I'm gonna drink that shit? This is from a café a few blocks over." She sipped her drink, her gaze flicking to the phone. "Chandler have any information for you?"

"No. I feel utterly blind to this enemy, and I hate it. It *has* to be Moreno. He was supposed to buy Hannah from James, who's now dead. He's the only remaining enemy we haven't dealt with. And if so, is he targeting her as a way to pay me back for killing his men?"

"Hey, I killed them too. If that were the case, he should be after me as well." She shifted her gaze to Hannah's room. "She's had a lot thrown at her in the last few months. Could this be connected to anything else from her recent past? Someone connected to Marco or Angelo? Hell, maybe someone connected to James?"

Erik shook his head. "No. Call it gut instinct, but this is either Moreno or…"

"Or what?"

"She has a foster brother who…disappeared. She thought he was dead, but he's not. He's alive, and he could be involved."

"Name?"

"Nicholas Spalder. Or Nico, to Hannah."

Rachel shook her head before sipping her coffee. "You'd really fucking hope her foster brother isn't out to get her."

A vein throbbed in Erik's temple. "Hope" was the key word there. "Yeah."

"How are you feeling about the pregnancy?"

They'd told Rachel about the baby this morning. He'd left the decision up to Hannah, and since Rachel was protecting her a lot, she'd felt the woman should know.

"Honestly…after thinking that I'd lost her, I realized I'd do everything in my power to be okay about this pregnancy for her. That moment changed me." In so many fucking ways. He glanced at Rachel. "I'm thinking of getting out."

Her eyes swung up, widening. "Fuck off…you're not saying out of…"

"The job. The work. The industry where we play God."

"But Erik, how many times have you told me that you *need* the job? That it's the air in your lungs that helps you breathe? That the work of ridding the world of assholes is what saved you all those years ago."

Yeah, he'd said that. All of it. And it had been true…until it wasn't. "Things have changed. *She's* changed me. I don't need it anymore."

Rachel frowned.

"All I need is her. And for Hannah, I want to be a different man. I want to be a man who doesn't have to work the edge of morally gray to survive. Who can tell people what he does for a living without having to lie. And as we navigate this new life, I want *her* to be my focus."

"Erik…what we do matters. We save people. We make a difference."

"I know. That's one of the reasons I've done it for so long. But I've done my part. And if I leave, someone else will just replace me."

Her brows furrowed. "You're the best."

"I thought that was *you*."

She rolled her eyes. "Okay, the second best."

"Someone else will take that title."

She looked at him like he'd lost his mind. Maybe because she lived and breathed her job and couldn't picture a life without it.

"What are you gonna do, then?" she asked.

"I don't know. I don't need money. I have more than enough."

"But you do need purpose."

His gaze rose to Hannah, every part of him wanting to be close to her. "I have my purpose."

A woman in a white coat wheeled a machine into Hannah's room. Erik straightened, turning to Rachel for a moment. "It's time for the ultrasound. I'll see you later, Rach. Thanks for coming today."

Erik stepped up beside Hannah as her friends left. She reached for his hand and squeezed. She was studying him closely, probably looking for any signs of anxiety or fear. Maybe she was scared he'd run.

He smiled down at her. "Ready to see our baby?"

Hope lit her eyes, and she nodded.

"I'm Kate, and I'll be doing your scan today. This is a trans-ducer," the sonographer said, setting the small device, already coated in gel, onto Hannah's lower abdomen. "It will help us hear the baby. It's still early, so there won't be a lot to see, but hope-fully we'll hear…"

She trailed off as small thuds sounded from the machine.

It took Erik two seconds to work out what they were. And when he did, the air in his lungs seized.

"That's your baby's heartbeat," the woman said quietly.

Something hot and heavy rushed through Erik's veins. He'd expected to feel fear. To have to fight the urge to run from the beating heart growing inside Hannah.

He didn't. He felt the opposite—hopelessly connected to both Hannah and his child. His family.

"And that," the woman said, pointing at the screen, "is your baby."

Hannah glanced up at him, tears in her eyes. "Our baby."

He tightened his fingers around hers. It barely looked like a baby, more of a dark circular shape…but it was *everything*.

He had another person to protect, and somehow, that didn't scare him. Because he knew he *would* protect them, with every single thing he was.

* * *

HANNAH TRACED her finger over the printed scan. The small shape was their *baby*. It felt completely surreal.

Her gaze rose to Erik, asleep on the tiny sofa across the room. It was three in the morning. She should be asleep as well, but she'd woken an hour ago and couldn't get back to sleep.

So many emotions bubbled inside her. Love for this child. A deep need to protect it. But also a bit of fear for Erik. He'd been so quiet during the scan. He'd held her hand, grazing her skin with the pad of his thumb, but he'd barely said a word or shown any emotion.

It scared her. Made her fear that, while he was trying to be okay for her, in reality, it was a mask.

Her heart did a sad turn at the thought. Could they really make this work? Could they be happy?

She shifted her gaze back to the photo. She already loved this baby so much, yet they hadn't even met. She wanted to give them everything she'd been denied growing up—security, safety, and a forever home they could always return to.

She was still tracing the photo with her finger when movement outside her room had her gaze lifting. She just caught the back of a man as he passed her room.

Her heart jumped, her breath catching in her throat.

She hadn't seen his face, but there was something so familiar about him. Something about the way he moved…

Nico?

Quickly, she sat up, then carefully tested her legs as she put a bit of weight on her feet. When they were steady, she took a small step forward, then another, pushing her IV machine with her.

When she reached the doorway, she saw the back of the guy as he turned the corner at the end of the hall. She took a step forward, intending to follow—but strong fingers wrapped around her arm.

She gasped and spun to see Erik standing behind her, looking tall and fierce and…angry. Yeah, there was definitely anger there. God, she hadn't even heard him move.

"What are you doing?" he growled, voice just above a whisper.

She wet her lips and shot a glance down the hall again. "Nico…"

Erik's eyes widened, his gaze flicking above her head before returning to her. "You saw him?"

"I don't know. I saw the back of someone and…" God, what was she doing? She dropped her head into her hands and massaged her temples. It had to be the drugs messing with her mind. "It probably wasn't him."

Right? Because why would her formerly dead foster brother be walking the halls of the hospital at three in the morning?

Erik's brows slashed together, and he opened his mouth like

he wanted to say something but then stopped. He bent slightly, slipping his arms under her before lifting her against his chest.

She grabbed onto him with her spare hand, still holding the IV pole with her other. "Erik. I can walk."

"You should be in bed." He pushed the door closed with his foot before moving to the bed and lowering her. He was just about to pull up the sheets when she grabbed his wrist.

"Hold me."

"Angel—"

"Please? Just for a little bit. I can't sleep, and having your arms around me makes me feel safe."

Emotion flickered in his eyes. There was a beat of silence before he toed off his shoes and climbed into bed.

"I just need to send a text." He quickly typed something into his phone.

She rolled to her side so her back was pressed against him, and right away, his arm came around her waist. Instantly, she felt it. The safety. The sanctuary. And the melting away of every fear and insecurity that had been plaguing her since she woke. Because Erik was holding her, and no matter the hurdle, they'd work it out. It was the two of them forever.

CHAPTER 11

$\mathcal{H}$annah let the cool air run through her fingers. After yet another week-long hospital stay, nearly back-to-back with the last one, she was well and truly ready to go home. She could admit it had been good to rest, but she'd also gone a little crazy.

Erik had been with her almost every second of this stay. The rare occasions he'd had to slip home, Rachel had been tasked with guarding her room.

She was lucky to have people looking after her and the baby, but she hated that she needed it. The sooner they found Moreno, the better.

Her hand slid to her belly. Erik told her more than once that he was okay with the pregnancy, but a part of her still wondered if he was just telling her what she wanted to hear. Because how could a person go from rebelling against the very idea of fathering a child to being okay with it so quickly? He said almost losing her had changed things. But what about in a few months' time when she started showing? When they had to set up the nursery and everything got more real?

Nerves fluttered in her belly, an anxious tingle running over her skin.

Erik's hand suddenly slid onto her thigh, gently squeezing. "Hey. You okay?"

Was she okay? Or was she making herself crazy with what-ifs? "Yeah. Just thinking."

"Wanna talk about it?"

"Not right now. I'm kind of enjoying just being out of the hospital."

He lifted her hand and kissed it, sending spirals of awareness down her arm. He'd been so gentle with her this last week. Every touch had been a soft cherish. Every kiss a sweet graze.

There had been moments that she'd seen other emotions flickering over his face. Emotions she was almost certain he thought she missed. Anger. Focus. Fear. Fear of what, exactly, she wasn't sure. She was just hoping it was fear of the enemy and not of their pregnancy.

"I can almost hear you thinking, Angel."

She shifted her gaze to him as they turned into his driveway. "And what am I thinking?"

"I can't tell you that." He pulled into his driveway. "But what you *should* be thinking about is how protected you are. How loved and safe you are."

Oh, God, this man. "I think all those things all the time."

She frowned when he pulled up in front of the house. "You're not parking in the garage?"

"I'll take it in later."

He slid out of the car and was around to her side before she could put her hand around the handle. He helped her out, sliding a hand to her lower back as he led her to the door. The entire walk, his gaze shifted around the house like he was expecting the enemy to jump out at any second.

He stepped in first, deactivating the alarm before she entered.

She was halfway through the living room when she stopped and frowned, her gaze falling on a photo that sat on the fireplace mantel. It was of her, Henry, and Brigid.

It usually lived in the living room of her house.

Slowly, she crossed the space, lifting the framed photo in her fingers. "What's this doing over here?"

Before he could respond, she glanced at the photo beside it. A picture of her at Emerald Lake. It had been taken a little over three years ago. She loved it because Nico had taken it.

She turned, looking around the room, noticing a few other trinkets from her house. Her favorite salt lamp. A cat-faced cushion from her sofa.

When she made her way into the kitchen, her pod coffee machine sat on the counter.

"Um, you hate pod coffee," she said softly, looking back at Erik. "I distinctly recall you telling me that it tasted like mud, and the best part about us being here, instead of at my house, is that you get real coffee every morning."

He shook his head, hands tunneling into his pockets. "I don't recall that conversation."

She laughed. "You don't recall me saying that I love pod coffee, and the machine's coming over here, and you responding with if it enters your home, it will meet an unfortunate demise?"

He stepped in front of her, a hand sliding behind her back. "Okay. Maybe I remember. And maybe I've changed my mind."

"About pod coffee tasting like mud or the unfortunate demise?"

"Pod coffee will always taste like shit to me." He kissed her cheek. "But...you like it. And because this is *our* house, you should have access to it in *your* home. Just like your photos should live here. And your salt lamp. And your cat pillow...even if I think the thing's creepy as hell."

She bit her bottom lip. "Our home?"

"Mm-hmm. I even brought your juicer, in case you wanted to give celery juice another go."

She threw her head back and laughed. She'd told him about her disastrous foot-sweat-tasting celery juice experiment. "That's not gonna happen. But thank you. I really appreciate it."

"Come on, I have something else to show you."

He slipped his fingers through hers and led her toward the stairs. For some reason, a new flurry of nerves began to skitter through her belly.

Upstairs, Erik stopped in front of the closed door of a spare room and turned the knob. The second they were inside, Hannah's feet ground to a halt.

The room was completely different. The full-size bed was gone. The oak bedside tables no longer there. Even the masculine light fixture had changed.

Instead, an oak crib sat against the right wall. There were pale green sheets hanging over the railing. To the left was a gray rocking chair, and beside that, a wooden set of drawers with an adorable lamp. There was even a little bookshelf hanging on the wall, with a few children's books already inside.

She stepped forward, almost sure her eyes were deceiving her. They weren't. It was all here, and it was real.

"You created a nursery," she whispered, voice thick with emotion.

When Erik didn't answer, she turned—and her heart crashed against her ribs.

He wasn't standing anymore. He was down on one knee.

Breathe, Hannah. Just breathe.

"Angel, I have been many things in my life. A soldier. A fighter. I've been a man who's had nothing, and a man with more than I need. I've been angry and alone. I have lived so many lives. And out of all of them, I choose *this* one. I choose you, and us, and everything we are together."

Tears welled in Hannah's eyes, her heart beating so hard against her ribs it was like it was trying to break free.

"Anyone else would have given up on me by now," Erik continued, gaze locked on her. "Anyone else would have walked away and found someone easier. But through everything, you've remained. You've fought for us. Every time I drop the sword, every time I'm too weak to wield it, you pick it up and battle for our survival."

"Erik…" she sobbed. "I'll always fight for us."

"I know. And I love you for that. I thought having a child would be the most terrifying thing in the world, but it's not. Losing *you*, losing our *family*, is unthinkable. So I'm choosing love over fear. I'm choosing you and our child…and I hope you choose me too."

"Always, Erik. I will *always* choose you."

He reached into his pocket and pulled out a small black velvet box. Her pulse quickened again.

"You're my refuge, Angel. And even though I'm less than the man you deserve, I promise that I will work on myself every day because I want to be everything for you that you are for me."

"You *are* everything," she whispered.

He snapped the box open, and her breath stuttered. Because there, nestled inside, was the most beautiful diamond ring she'd ever seen.

"Hannah Jacobs, I love you. I will always love you. And I will *always* choose you. Marry me."

* * *

ERIK THOUGHT he'd feel nervous being on his knee in front of Hannah. He thought his entire world would feel like it was on the edge of a precipice, about to tumble over. He'd pictured this moment in his head so many times, and each time he saw fear paralyzing him.

But it didn't. Everything about this felt too right to be nervous. *She* felt too right. If anything, he felt relief that he was finally asking Hannah to be his in the best possible way.

Tears gathered in her eyes. "Erik, I love you. I've loved you since the day I met you. You're it for me. You always have been. In my mind, it's always ended with us." A tear trickled down her cheek. "Yes. I'll marry you."

The words arrowed into his chest, straight to his heart.

"You'll marry me?" Even though she'd said the words, they didn't feel real. This perfect woman who could have anyone in the world…she was choosing *him*?

"Yes," she whispered.

His breaths soared through his lungs as he carefully extracted the ring. He set the box on the floor before gently sliding the ring over her finger.

Perfect. It fit perfectly.

Something inside him sparked to life. A flicker of light. An explosion of energy and feeling of rightness.

He rose to his feet and tugged her close. "I love you, Hannah Jacobs. God, I love you so much it hurts."

"I love you more."

Not possible.

His mouth crashed to hers, taking her lips in a life-altering kiss. And God, the pleasure slid into his bones. His blood. Shifting him. Changing him.

Hannah's mouth opened and he dove in, tangling his tongue with hers and tasting her. In one swift move, he lifted her off her feet and turned, moving down the hall to their bedroom.

When he reached the bed, his mouth only separated from hers long enough to lay her on the sheets, but they never left her skin. They trailed down her cheek, her neck.

He reached for the bottom of her sweater and T-shirt, lifting both over her head and dropping them to the floor. He latched onto one pebbled nipple through the bra and sucked.

Hannah arched and moaned, her fingers slipping through his hair, tugging and pulling. Every sound she made was nectar. He wanted to bottle it up, savor it when he was lonely.

But he didn't have to. She was his forever.

He slipped his hands behind her and unclasped her bra. Her breasts sprang free, and for a moment, he was still, taking her in. "You're so fucking perfect, Angel."

He took one of those bare buds into his mouth. She sighed his name as his tongue flicked the hard nipple back and forth. As his teeth grazed her flesh. He reached down and slid his hand inside her yoga pants and panties, finding her clit.

Another perfect fucking moan from Hannah. He circled and rubbed, his mouth releasing her nipple to move down her chest, her stomach. When he hovered at the V between her thighs, he pushed down her yoga pants and panties.

The first swipe of tongue against clit had her body jolting beneath him.

"Erik…" His whispered name on her lips was everything. The damn air in his lungs. The warmth on his skin.

He licked again and again. Hannah writhed, her body moving and swaying with each touch. When he brought a finger to her entrance, her body stilled. He pushed inside, and she cried out.

Fuck, she was so wet for him. He continued to suck and lick, to thrust into her while she moaned. It was only at the tugging of his hair, the pleading from Hannah, that he finally rose to his feet.

He claimed her with his eyes as he tugged his shirt over his head.

She looked so damn gorgeous lying there, trust and love mixing in her blue eyes. He reached for the buckle of his jeans and had just stepped out of them when Hannah rose to a seated position and scooted to the end of the bed.

"Hannah—"

The words cut off in his throat when she reached for him, wrapping her fingers around his cock and leaning forward. The second she took him into her mouth, blood roared between his ears, his entire body turning to stone.

She moved her mouth up and down his cock, swirling her tongue over his tip, her fingers pumping his base.

He gripped her shoulder, using every fucking scrap of restraint he had to stop from tipping over the edge. It was only when she started to pump her hand at a faster pace, her tongue teasing and tormenting the head, that he tore himself away from her. Grabbing her hips, he moved her to the center of the bed before positioning himself between her thighs.

"I need you." Three whispered words. That was all he got out before he slid inside her.

Her eyes darkened to the color of the ocean when it was too deep to see to the bottom. But they didn't close. She gripped his arms and wrapped her legs around him, tugging his head down and nipping his bottom lip.

"Take me."

Fuck.

He lifted his hips and drove into her. It was heaven. It was salvation. It was fucking refuge.

He thrust again and again, casting every moan and cry to memory. Letting them dig their claws into his skin and become a part of him.

He cupped her breast, flicking her nipple with the pad of his thumb as he lowered his head and took her mouth.

Her walls began to tighten around him, her fingers clenching his hair. "Erik…I can't!"

"Then don't. Let go, Hannah."

One more graze of her nipple and she arched, her scream echoing through the room as her body clenched around him.

Every emotion that flickered over her face was magic. It was the real and the raw Hannah. And she was all his.

He tried to hold off. Fuck, he tried hard, but too soon, his body tensed and his orgasm exploded. He lowered his head and took her lips as his world narrowed to just the two of them.

He kept thrusting, kept moving until finally there was still-ness, and all he could do was hold her. Hold the woman who was going to be his wife. The mother of his child. The woman who'd pulled him out of the depths of hell and saved him.

CHAPTER 12

Erik hit the bag hard. It shook upon impact.

For once, he wasn't working out as a way of releasing any tension or anger. He wasn't letting the danger that surrounded him and Hannah threaten to blacken his world. And he wasn't focusing on the nightmares of his past mission all those years ago.

Hannah had said yes. She wore his ring on her finger. She was going to marry him.

He threw a cross punch, a smile tugging at his lips.

She'd said yes a few nights ago and it still hadn't set in. He was the luckiest son of a bitch on the planet. He'd told his parents and Andi, all of whom had lost their minds and come over yesterday to congratulate them. They'd also received visits from Brigid, Henry, and Leo.

He was getting married to the woman he loved. Not only that, but he was going to be a father. *That's* what he was choosing to focus his energy on.

There were still moments when the world got quiet and his mind got loud, taunting him with reminders that he'd failed before in keeping those he loved safe. The fear wove its way into his limbs, causing acid to crawl up his throat.

But then he refocused. He reminded himself that the past wasn't going to repeat itself because he wouldn't let it.

He'd had his first therapy session last night via Skype. Ryker was right, the guy was good. Erik had thought he wouldn't want to talk about the horrors of his past with a stranger. And there was no pressure on him to talk about anything painful. Maybe that's why he'd been able to. Because without the pressure, it didn't feel like he was opening old wounds. It just felt like…talking.

Erik had just thrown a jab when he felt the tingle at the back of his neck. He dropped his hands and turned.

Every time. Every damn time he saw Hannah, it was like he was seeing her for the first time. And the impact…a complete loss of how to function.

She stood by the stairs wearing yoga pants and an oversized T-shirt. Her hair was down and flowing over her shoulders. And there was just a hint of a smile on her face.

"I like it when you do that," he said quietly.

She frowned. "Do what?"

"Smile. I haven't seen it nearly enough on you lately."

She wet her lips and took a step toward him. "There's a lot to smile about." She stopped in front of him, reached for his right glove and began to unstrap it. "I'm marrying the man I love. We're having a baby. And we're focusing on the positive."

Absolutely.

She dropped the glove and switched to the other hand.

He slipped his free hand around her waist and tugged her into him. "You're right. There *is* a lot to smile about." When the second glove was off, he reached up and brushed some hair from her face. "There's something I've been meaning to talk to you about."

Trust…that was the only thing in her eyes as she nodded. "Okay."

"After you thought you saw Nico in the hospital hallway, I got Chandler to access the security cameras."

Her chest rose and fell before she answered. "And?"

"There was a guy who fit his description. His head was down, though, so we couldn't see his face or confirm his identity."

"So it could have been him? He could have been in the hospital that night, just like he could have been in the bar?"

"Yeah, Angel. We're searching all local accommodations trying to find him."

Her bottom lip disappeared between her teeth. "Do you think, maybe he got involved with Moreno again?"

He hated the uncertainty in her voice. The fear. "I don't know. I don't know him like you." But, fuck, the coincidence was a big one.

"A few months ago, I would have said no. But now…I'm not sure."

"We'll find him and get to the bottom of it."

She nodded quickly and was about to turn when he tugged her back. "There's something else I want to share."

This time, worry glazed her eyes.

"I'm thinking of leaving my job."

Shock seemed to render her speechless for a moment. "Why? You love what you do."

"A few reasons. For one, I want to be with you more. I don't want to leave you for days if I get a job across the country. Hell, I don't want to leave you overnight, period." He wanted this woman in his arms every damn night. He lowered his head and kissed her cheek. "Two, I don't need it anymore. I don't need the purpose it gave me. I only need you and our baby."

Another kiss, this time behind her ear.

She shuddered. "Is there a three?"

She knew him too well. "That world can be a dark one…and right now, I only want light. *You're* that light."

"You know you're my light too. But are you sure? What will you do?"

"Be with my family. Raise my child. Live."

She cupped his cheek and pulled his head up. There was worry in the depths of her blue eyes. "What if that's not enough for you?"

Was she serious? "You're worried you won't be enough?"

"Me. The family life. The lack of excitement."

This time he laughed. "You *are* my life. Our baby is our life. And you are so much more than enough, Angel. You're everything." He lowered his mouth to hover over her lips. "And that's the most exciting damn thing in the world."

He kissed her, slipping his tongue between her lips and tasting her. He was about to turn them. Press her to a wall and show her exactly how much he meant what he said, when the ringing of her phone cut through the room.

Hannah started to pull away, but he growled, tightening his hold.

She laughed. "Erik, I need to take the call. It's either Brigid or Henry. And I actually just came in here to tell you I'm going to take a bath."

"A bath?" His dick twitched at the thought of her naked body submerged in water.

She tugged his head down, her lips brushing against his ear as she whispered, "Join me once you're done."

He groaned as she turned and left the basement.

It took a lot of self-restraint to put his earbuds back in and strap on his gloves instead of following her. He'd planned to do another hour, but fuck, he wasn't sure he'd last that long.

He turned to the bag and threw his first punch.

* * *

"How's the second day of being engaged going?"

Hannah laughed as she stepped into the bathroom. It was Brigid. Of course it was Brigid. Her best friend was just as excited about this engagement as she was. Hell, at times it felt like she was more excited.

"Same as yesterday, but fewer visitors."

"I could always change that. I could come over, and we could do some wedding planning."

Hannah bent down and turned on the tap. "Uh, I think it's a bit early for that. Right now, I'm happy to just be engaged."

"Han, there's a lot to do! We've got to talk color scheme. Venue. Guest list. We need to narrow down what you want in a dress and shoes and makeup. It all has to be just as big and fancy as that diamond of yours."

Her gaze lowered to the ring. It *was* big and fancy. If anything, it felt like too much. She would have been happy with a small stone. Hell, a simple band around her finger.

"Let's not go crazy. Something small and intimate will do me fine."

"Is an ice sculpture in the form of an angel spouting water out of its mouth crazy?"

Hannah really hoped her friend was joking. "Way, way crazy."

"Pfft, you spoil my fun."

Hannah was just shaking her head when a noise sounded somewhere outside the bathroom. She turned off the tap before looking through the doorway. Was Erik cutting his workout short to join her?

A small smile tugged at her lips. "Brig, I have to go."

"What?" Brigid whined. "I have so many ideas to run past you!"

"Luckily, we have plenty of time on our hands. Chat soon." She hung up and stepped into the bedroom, pausing when she saw it was empty.

Okay, maybe he wasn't joining her.

She was about to turn back into the bathroom when something had her pausing. She wasn't sure what. Maybe a small rustle of movement. The creak of a floorboard.

"Erik?"

Slowly, she moved toward the hall.

She'd just stepped out of the room when a hand clamped over her mouth, a body pushing her into the wall. For a moment, shock and fear rendered her still. Then, something sharp touched her stomach.

Her world slowed.

"This is what's gonna happen," a low, deep voice whispered into her ear. "You're going to remain quiet as we go down the stairs. If you make a sound, even the smallest protest, I gut you. Got it?"

Her heart hammered in her chest, terror whipping through her limbs. Not just terror for her, but for her baby.

At her hesitation, pain pricked at her stomach as the knife pushed a fraction into her skin.

"Nod if you understand," the man growled.

She didn't want to nod. She didn't want to *move*. But she forced the smallest dip of her head.

With enough force that her teeth clacked together, she was pulled from the wall and tugged toward the stairs.

How had this man gotten into the house without the security system alerting Erik? He had the best system money could buy. Hell, he had *numerous* security systems.

Had someone deactivated them? Moreno? Did he have that kind of skill set?

Nausea rolled through her belly as the man pulled her down the stairs, his hand still covering her mouth, and while she couldn't feel the knife anymore, she knew it was still there.

All she wanted to do was bite down on the hand and scream for Erik. But it would take a single moment for the guy to stab her and run. It was a risk she couldn't take.

On the first floor, she expected him to lead her toward the front door. Instead, he moved to the back.

Her pulse picked up as they stepped outside, and she saw two more men waiting at the back fence between her and Erik's properties. They both wore black clothing. One had a scar across his right cheek. Both held guns so big that every part of her wanted to run and hide.

Without a word, they climbed over the fence, forcing her over with them. Every step away from Erik had her heart beating faster, the fear inside her multiplying. She tried to dig her heels into the ground. Leave tracks as they moved.

"Please," she begged, grateful the hand was no longer over her mouth. "If you work for Moreno and are doing this for money, Erik has money. He'll pay you whatever you want."

"Shut up," the guy with the scar growled.

When she shifted her gaze over her shoulder, she received a shove in the back and stumbled, almost falling to her knees.

She chanced a glance at the guy with the scar. "You know he'll kill you, right? He'll kill anyone who touches or hurts me."

The guy with the scar lowered his head, almost causing her to cower. "You say another fucking word, and I hit you so hard I knock you out. Got it?"

She swallowed and nodded, forcing the fear to remain inside her instead of tumbling out into the world. Another shove in the back and she stumbled forward. She used all her energy to focus on putting one foot in front of the other.

They'd just reached the wooded area behind her house when the man in front stopped and held up a hand. "You hear that?"

The guy with the scar frowned. "What?"

There was a small pause, and in that pause was complete silence. The first man took one step forward—

Two bullets rang through the air.

Her breath stopped, her world slowing as two of the three men instantly dropped to the ground.

The guy with the scar pulled her behind a tree.

"What the fuck is going on?" he growled, almost to himself as he pulled out his gun. "Show your fucking face!" he shouted.

Only silence followed, and that silence filled Hannah with terror. Was this *another* threat? Someone else who was after her? Would they kill this guy *and* her?

Instinctively, she put a hand over her belly, closed her eyes, and focused on her breaths. On remaining calm, even as a bullet ricocheted off the tree.

"Fucker gave away his position," the guy whispered under his breath.

Suddenly, she was tugged out into the open, her body pressed to the man's front. The muzzle of a gun touched the side of her head. "Come out or I shoot her! That's what you're here for, isn't it? To save this bitch? Either that, or take her for yourself?"

He dragged her a few steps to the right. "My boss is pretty set on getting his hands on her. He's pissed as hell that her little friends killed most of his guys. Come on. Come out and maybe we can negotiate."

More silence, and for some reason that silence made her stomach cramp.

The guy growled. "All right, if you're not gonna play ball—"

A gunshot cut him off. The man holding her dropped. Then a man stepped out from behind a tree—and everything faded but him.

"Nico…"

CHAPTER 13

$\mathcal{E}$rik pulled off his mitts and took out his earbuds as his phone lit up from where he'd set it on the bench, Chandler's name flashing on the screen.

"Chandler, what—"

"Your alarm's down!"

The muscles in Erik's body tensed. *"What?"*

"Someone hacked the system. Someone so fucking good, they deactivated the alarm *and* the sensors at the back of the house."

Erik's chest seized, terror filling his lungs.

Hannah.

He ran out of the basement, then up the stairs to the bedroom. The entire way, he prayed she was okay. That whoever had messed with his home security system hadn't reached her first.

He'd almost made it to his bedroom when he saw the cell on the floor in the hall—Hannah's cell.

Fear catapulted his heart into his throat. He pushed it down, moving into the bedroom, then bathroom. Shallow water pooled in the tub, but Hannah wasn't in the room.

"She's not here," he growled to Chandler before returning to the bedroom and taking a gun from his safe.

"I'm calling the police," Chandler said quickly. "The person would have taken her through the back. Go."

Erik sprinted down the stairs and out the back door. If the assholes had only deactivated the cameras and alarm at the back of the house, it meant they'd likely gone through Hannah's yard to get out, and probably through the woods to eliminate any chance of Erik hearing or seeing their cars.

Why the hell had he worn earbuds? But he knew the answer to that question. Because he had the most advanced security system available. No one should have been able to penetrate it. It should have held up and alerted him the second someone had encroached on his property.

He leaped over the fence and sprinted past Hannah's house. He couldn't be too late. He had to reach her. Anything else wasn't an option.

* * *

HANNAH STUMBLED BACK A STEP, her heart warring with her head.

He was here. Nico. Her brother. He looked the same, but he also looked...different. Harder.

His eyes held hers, so intense and memorable that her knees threatened to buckle.

"Hey, Cloud."

His voice... God, it was so achingly familiar. "You let me think you were dead!"

"I know. I'm sorry. I did it for both your protection and mine, so that I could get out."

Her heart stuttered. "Out...as in...out of the trafficking ring? They were telling the truth? You really were part of it?"

Every part of her begged him to say no. To deny his involvement and tell her Erik's information was wrong.

"Yes."

The word hit like a physical blow. It knocked the air from her chest.

He stepped forward. "But it's not what you think."

She held up her hand. "Stop! I don't...I can't have you near me." Tears built in her eyes. "You *hurt* people. Women! You took their lives from them!"

"I didn't know what I was getting into until it was too late. Then I did everything I could to get out, and I've been trying to fix their damage ever since." He shook his head. "I don't hurt people. And I would never hurt *you*, Cloud. You don't need to fear me."

She wanted to believe him. God, she wanted to believe him so badly. But she didn't know him...not really. Not anymore.

Nico took another a small step toward her, gun still in his hand but lowered at his side. "Are you okay?"

Was she? She'd almost been kidnapped, her abductors were dead, and a man she loved like family had just reappeared in her life. A man she'd thought for so long was dead. A man who'd admitted to being part of a human trafficking organization.

"No," she whispered. "I'm not. I lost you, Nico. You were the only family I had, and you let me believe you were dead. You got involved in a group of *human traffickers*. Are you...are you back working with the trafficking group? Are you working with Moreno?"

His eyes hardened. "No. I'm here to help you."

Slow steps drew him toward her, closing the distance between them. A part of her still wanted to pull back. But another part of her, the bigger part, couldn't. "I don't know if I can trust you."

"I'm not the bad guy in this story. I would have given anything to be able to tell you the truth and take your grief away." He stopped in front of her. "But I knew you were strong. That you could handle my loss. So it was a sacrifice I made to protect you. That's all I've ever wanted to do...keep you safe. If I'd have just left, they would have targeted you to get to me."

He reached up and swiped a tear from her cheek with the pad of his thumb. And even though she'd just gone through hell—even though bodies surrounded them, and she'd just admitted to not trusting him—she leaned into that touch. Because it was Nico. Her first protector. Her longest family member.

"I missed you, Cloud. I missed your laugh. Your smile. The way you used to force oat milk on me."

Despite everything, she laughed.

Suddenly, his head snapped up. She followed his gaze—and her breath caught when Erik came into view, his eyes narrowing and gun rising, taking aim at Nico.

She moved on instinct, stepping in front of Nico and holding up her hands. "Erik—don't shoot!"

"Hannah. Come here," Erik growled.

She took a small step forward, keeping her body positioned in front of Nico. "It wasn't him. The three men on the ground took me from the house. Nico shot them. He saved me. He doesn't mean me harm."

"I don't believe that for a fucking second." Erik took predatory steps toward them, his gaze never leaving Nico. "How are you here at the exact right time? How did you know she needed saving?"

She turned her head, noticing Nico hadn't lifted his gun. But the look he was giving Erik wasn't friendly. "I've been in town since Hannah became a target for Moreno. I had a guy on the inside who told me they were making a play for her. You killed him. I know because I was there that night you killed Moreno's guys, ready to intercept her."

"You weren't there."

"I was. I was armed and ready. I would have shot every man who tried to touch her."

Erik's gun remained raised. "Let's say I believe you. How are you here now? Your inside died."

"When my guy died, Moreno went underground, and even

with all my resources, I couldn't find him. So I switched my focus from him to her." Nico's voice hardened. "Which was pretty damn lucky, considering if I *hadn't*, they would have taken her."

Accusation pulsed through Nico's tone.

Hannah swallowed. "Maybe we should talk about this inside."

"Fuck no," Erik barked. "He's not coming into the house. He can explain to the damn police what he's doing here. Hell, he can explain why he's *alive*."

Nico almost looked amused. "I have no problem telling the police who I am. I have a new identity and they won't connect me to the man who died two years ago. I also have no problem telling them I was here to visit Hannah, an old friend, and I saved her from being kidnapped."

Something niggled at Hannah's mind. A memory. The headlights… Then the body against her own.

"You're safe, Cloud."

She gasped and spun, pinning all her attention on Nico. "It was you! You pulled me out of the car after the crash."

Erik hissed out a breath. "You ran her off the fucking road?"

Nico didn't flinch. "I was following her. Watching her. I saw the crash, pulled her from the car, and called the paramedics."

"If that's the fucking truth, then why did you just disappear?" Erik asked.

"Another car was coming up from behind, so I hid, made sure she was safe, then went after the car. I've been chasing Moreno since I got here but can't seem to get him."

He made it sound like he was working toward the same goal as them…finding Moreno and taking him down. But was he?

"Why should I believe you?" Erik asked.

"Because it's the truth."

When Erik was within touching distance, he reached out and slipped his fingers around her wrist and tugged her behind him. "Why isn't your weapon pointed at me?"

"Because I know you won't shoot."

Hannah frowned in surprise.

"I've been watching you two together," Nico continued. "You love her, and you spend ninety-nine percent of your time making sure she's protected. Shooting me would *hurt* her. So would trying to tell the police who I really am."

Sirens wailed in the distance.

Hannah wrapped her fingers around Erik's forearm. "Please. The enemy is Moreno and his men. Let's focus on that. We have time to deal with Nico later." When he didn't respond, she stepped closer and lowered her voice. "Erik, please...for me."

CHAPTER 14

"Erik, please relax. It'll be fine."

Erik heard Hannah's words but just couldn't fucking heed them. They'd spent hours with police yesterday, and the entire time, Erik hadn't been able to take his eyes off Nico. The asshole had been here for weeks. A former fucking human trafficker. Watching Hannah. Apparently searching for Moreno. And now, they were meeting him for a damn *coffee*, when what they should be doing was putting the guy in a cell.

The meeting spot was a public space, but that wasn't good enough.

"I don't like you being around him," Erik said through gritted teeth.

She tugged his hand over to her lap, slipping her fingers through his. "He saved me yesterday."

The muscles in Erik's forearms bunched. Yeah, he knew that. Nico had saved her because Erik hadn't gotten there in time. He hadn't even heard the intruders in his own damn house. *Fuck*, he wanted to kick his own ass. He still didn't know how the hell Moreno had accessed his security system.

"And more than that, I don't believe Nico would ever hurt me," Hannah finished.

Erik was tempted to tell Hannah that she couldn't be so sure of that conclusion. That a few months ago, she never would have dreamed the guy would be part of a human trafficking ring. Her foster brother wasn't the kid she remembered growing up with anymore.

It felt like too big of a coincidence that for two consecutive attacks, he just happened to be there to save her.

But he kept his mouth shut because sharing those thoughts would only hurt her.

"If I say leave—"

"I know," she said quietly. "We leave. But nothing's going to happen."

Yeah, nothing would happen because Erik was armed and ready for whatever would be thrown at them. Not only that, but he'd asked Rachel to come to Black Bean and sit at the counter so there was a second set of eyes on both Nico and their surroundings.

When they pulled into the coffee shop's parking lot, Erik's knuckles were white around the steering wheel.

"Hey."

He turned to look at Hannah at her soft word.

"It'll be okay. Trust me."

It wasn't *Hannah* he didn't trust.

Without a word, he lifted her hand to his lips for a kiss. He didn't have the same level of trust in Nico—or any trust, really—because he'd seen the depth of evil in the world. He'd seen how someone would say whatever the fuck they wanted to make themselves look like one person, when really, they were someone else entirely.

He climbed from the Corvette and stepped around to her side to help her out. His gaze never stopped moving around the parking lot as they walked toward Black Bean.

Inside, Rachel was the first person he saw. She sat at the counter, coffee in front of her. When she met his gaze, he gave her a small dip of the chin.

Nico sat at a table in the middle of the café. He was pretty sure Hannah didn't even notice Rachel. She only had eyes for her foster brother. He touched a hand to the small of her back and led her to the table.

Nico's eyes narrowed on Erik before shifting to Hannah and softening. "Hey, Cloud."

"Hey." She lowered into the chair opposite Nico, and Erik sat beside her.

Nico shifted his attention back to Erik, the slight smile slipping. "Everything okay after I left yesterday?"

"It was fine. My security guy got everything back up and running."

"It should never have been taken down to begin with."

A muscle ticked in Erik's cheek. "I know that. Moreno must have hired someone really fucking good with technology to manage to penetrate it."

"Maybe. Or maybe you need a better system."

Erik's hands fisted and Hannah slid her own beneath the table, over Erik's thigh.

She gave Nico a small frown. "Erik has an excellent security system. I heard you run a business now. You find missing people?"

"That's right. People privately contract my company to find missing loved ones when law enforcement fails them. Or sometimes they come straight to us."

"That's impressive. What made you start that?"

There was a flicker of emotion in the guy's eyes. "I was motivated to find the women who were taken during my time with the trafficking ring."

Hannah's fingers tightened around his thigh.

"And did you?" Erik asked.

"Every one of them. Although they were just the women who were taken while I was part of the group. More have been taken by Moreno since." Nico leaned forward. "Just to be clear, I didn't know what they were when I joined the trafficking ring. I was told the job was security. By the time I realized what was going on, I was promoted to a recruiter—but I never took a single woman. And I realized the only way to get out was to disappear. Since escaping, I've dedicated my time to finding missing persons. In particular, women and children."

"It's turned quite the profit for you," Erik said quietly.

If the thinning of Nico's lips was anything to go by, he didn't like the comment. "It's not about the money. In fact, we do more than our share of pro bono jobs."

Hannah's brows drew together. "Nico, that's amazing. You must be helping so many people."

Rita came over to the table, drinks in hand. "I have one macchiato." She set it in front of Nico. "A lavender oat latte for Hannah, and black for you, Erik."

"Oh, we haven't—"

"I ordered for us," Nico said, cutting off Hannah's words. "I knew what Hannah drank, but made a guess with you, Erik."

A guess? Or he'd been watching longer and more often than they thought?

When Rita left, Hannah wrapped her fingers around her mug. "You guessed right. He's definitely a straight-black kind of guy. Have you spoken to Becca?"

Becca…Hannah had mentioned the woman before. Nico's girlfriend at the time of his disappearance.

"No. She helped me get away, but she couldn't know where I was after that. It wasn't safe."

Hannah reached across the table and touched Nico's hand. "I'm sorry. I know you really cared about her."

A vein throbbed in Erik's temple at the way she touched him. Fuck, all he wanted to do was tug her hand away.

Hannah and Nico talked about their time in foster care for a while, until her watch vibrated. "Crap. I need to eat. I'm going to order some food. Anyone want anything?"

"I'll come with you," Erik said, pushing his chair back.

She shook her head with a smile. "That's okay. I'll probably take a while looking at the cakes Rita has in today."

"All right. Nothing for me, Angel."

Nico shook his head.

It wasn't until Hannah had walked away that Nico broke the silence. "Who's the woman at the counter?"

"What woman?"

Nico raised a brow. "The one with the gun in the concealed holster and the knife on her ankle, who's watching both us and this place like she's a moment away from blowing it up. She's also been around Hannah a lot recently."

Erik still couldn't fucking believe this guy had been watching them. No wonder he'd felt eyes on him more than once. "She's a friend."

"A friend willing to kill for you?"

Erik's back teeth ground together. "You really here for the right reason?"

"I'm here for Hannah," Nico replied, not missing a beat at the change of conversation. "To make sure she's okay."

"So you're gonna help find Moreno?"

"Fuck yes, I am. It's what I do. What I'm *already* doing. But the guy's clearly good at staying underground."

"Then you disappear?"

The right side of Nico's mouth tugged up, but there was no humor in the half smile. "It really pisses you off that I'm here, doesn't it?"

"What pisses me off is that you have a questionable past. I don't trust you. But Hannah loves you."

"Unfortunately for you, I have no plans to leave anytime soon."

Yeah, that's what Erik had thought.

Nico leaned forward, his eyes narrowed and his voice hardening. "I know what you did."

Erik was careful to keep his expression as it was. "And what exactly did I do?"

"You're the person who shot me that night. You tried to kill me."

"How would you know that?"

"The second I saw you with her, I did a full background check."

"That information isn't available to the public."

"You're right. It isn't." Nico shot a look over Erik's head, presumably at Hannah, before looking back to him. "You might not like me, but I don't like you either. And not just because you put a bullet in me, although yeah, I'm pretty fucking pissed about that."

Erik could have laughed. Did the guy really think Erik cared if he liked him?

"I don't like you," Nico continued, "because you're dating my sister, and I don't think you're good enough for her, but then, no one's good enough. I don't like you because you've let her get hurt while under your protection—more than once."

"At least I've *been here* to protect her."

Nico didn't seem fazed by his jab. "Guess she's got us both now."

Hannah's fingers flew across the keyboard. The contract was taking far longer than it should to finish because her mind was elsewhere. On Nico.

Of course, it was on Nico.

What was he doing today? When would she see him again? How long would he be in town?

He'd told her he was staying until Moreno was taken down. That he'd use his resources to help find the man. But that could be tomorrow, or it could be in two months' time. And then what? Would he leave again?

She read back over the sentence she'd typed, cursing when she realized she'd misspelled three words.

Dammit, she had to concentrate. It was only eleven in the morning.

A knock came at the door, and she looked up to see Reuben.

"Hey, Han. Just heading out to a client meeting. Taylor's out too, but Leo's in his office if you need anything."

She smiled at her boss. "Thanks. Good luck with the meeting."

He stepped out of the office, and Hannah turned back to her

laptop, groaning when she noticed more mistakes and spelling errors throughout the document.

With a sigh, she went back and fixed each mistake.

Unfortunately, with everything that had happened recently, she'd had to shift over a few of the properties she was selling to Leo and Taylor. The only good thing was that she had the most understanding boss in history. Even after all the days off in recent months due to attacks, illness, and hospitalization, he'd welcomed her back yet again.

She glanced at her phone. Nico had given her his new number, and she itched to text or call.

Argh. Concentrate, Hannah.

Forcing her attention back to the screen, she managed to get a bit more work in. A few hours passed, everything still taking far longer than it should have. It was only when she heard the office door opening, followed by Henry's voice, that she finally took a break.

She rose from her desk and headed down the hall. Henry stood on the other side of Leo's desk, Leo in his chair.

The second she was beside him, Henry pulled her into a hug. "Hannah! Show me the ring again." He pulled back and lifted her hand. "*Fuck.* It hits me every time. You're actually getting married! And that is a hell of a rock."

"It really is. I keep needing to pinch myself that it's mine."

He kept an arm around her shoulders. "You doing okay?"

"No. I can't work."

Leo's gaze softened when she glanced at him. "Henry told me you had a family member come back into your life."

Ha. That was a very simple way of putting it. Henry and Brigid had almost lost their minds when she'd told them about Nico. She'd already told them that Erik had found out he was alive, but, well…knowing someone was alive and having them show up at your home were two very different things.

"Yep," she said quietly. "And now my concentration is shot. Gone. Nonexistent."

"You've had a lot going on," Henry replied. "Are you okay after the attack at your house?"

"It's strange, but I haven't thought about it at all. Nico's appearance has just completely overshadowed it." She scoffed. "Or maybe it's that I've been attacked so many times, I'm used to it now."

"I'm guessing someone's watching the office?" Leo asked.

She looked toward the door. "Yeah. I'm not sure who. Erik tries to be that person most of the time, but today, he's got errands to run and then he's working out. Which means it's either Rachel or some other guard." Probably Rachel. She was as badass as they came, and Erik would always choose her over anyone Chandler arranged. She flicked her gaze between Henry and Leo. "How are you two doing?"

The men smiled at each other, true affection in their eyes.

"Good," Henry answered. "Leo's been speaking my love language by getting me coffee most mornings."

Leo's lips twitched. "And Henry's been speaking mine by watching long wildlife documentaries with me."

Hannah's nose wrinkled. "Wildlife documentaries?"

"I find them fascinating," Leo gushed.

Well, that definitely wasn't her thing, and she knew Henry well enough to know it wasn't his either, so if anything was an indication of true love, it was that.

Suddenly, voices sounded from the front of the building. Loud, angry voices.

She frowned. What the hell?

She ran out of the office and down the hall. When she stepped outside, her jaw dropped.

Rachel stood close to Nico, blocking his entrance into the building. Both looked ready to kill.

"What's going on?" Hannah asked, attempting to step forward.

Rachel crossed her arms. "He won't show me that he isn't armed."

Nico almost looked amused. "You're armed."

"I'm her protection," Rachel growled.

Hannah touched Rachel's arm. "Hey. It's okay." She looked up at Nico. "You want to chat?"

His eyes softened as he looked at her. "Yes."

"I could actually use a walk."

"I'm going too," Rachel said through gritted teeth.

Nico's eyes narrowed. "I can protect her."

"I'm still coming."

Hannah's fingers tightened around Rachel's forearm. "Guys… please. Rachel, if you'd like to join us, you're welcome."

Anger glittered in the other woman's eyes, but at least she nodded.

Hannah's chest felt unbelievably tight as she stepped forward, Nico moving to her side. Rachel remained at least five feet behind, probably with a hand close to her pistol.

Hannah peeked up at Nico. "You were really going to start a fight with a former Marine turned government killer?"

Erik had already shared that Nico knew what Rachel and Erik did for a living. To be honest, Hannah was kind of relieved. It saved them from having to figure out how to tell him that Erik was his shooter.

"If she was going to make me hand over my weapon, yes. I've had meaner opponents."

Hannah cocked her head, not sure if he was underestimating Rachel and what she was capable of, or *she* was underestimating the life her foster brother had lived.

"How are you?" she asked quietly. "Really?"

He shoved his hands into his pockets. "I'm okay. I love what I do. I'm alive. And I'm better now that I'm with you."

She wanted to ask so many follow-up questions. Like why he hadn't just figured out a way to tell her he was alive years ago. Or tried to return to her sooner. She asked neither. "I didn't believe it when he first told me, you know. I was so sure that their intel was wrong. That you couldn't possibly be that person."

His jaw visibly clenched. "I hate that I was ever part of that group. I hated myself so much for being so gullible, I put everything I had into building the business I have now and getting missing people home."

She touched his arm. "We all make mistakes. And once you realized yours, you fixed it. You're a good person at heart, Nico."

She'd always believed that. Of course, there'd been moments when she'd wavered, but deep down, he was always her foster brother. The guy who'd stood up for her when she needed a protector. Who made sure she had food in her belly as a child. Who'd loved her when no one else did.

He glanced down at her, emotion in his eyes. "I think you're the only person who's ever believed that."

She gave him a soft smile. "I doubt it."

"Thank you." He slipped an arm around her waist, giving her a side hug before releasing her. He glanced over his shoulder. "I see GI Jane's not far behind."

"I missed you."

His attention swung back to her at her words.

"So much," she continued.

"I would have come to you earlier. Fuck, all I wanted to do was tell you that I was okay. But while the trafficking ring was still running, it was too dangerous. I needed you safe more than I needed you to know I was alive. You're my only family, Cloud."

She swallowed.

"Is he treating you right?"

The corners of her lips twitched. "Yes. It hasn't been an easy road for us, but I've never loved a man like I love him. And I think it's the same for Erik."

"That's a nice rock on your finger."

She nibbled her bottom lip. "I'm also pregnant."

He stopped walking. "No shit?"

"It's still early, but yeah, we're having a baby."

"Now I *really* can't kill him."

She hit his shoulder playfully. "No. You can't."

He tugged her into his chest. It was the first hug they'd shared since he got back, and immediately, her arms slipped around his waist, and she leaned into it.

God, he felt familiar. And his scent, woodsy and masculine… He smelled like home.

* * *

EXHAUSTION PULLED at Erik's limbs as he did the last of his pull-ups. He'd been here at Hendrix for over an hour, using the machines to exhaust his body. Rachel was watching Hannah, so he knew she was safe.

Half a dozen people were in the gym. Mostly men. When the entrance door opened, he didn't pay any attention to who walked in. Instead, he completed his set, welcoming the ache to his muscles, before tugging out his phone and texting Rachel.

Erik: Everything okay?

It was only when he felt someone standing behind him that he stopped and turned.

Every fucking bone in his body turned to stone as he was immediately thrust back eight years.

"Hey, Hunter."

Erik worked hard to keep his breaths steady. "Jake. What are you doing here?"

"As you know, my grandmother had a house in town. I came to visit a couple months ago when she was sick, and I actually decided to move here."

"You live here?"

"Yeah. I own this gym."

Erik frowned. "No shit?"

He chuckled softly. "Mom and Dad don't live far, and you always spoke well of Redwood."

Jake's parents lived in Leavenworth, so yeah, really close. Another reason he should have expected to see the man around at some point.

"That's why you were calling me," Erik said, almost to himself.

"Yeah, I was checking if you were home and wanted to catch up." There was a beat of silence before emotion flickered in Jake's eyes. "You cut us out after that last mission. You didn't even go to the funerals."

Guilt pressed at Erik's chest. "I wasn't in a good place."

"I know that. None of us were. We all lost our brothers, but you had the extra burden of losing Vicky and the baby. We wanted to be there for you." Jake stepped closer. "I've been wanting to tell you since that day that none of us blame you for what happened, Erik."

"I was the team leader. It was my job to keep us safe and bring everyone home."

"You did everything right. It was Charlie who broke rank. *Charlie* who fucked up and gave away our location."

"I knew he was bad news."

"You couldn't have known what he'd do. I'm his damn cousin, and even I didn't know. And we all knew the risks of the job."

A pulse beat in Erik's temple.

"I'm sorry you've had to see him again. He's helping me sell the house. But while I'm here to stay, he's not. He'll be gone soon." Jake wet his lips. "For what it's worth, he got therapy after being discharged."

"I can't forgive him." Not right now, anyway. The anger was still too hot, even almost a decade later.

"And that's your right. How are you doing otherwise?"

"Good, actually. Better than in a long time."

A small hint of a smile tugged at Jake's mouth. "Good. I'm

happy for you, man. And you're welcome here anytime. To work out. To spar with me. Get your ass beat."

Despite everything, the corners of Erik's mouth lifted as well. "Appreciate it. You come here with anyone? Wife? Partner?"

Jake laughed. "Nah, I'm a lone wolf. No one's been able to break down my walls. What about you? Any great loves in your life?"

"Yeah. We're engaged, actually."

"No shit? Lucky woman. Maybe I'll get to meet her sometime."

"If you're here to stay, I'm sure you will."

Erik's gaze shot down to his phone in his bag as it beeped. He pulled it out to see a message.

Rachel: All's been quiet. Hannah's walking with Nico right now and I'm trailing them.

His jaw tightened. "I have to go, Jake."

His friend nodded, watching him closely. Erik lifted his bag just as he spoke.

"Promise me you'll answer my call next time."

He looked up, taking a breath before dipping his head. "I'll answer."

Once he was behind the wheel, he sent a text to Rachel.

Erik: Where are you?

A part of him knew that Hannah was allowed to spend time with Nico. He was family to her—of course she was. But, fuck, Erik didn't trust or like him. And he didn't want her anywhere near him when he wasn't around to protect her.

Rachel sent a pin of their location. Around the corner from her work. Good. They weren't far.

He drove too fast, reaching her office in half the time it should have taken him. When he turned onto the street, he saw them immediately, Hannah and Nico walking closely together, with Rachel not far behind.

He pulled over and climbed out of the car. Hannah frowned

when she saw him, and Nico's lips tightened. She opened her mouth to say something, but a loud motorbike passed them on the street.

The rider's hand stretched out, a pistol in his grasp.

Nico saw the asshole at the same time as Erik, throwing his body on top of Hannah's and sending them both to the ground.

Erik rolled behind a car just as the first shot fired. Rachel fired back. Fuck, why didn't he put his holster on when he left the gym? He looked up as the bike sped away, but there was no license plate.

The second it disappeared, Erik rose and ran to Hannah. Rachel still had her gun at the ready, her gaze on the street.

Nico climbed to his feet, and Erik grabbed Hannah, scanning her body. "Are you okay?"

She nodded, eyes too wide. "The bullets didn't hit me. Is everyone else okay?"

Erik nodded and looked over to Rachel, who also appeared unharmed.

At Hannah's gasp, he followed her gaze back to Nico. Blood seeped through his shirt at his side.

Nico lifted the material. "It's just a nick."

Sure enough, the wound was small.

Hannah reached out. "You need medical attention!"

"I'm okay."

"Nico—"

"I'll go with you," Rachel interrupted. "We need to alert police anyway."

Nico almost looked amused. "You gonna protect me, GI Jane?"

She rolled her eyes. "Shut up." Her gaze moved to Erik. "I'm guessing that was one of Moreno's guys."

"Had to be," Erik said, a vein throbbing in his temple. "But was he shooting at Hannah? Or at us so he could *take* Hannah?"

Everyone was quiet. Because no one knew the fucking answer to his questions.

CHAPTER 16

*H*annah moved into the bathroom, worry pressing at her chest. Worry for Nico. For her baby. For the danger that constantly seemed to surround her.

It was never-ending. When would she be safe? When would those she loved be able to stop putting their lives on the line to save her?

Yes, the wound in Nico's side had only been a graze, but it could have been worse. Hell, today could have gone worse in so many ways. All she'd wanted to do was go for a walk with Nico. She couldn't even do that much.

Her gaze moved over her reflection in the mirror as she pulled the band out of her hair, locks falling over her shoulders.

She was trying to be positive. She and Erik were engaged, expecting a baby, and in a good place. Nico was back in her life. But after today, all she could seem to focus on was how much more she had to lose now.

Her watch vibrated, and she looked down to see her sugar levels were slightly high. Not a surprise. Stress often pushed her numbers, not to mention the pregnancy messed with her levels. But at least she was working with a good endocrinologist.

She stripped off her clothes and had just turned on the shower when a small cramp had her breath catching in her throat. She paused and pressed a hand to her belly, her heart picking up its pace.

What was that? Was it normal? She stood completely still for a moment, waiting to see if another came. It didn't. Instead, her phone vibrated from the bathroom counter. At the sight of Nico's name, her mind switched to him, and she snapped up her cell.

Nico: Hey. Just letting you know I'm all stitched up. I know you worry, but you don't need to. GI didn't leave my side. In fact, no matter how many times I told her to go find an innocent victim to save, she wouldn't. Doctors took good care of me. Get some rest.

Some of the worry slipped from her chest. Thank God.

Hannah: I'm glad you're okay. Remember, if you want to stay in my house instead of the hotel, it's empty and you're always welcome.

Nico: Thanks. I'm not sure Mr. Hunter would like that, but I'll think about it.

She nibbled her bottom lip. He was right—Erik wouldn't like it, and she hadn't run it past him. But she wanted Nico close, so offering felt right.

Hannah: K. Well, the offer is always there. Look after yourself, Nico.

Nico: You too.

She lowered her phone and stepped into the shower. Let the warm water cascade over her shoulders. Her entire life, she'd made the conscious effort to see past her problems. But right now...man, that felt like the hardest thing. Maybe it was the pregnancy hormones. Or maybe she was just tired. Whatever it was, she was more than ready to live a white-picket-fence life, devoid of any problems. Was that even a thing anymore?

* * *

"WHAT THE FUCK did I just receive from the boss?"

Erik leaned back in his desk chair, his lips curving at Chandler's question. "I assume you're talking about my letter of resignation."

"You're shitting me, right? You're leaving?"

"I'm not leaving *you*. I'm leaving the job."

"Same fucking thing."

Erik rose and moved to the window, looking out over the front yard. "I've been doing this job for years. It's time."

"You say that like you're eighty damn years old. You're not. You're thirty-six and you're the best contractor we have. You take out our hardest, most dangerous targets."

"Others can handle it." He watched the leaves rustle in the trees. The way the wind lifted the branches. "Hannah's pregnant."

There was a beat of silence. "*Wow*. Okay. Now I get it. How do you feel about that?"

"At first I had no idea how to handle it. I thought there was no way I could be a father. But now...now all I want is to be with her. And when the baby comes, be with him or her. It's accelerated things. Made me realize I want to live a different kind of life for my family."

Chandler blew out a breath. "That's huge. Fuck, I'm happy for you, Erik."

"Thanks." He always knew his friend would be, once he got over the shock of Erik quitting. His fingers tightened on the phone. "There was another attack today."

"Shit. Is everyone okay?"

"Someone on a motorcycle did a drive-by and shot at us." The muscles in his forearms clenched, even the memory making the fury return. "Nico dropped on top of Hannah and got grazed by a bullet. They're both fine though."

"You get plate numbers?"

"Nope. There wasn't one."

"Asshole."

That didn't come close to describing the guy. "What I don't

understand is, are they trying to *take* her or *kill* her? Because today, and when she was pushed into the fucking hole, it appeared they were trying to hurt or kill her. But when they hacked my security system, they were trying to kidnap her."

"Maybe Moreno doesn't know what he wants. Just that he needs you to suffer."

He was definitely doing that. "You still haven't found any clues as to where he might be?"

"No. It's frustrating. I did identify the men who killed your security and took Hannah."

Erik's chest tightened. "Tell me."

"Hired thugs. The leader's name was Jacob Waterhouse but goes by the street name Wolf. He was well known for his tech skills and muscle."

"So Moreno's run out of men and is hiring help now."

"Yep. Probably hiring more to help him remain hidden as well."

Fuck.

"What about her foster brother?" Chandler asked. "You said he appears to be looking for him too. He found anything?"

"He *says* he's looking and claims he's on our side." Not that Erik had started trusting Nico.

"Give me his number."

Erik's brows slashed together. "What?"

"If he does have good intentions, he'll want to work together on this."

"We can't trust him, Chandler."

"I'll double check any information he brings me. Come on, Hunter, we have nothing to lose at this point."

Shit. He didn't like it, but Chandler was right. She'd already been attacked too many times, so they didn't really have a lot to lose. "I'll send it to you."

"Thanks. Send me the location of the shooting too. I'll see if I can get access to local cameras. If he was wearing a helmet and there wasn't a plate, there might not be much I can do, but I'll try."

"Thanks, Chandler. I appreciate everything you do. I'm gonna go check on Hannah."

"She doing all right with everything?"

"She's so fucking strong. Any other woman would have folded by now, but she's still standing."

"You look after her and yourself, okay?"

"Always."

He hung up, but before going upstairs, he checked all the doors and windows on the first floor, as well as his security system. Since the security breach, Chandler had been checking and double-checking it for them daily. Erik already had the best system money could buy, but if it had been penetrated once, it could be again. The fact was, Hannah wouldn't be safe until the threats were taken care of.

He hadn't done a workout in his basement again. In fact, if he wanted to hit the bags while he was home with Hannah, he'd already made the decision that he'd take her to Hendrix with him.

Once he was satisfied the home was locked and alarmed, he climbed the stairs and went into the bathroom. The second he saw her in the shower, his heart did that thing it always did around her. It stopped, then started again, but at a faster, less natural rhythm. She stood under the stream of water, eyes closed and head turned up toward the spray.

How one person could make him feel so much, he had no idea. She made him want to exist just for her. To be her partner. Her protector. Her light when there was only darkness.

He stripped off his clothes and stepped in behind her, slipping his arms around her waist.

She gasped and spun, then her eyes softened. "Erik. I didn't hear you come in."

"I can be quiet." He kissed her cheek, then her ear. "Is it okay that I join you?"

She leaned into him. "It's more than okay. I need your arms around me."

He lifted his head, frowning at what he saw. Gently, he grazed a dark circle shadowing her eye with the pad of his thumb. "You're tired."

"I am. But not just in a physical way. In a whole body, emotional and spiritual way." Tears gathered in her eyes, and they fucking shattered him. "I'm so tired of looking over my shoulder. I'm worried about the people around us, like Rachel and Nico. I'm worried about you getting hurt or putting yourself in danger to save me. And I'm worried about our baby."

Something primal and protective rattled in his chest. "*Nothing* is going to happen to anyone we love. Rachel and Nico can both handle themselves and will be okay. *I* can handle myself and will be okay. And you and our baby are sure as hell safe and protected because you have a team of people making sure of it." He lowered his hand to her stomach, spanning his fingers over her skin. "That's a promise I make to you today, tomorrow, and every day after."

"You can't promise that, Erik."

"Angel, I will do everything in my power to ensure your safety." He swiped his thumb over a tear that trickled down her cheek. "Trust me."

"I do. I trust you more than anyone else in the world." She wrapped her arms around his waist, pressed a single kiss to his chest, right over his heart, before laying her head against him. "I just worry because I love you."

He pressed a kiss to the top of her head, tightening his hold around her. "I was made to love you, Angel."

CHAPTER 17

*H*annah paused in typing an email to massage her temple. A headache had started thumping at the backs of her eyes about an hour ago. She knew it was stress. She needed to get better at managing it. Yes, there was danger surrounding her, and yes, being pregnant made that danger scarier, but stressing about it wouldn't help.

She had just finished the email when an alert came through on her laptop.

Meeting with Jake and Charlie Moore in ten minutes.

She frowned. What the heck? She hadn't set up that meeting. Was Charlie Moore *the* Charlie? Erik's ex-teammate Charlie? And Jake… Erik had mentioned Charlie had a cousin who was also on his team and now running the new gym in town. Was that him?

Quickly, she rose from her desk and walked down the hall to Reuben's office, only the room was empty. Crap. And Leo and Taylor were out too—Leo for a showing and Taylor for a client meeting at a café.

She hurried back to her desk and lifted her phone. Reuben answered on the third ring.

"Hannah, hey, everything okay?"

"Hi, Reuben, I appear to have a meeting on my calendar today with a Jake and Charlie Moore at eleven. I was wondering if you set that up?"

"Yes, I did. Sorry, I meant to mention it. Charlie contacted the office and asked for an appointment for him and his cousin to sell their family home. He requested this morning, and Leo and Taylor were both scheduled, so I put him with you." Wind blew over the line. "Is that okay?"

She nibbled her bottom lip, her gaze rising to the door, then dropping back to the desk. She wanted to say no. Erik would likely hate it because, well, he hadn't exactly forgiven Charlie for what had happened all those years ago. But how could she? There was no one else here to take the meeting, and it was too late to cancel. Not to mention it would be unprofessional of her to send the men away last minute.

"Of course it's fine." The second the words were out, she wrinkled her nose.

"Great. I'll probably be back in the office in an hour."

"Okay. Thanks. See you then."

She hung up and lifted her cell, then started a text to Erik before deleting it. She did that about three times, then switched her text to Rachel. Yeah, she was a coward.

Hannah: Jake and Charlie Moore are coming in for a meeting in a couple minutes.

There was a short pause before Rachel responded.

Rachel: Got it.

It was several minutes later when she heard the door to the building open and footsteps pad down the hall. Charlie walked in first, closely followed by who she assumed was Jake, then Rachel. And by the thin line of her mouth, she wasn't too happy.

Hannah rose from her desk. "Hi, Charlie. It's nice to see you again." She reached out and shook his hand before turning to the other man. "I'm Hannah."

"Jake. It's nice to meet you. I've heard a little bit about you from Erik."

She smiled. "Good things, I hope."

One side of his mouth lifted. "Only the best."

Both men were tall, well over six feet, and so incredibly broad. God, it was like all these men from the military were cut from the same cloth.

Hannah glanced at Rachel. "Thank you for showing them in."

"I can stay if you need."

"We'll be okay." She couldn't allow the woman to sit in on a client meeting, even if she wanted to.

Rachel's gaze moved to Charlie, almost shooting daggers into his back, before returning to her. "I'm gonna be right outside your door."

Rachel stepped out, closing the door with a loud thud.

Hannah cringed as she shifted her attention back to the two men. "Sorry about that. She's a little protective. Have a seat."

"Is everything okay?" Jake asked.

"Yeah, we've just had a bit of trouble recently. Nothing we need to discuss today. So, you have a family home to sell?"

Charlie nodded. "It was our grandmother's. She left it to the two of us, as the only grandkids, and we'd like to sell it. The place is old but big. Four bedrooms. Three bathrooms."

"What makes you want to sell and not keep it?"

"Not really our style," Jake said. "Plus, even though I'm staying in town, Charlie isn't."

Charlie lifted a shoulder. "I get bored and change jobs a lot. I've spent a bit of time in gyms and construction work. I drove trucks for a while. But I'm currently doing some online sales stuff as well as a couple shifts at Jake's gym."

"Sounds interesting."

"I get restless."

"Nothing wrong with that." She smiled at them. "Well, thank you for coming to us to sell your property. I'll go through how we work, and after talking about the property and expectations, we can arrange a time for me to see the house."

Charlie nodded. "Sounds good." He was silent for a moment before asking. "How's Erik doing?"

"Charlie—" Jake started, but his cousin cut him off.

"What? I've seen the guy twice, and both times he was mad as shit at me. I just want to know that he's okay."

She swallowed. "He's doing well."

Charlie's gaze lowered to her left hand. "Congratulations."

She glanced at her engagement ring. "Oh, um, thank you. It's still so new, I forget I'm wearing it sometimes. But we're happy. Both of us."

"I'm glad. Before I came here, I got in contact with a few of the guys on the team to apologize to them as well. I asked them about Erik, and they didn't know much but didn't think he was doing too good."

"He's doing well," she said softly.

"That's good." Charlie nodded. "And I'm glad he has you to look after him."

She laughed. "Trust me, it's him who does all the looking after. I'm incredibly lucky to have him. Now, is it okay if I get some more information on this property?"

She'd just twisted slightly to glance at her computer screen when a small pain cramped her belly. She gasped, her hand covering her stomach.

Charlie frowned, and Jake leaned forward.

"Are you okay?" Jake asked.

"Um…yeah, I'm okay." She nodded quickly when really, worry skittered down her spine. This was her second cramp in two days. Was something wrong?

She cleared her throat. "Okay, could I have the address of the property?"

Over the next half hour, she forced her mind to remain on the meeting. To take down all the details of their property and give the men a rundown of the sales process.

They were just finishing up when a knock sounded at the door. Nico stepped in, his eyes narrowing on Charlie and Jake before shifting to Hannah.

"Hey. We still doing lunch?"

Crap. She'd forgotten. She checked the clock, noticing she was ten minutes late for their scheduled time. God, she was so disorganized these days.

Charlie stood. "Thank you for your time, Hannah."

"Yeah, thanks, Hannah," Jake added.

"Thank you both. I'll email you some suggested times for me to come look at the property."

When it was just Nico and Hannah, he pushed his hands into his pockets. "Sorry, I texted but…"

"No, it's my fault. I didn't realize I had that meeting and it threw my morning out of whack. Ready to go?"

He nodded. "I'm guessing GI Jane will be joining us?"

She rolled her eyes. "You need to stop calling her that."

"I don't mind," Rachel said from the doorway. "It's better than any of the names I call him."

"Like Gladiator?" Nico said with a mischievous grin on his face. "Hercules? Man, I'd like to—"

"Okay!" Hannah interrupted. "Let's go. It's lunchtime and I'm hungry."

She moved past them into the hall. Once they were on the street, as usual, Rachel stayed at a distance behind them. She was tempted to tell the woman she could walk with them but knew it was no use. Rachel would refuse, probably because she knew she'd fight with Nico.

Nico nudged her hip. "You doing okay?"

"You want the truth?"

"Always."

"Not really. I feel really stressed about everything. I keep telling myself to relax, but I just…can't."

He frowned. "Why? Because of yesterday? I'm fine. And nothing's going to happen to you."

"Erik said the same thing, but you can't guarantee that. Moreno is out to get me, and he hasn't made any secret of it. He wants to punish Erik for killing his team." Saying that out loud made more anxiety spider through her limbs. "He's already gone to such extremes. And until we find him—"

"That's the thing. We *will* find him. And there's no way in hell we'll allow him anywhere near you before then."

He sounded so sure. And she'd needed that. She linked her arm through his. "Have I told you how much I missed you?"

"Yeah, but you can tell me again." He kissed the top of her head. "I missed you too."

She swallowed, wanting to ask the next question but also scared.

"What is it, Cloud?"

Her gaze shot up. "How do you do that? Always know when something's on my mind?"

"You wrinkle your nose and you purse your lips. It's your tell."

She had a tell? "Okay. I was just wondering…once we do catch Moreno, are you going to leave?"

His pause was heavy, and it stretched so long that she already had her answer. "You are."

"Hey." He stopped outside Black Bean. "I haven't decided what I'm doing. My business is based in Chicago, but I can work from anywhere. Regardless, I'm alive, and we're back in each other's lives. If I leave, it's not forever. We can visit each other whenever we want."

It wasn't the same. But she didn't say that out loud. Instead, she nodded, taking hope from the fact that he had no solid plans to leave yet. "I'm glad you're here now."

"You have no idea."

They stepped into Black Bean and were halfway across the café to the counter when another of those cramps hit her lower abdomen. This one was so strong, it cut off her breath, almost causing her to double over.

Nico set a hand on her back. "What's wrong?"

"I, um, I'm not sure. I'm just going to pop into the bathroom."

She didn't wait for a response. Her knees shook the entire way across the room, fear making her heart beat too fast and panic coil in her belly. She stepped into the bathroom and moved straight to a stall.

When she saw the crimson blood on the toilet paper, her world slowed, a new terror like she'd never felt before settling inside her chest, paralyzing her.

Oh, God.

Blood rushed between her ears, the buzz blocking out all other sounds.

The panic was just seizing her when she heard the door to the bathroom open, then Rachel's voice sounded.

"Hannah? Are you okay?"

Her mouth opened and closed a couple of times in an attempt to respond, but no words came out.

"Hannah!"

Finally, she cleaned up and forced herself to rise. She had to lock her knees to keep herself upright. When she opened the door, she wasn't sure what Rachel saw, but her features immediately turned to a combination of concern and fear. The fear looked odd on the woman. Out of place.

"What is it? What happened?" she asked.

Again, Hannah opened her mouth, but dammit, words still weren't working.

Rachel gripped her arms. "Hannah, breathe. Talk to me. You can do it."

"I need you to drive me to the hospital."

$\mathcal{E}$rik ran through the hospital hallway, his heart beating so damn hard he could just about hear it. He'd been at a therapy session this morning. He should have been with Hannah. He'd known she wasn't okay last night, dammit.

Rachel was the first person he saw. She stood in the hall outside an open door.

"Is she okay?" Erik asked before he'd stopped running.

Rachel nodded, tilting her head toward the room. Inside, Hannah was on the bed, Nico beside her, holding her hand as the technician set up the ultrasound machine.

Anger tried to pulse through his veins at the sight of Nico standing where he should be. But he forced the emotion down and focused on her. Her pale features. Her too-wide eyes. He should be glad she had her brother and she wasn't alone.

He crossed to the bed. Nico stepped back and quietly left the room while Erik took his spot, lifting her hand. "Are you okay?"

"I don't know. I got some cramping...and there was blood. Erik...I'm scared."

Her words were like a fist around his heart, squeezing. "It'll be okay."

He knew he had no fucking right to say that, but he couldn't have stopped himself if he tried. He needed to offer her some sort of reassurance that everything would be all right.

It was the same sonographer as last time. She put gel on the transducer before pressing it to Hannah's lower abdomen, where there was the smallest hint of a bump.

The second the heartbeat sounded through the machine, the air rushed from Erik's chest and tears filled Hannah's eyes.

"Heartbeat sounds good," the sonographer said confidently, pressing a few keys on her machine. Suddenly, an image popped up on the screen. "And there's your baby."

Hannah's fingers tightened around his hand. "And the baby's okay?"

"Yes. Everything looks as it should."

Hannah's eyes closed and Erik leaned down, kissing the top of her head, lips lingering.

The sonographer lifted the transducer and wiped her stomach. "I'll email these to your doctor and send her down."

When the woman stepped out of the room, Erik helped Hannah sit up.

"I'm sorry," she said quietly.

"You do not need to apologize. Ever. If you think something's wrong, I want you to come here."

"I made you worry."

"I worry about you regardless of where you are or what you're doing."

She leaned her head against his chest, and he just held her. They didn't speak as they waited for the doctor. It was like they both needed the quiet time to just hold each other.

When the doctor finally walked in, Hannah straightened. The woman gave them a warm smile. "Hi. I've just looked at your scans and read through the notes, and it appears everything is going well."

Hannah frowned. "But what about the cramps and bleeding?"

"It can happen during pregnancy." Her eyes turned sympathetic. "Sometimes external factors like stress can contribute to these things."

Erik's muscles locked. Of course she was stressed. A fucking human trafficker was after her, and Erik couldn't track the asshole down.

The weight of his failure pressed on his shoulders.

"Hey." Hannah's fingers wrapped around his arm, her voice barely above a whisper. "The doctor said our baby's okay."

He nodded, hating that *she* was comforting *him*. He forced his features to soften. "Good."

She studied him too closely before turning back to the doctor as she talked to them about supplements and rest. Before she left, her mouth spread into a smile. "As part of the blood test, we also discovered the gender of the baby. Would you like to know?"

Hannah's brows shot up, and she looked at him. "What do you think?"

"It's up to you, Angel. I don't mind either way." He loved the child regardless of whether it was a girl with Hannah's blond hair or a boy with his attitude.

She nibbled her bottom lip.

"How about I write it down and put it in an envelope for you both, and you can think about it," the doctor suggested softly.

Hannah nodded. "That sounds great."

When the doctor left, Hannah leaned her head back, hand on her stomach, and closed her eyes. "Thank God."

He kissed her forehead. "I'm just going to talk to Rachel."

Her eyes popped open. "Are you sure you're okay?"

"Yes. Rest. I'm fine."

She nodded, not looking like she believed him for a second.

He stepped into the hall to see Rachel and Nico standing close as they talked. Probably more like arguing.

Rachel's gaze rose to Erik, and she stepped toward him. "How is she?"

"She's okay. So's our baby."

Nico immediately stepped toward the room, but Erik grabbed his arm.

"Take your hand off me," Nico growled.

Fuck, he hated this guy. "Don't take long. She needs to rest."

He pulled his arm from Erik's grasp and entered the room. Erik's hands fisted, and he had to forcibly stop himself from going after the asshole.

"Hunter."

At Rachel's voice, Erik turned back.

"I think she's safe with him," she said softly. "The guy pisses me off too. Hell, I've been a second away from shooting his ass a number of times, but I've been watching them together, and he really cares about her."

He knew Nico cared about her. People still hurt those they cared about, though. "I don't trust him." How many fucking times had he said that? Didn't matter. He'd keep saying it.

"Well, considering you tried to kill him, I'd say the feeling's mutual."

Despite everything, he almost laughed. Trust Rachel to pull that out of him at a time like this.

She stepped closer. "I'm glad Hannah and the baby are okay. Are you?"

Was he? "I need to find him, Rach. I need to make sure he's not a threat to her anymore and she's safe."

"I know. We're working on it."

It wasn't enough. This had gone on for too fucking long.

Rachel grasped his arm. "Have faith that we'll get there, and that we'll keep her safe until we do."

Maybe that was the problem. He had no damn faith.

* * *

"I CAN COME STAY over if you need me?" Brigid asked over the phone. "I can bring Frosted Flakes and Cocoa Krispies. Ooh, I could bring Froot Loops. We haven't had those in a while."

Hannah smiled, glancing at her reflection in the dresser mirror. She'd barely had time to pull on her black panties and bra after her bath before Brigid had called. "Thank you, Brig. But I'm okay. I am officially working on lowering my stress with baths, meditation, and yoga."

"I'll join you for yoga."

Hannah barely held in the laugh. "No, you won't."

"Why not?"

"Do you remember that last time you joined me? You talked the entire time. I thought the instructor was going to kick us out. Either that or ban us for life."

"It was like one conversation."

"A conversation that went for sixty minutes! You talked the entire time about your dislike for Owen."

"And I was right, wasn't I?"

Well…yeah, she was, but that wasn't the point. "Yoga's supposed to be a silent activity where you go inward."

"It's also supposed to be good for the soul, which, hello, so is chatting with friends. I was just combining the two."

She laughed. "I'm doing yoga alone."

"Can I at least bring something to you tomorrow? Cupcakes? Soup?"

"I would love one of Rita's lavender oat lattes in the morning."

"Done. And we can talk all things wedding."

Hannah laughed. No matter how many times she told her friend it was too soon, there was no stopping her. "Okay."

"Oh, and we can invite Henry. And Andi, too."

"That will be nice. I think Andi would really like that. Although no mentioning swimming lessons. Erik keeps telling me he's going to teach me in Andi's pool."

"Han, that's awesome!"

"No, not awesome."

She could almost see her friend frowning. "Why not?"

"Because water and I do not mix."

"Because you can't swim. Lessons will change that."

When had Brigid become the rational one? "Okay, enough sense from you. I'll text you tomorrow. I love you, Brig."

"Great. Love you more, Han."

She hung up and set her phone on the counter. Taking a deep breath, she glanced at her reflection, her gaze roaming over her belly. The bump was small, but already she couldn't stop looking at it.

She slid her fingers over the bare skin. Everything was okay… thank God. Today had scared her. Like, really scared her. She wasn't sure she'd ever felt fear like that in her life.

Footsteps sounded from the hall. Erik entered and stood behind her. Immediately, she leaned back into him, loving how his hands curled around her body, sitting on top of hers.

He lowered his head and kissed her cheek right beside her ear. "How are you feeling?"

"Good. I just had an Epsom salt bath and lit a candle. I feel nice and relaxed."

A small growl reverberated from his chest. "Exactly the way it should be."

She watched their reflections in the mirror, studying their differences. He dwarfed her, and where she had fair skin and hair, Erik was tanned, his hair dark. Opposites in every way.

She lowered her gaze to his hands on her belly, sucking in a breath. "It's crazy that a year ago, my entire focus was work and paying my mortgage, and now I'm engaged and pregnant."

"Things move fast when you find your person."

Her heart softened. He was right, they did. "Your person…I like that."

"You *are* my person. And I'm yours." He kissed down her neck. "Have you thought about taking some time off work?"

She cringed. "I've taken so much time off in the last few months, I'm lucky I still have a job."

"You don't have to work, you know. I can support you."

"Work's not just about the money for me. I like my job and I like to contribute financially."

"That's understandable. But remember, if you need to take a hiatus, I think Reuben would understand."

Of course he would. Reuben was great. "It's okay. Work's not really that stressful. I mean, Charlie and Jake's appointment kind of threw me today, but—"

Erik's head shot up. "Charlie?"

Crap. How had she forgotten that Erik didn't know? "Yeah. He, um, contacted the office and Reuben gave him and Jake an appointment with me to talk about me selling their grandmother's house."

His whole body tensed against her.

She turned and cupped his cheek. "Hey, it's fine. The meeting went smoothly, and Rachel was right outside my office."

"I just have to process that."

Because he wasn't okay with her spending time with Charlie…not a surprise. "I couldn't get out of the meeting today, but I could ask Leo or Taylor to take the property?"

He shook his head. "No. It's okay."

"Are you sure? I don't mind."

"I'm sure."

Hm. She wasn't sure she believed him. She tilted her head. "I never asked…how was your therapy session this morning?"

"It was good. The guy's easy to talk to, and I felt heard and validated."

She couldn't help the little skip of her heartbeat. God, that made her happy. "That's good." Pausing for a second, she nibbled her bottom lip. "Can I ask you a favor?"

One side of his mouth lifted. "Angel, you know that I would sell my right fucking kidney for you."

Yeah, unfortunately, that might be easier than what she wanted. "I really want you and Nico to get along."

The humor slipped from his eyes, a muscle ticking in his cheek.

"I know it's asking a lot," she continued. "The history between you two is complicated and messy."

"Not really. It's actually pretty simple. I tried to kill him because he was part of a human trafficking ring."

Her lips turned down, the hope dying in her chest.

He sighed. "I'm sorry. I shouldn't have—"

"It's okay. It's true. But I believe him when he says he didn't know who they were when he joined, and that he started his business to help the women who were hurt." She grazed her fingers down his chest. "Nico's important to me. And so are you. I need you two to be okay together."

He lowered his forehead to hers, the sigh from his lips brushing over her face. "For you, I'll try."

She cupped his neck. "Thank you. That's all I ask."

When his mouth dropped to hers, all the heaviness in her chest, all the fear of the day and the panic, faded away. Because that was the effect Erik had on her. He was her calm in the storm. Her refuge.

CHAPTER 19

"*R*emember, if you get tired and want to go home to rest—"

"I'll tell you," Hannah finished for Erik, tightening her fingers around his hand as they made their way into Hendrix. "I'm okay, Erik."

He lifted her hand, kissing the back of it, concern glazing his eyes. "I worry about you."

She knew that. Heck, you just had to look at him to know. "But you don't need to. The doctor said all is okay. I've been resting and meditating and feeding my soul with a lot of 'us' time. I feel really good."

It wasn't even a lie to ease Erik's worry. She really did feel good. It was amazing what a few days of intentional rest could do. Not to mention, a few days of no attacks.

She rose to her toes and kissed Erik's cheek before they pushed inside the new gym. The place looked like it had been a warehouse at one time. It was a huge open room with high vaulted ceilings. There was gym equipment on one side and boxing stuff on the other, including bags and a ring.

"This place looks great," Hannah said quietly. "I wouldn't have thought there'd be enough demand in a small town like Redwood." Obviously she was wrong, because the gym was packed.

Erik tugged her forward just as Jake stepped behind the desk. "Hey. Good to see you back."

"Hey, Jake. I believe you've met my fiancée, Hannah."

Her skin tingled at being referred to as Erik's fiancée. Definitely not something she was used to yet.

"And Hannah," Erik continued, "you've met my former teammate, Jake."

Jake's grin widened. "We've met. How are you doing?"

"Good. Sorry we haven't set that date to look at the house yet. I've had a couple of days off."

"You don't need to apologize. We're not in a rush. Are you here to work out too?"

She laughed. "Uh, no. I'm going to work on my laptop while Erik hits the bag, if that's okay?"

"Go for it." He cleared his throat, gaze returning to Erik. "I should warn you, though—Charlie's here."

Even though Erik didn't outwardly react, she felt the shift in him. It was a subtle tightening of his hold on her hand. A small clenching of his jaw.

They both followed Jake's gaze to one of the machines. Charlie paused in his workout, dipping his head toward Erik and Hannah.

She offered a small smile, while Erik just turned back to Jake.

"It's fine," he said quietly.

"Okay. Great." Jake led them over to a bag in the corner of the gym that was near a bench against the wall.

Hannah lowered to the bench as the two men shared a couple more words. She waited for Jake to leave before turning to Erik. "You said you didn't keep in contact with Jake when you left?"

Erik dropped his bag beside her before unzipping it and pulling out gloves. "No. I didn't keep in contact with anyone."

That made her sad. The team was likely close, and not keeping in contact with the teammates who'd survived the mission would have just added to Erik's losses.

"He's a good guy," Erik continued as he pulled on his gloves. "He was always the most levelheaded one on the team."

She looked up, watching as Jake moved around the gym to help others. He paused in front of Charlie, and the two men talked for a moment.

When her phone vibrated, she tugged it out of her pocket.

Brigid: Okay, I just got to your house, but you're not here.

She frowned. Shouldn't her friend be at her shop today?

Hannah: Sorry, we're at the new gym in town, Hendrix.

Brigid: On my way.

Hannah chuckled. Looked like she wouldn't be getting much work done after all.

She was just logging onto her computer when Erik threw the first punch. Her breath caught. She'd seen him box so many times. She should be used to the power behind his hits, but she was starting to think nothing would ever prepare her.

He boxed with such ease but also so much power. Every shuffle of his feet. Every hook and jab at the bag…it was like he exerted little to no effort, while his impact was huge.

She forced her gaze down to her laptop screen.

Concentrate, Hannah. You have emails to respond to and contracts to write.

For a while, she did some work. But then the door to the gym opened and Brigid stepped in. Jake walked over to greet her.

Hannah grinned when her friend's cheeks reddened. She didn't blame her. Jake was tall and muscular, with perfect white teeth and blond hair that fell into his eyes.

He was definitely cute.

As Brigid crossed the room, she cast a quick glance over her shoulder at Jake before lowering beside Hannah.

Her voice was low. "Oh my God…that guy is *hot*."

Hannah bumped her shoulder. "He looked quite transfixed with you too."

"He didn't." She dragged her gaze from Jake to Hannah. "Did he?"

"He did. He didn't take his eyes off you as you walked over here."

That red in her cheeks darkened, then she shook her head. "It's too early for me to date someone else. I need to learn to be on my own for a while."

"Is that how you feel, or how you *think* you should feel?"

Brigid lifted a shoulder. "A bit of both. I was with James for years. Besides…I think a part of me is a bit scared to move on in case…"

Hannah frowned. "In case what?"

"I fall in love again and the guy turns out to be a drug-addicted psychopath."

Hannah slipped her fingers through her friend's. "Brigid… James turned out to be the worst kind of guy. And I'm so sorry for that. But don't let that scare you off from finding your person."

Brigid nibbled her bottom lip. "Maybe. You and Erik give me hope."

"Good." She kissed the side of Brigid's head.

"I grabbed these from Black Bean for us to share. Now we get food and a show—your show being Erik, mine being Jake."

Hannah looked at the box in Brigid's hands. She lifted the lid and immediately salivated at the array of cookies. "Oh my gosh, they look amazing."

"I got a bit of everything," Brigid said, shuffling through the box. "Peanut butter, chocolate chip, snickerdoodle. Even some of your favorite sugar cookies."

"Oh my Lord…I love you. Have I told you that today? I do."

"You can tell me again." She handed Hannah a sugar cookie,

and Hannah bit into it just as the gym door opened and Nico walked in.

* * *

ERIK SAW him the second he stepped into the gym. Every fucking muscle in his body tensed, his fist stopping mid-strike.

Nico was dressed in shorts and a T-shirt, with a workout bag slung over his shoulder. His gaze narrowed when it hit Erik but then eased when it trailed behind him to Hannah.

It was probably irrational, but fuck, he hated the guy even looking at her.

Hannah rose, and Nico crossed the room and pulled her into a hug. Erik went back to hitting the bag, but this time with more force. Every punch, every jab sent the bag trembling.

Nico moved to stand beside him. "Hey."

"Wasn't expecting to see you here." Erik didn't stop hitting the bag.

Nico lifted a shoulder. "It's the only gym in town."

True. So he probably *should* have expected Nico, and hell, even Charlie. Maybe Moreno would show up next and they could have a fucking party.

"Wanna go a round in the ring?"

Erik's fists paused, his gaze shooting to Nico at his words. "You wanna fight me?"

"Why not?"

He could think of a shit load of reasons why not. "No."

Nico raised a brow. "Scared I'll beat you?"

"I was a professional boxer, and before that, I was a Marine."

"I can hold my own." He tugged off his shirt, and the first thing Erik saw was the scar on Nico's chest. The bullet wound... the bullet Erik had fired.

Nico strapped on his gloves. "But if you're afraid of losing to me..."

143

Fuck off. "If we step in there and I hurt you—"

"That's on me."

Nico moved to the ring first, climbing through the ropes before turning and looking at Erik with a challenge in his eyes.

A muscle in Erik's jaw clenched, but he stepped forward.

"Erik." He turned to see Hannah rushing to her feet. "What are you doing?"

Before he could answer, Nico did. "I asked your fiancé for a round in the ring."

She shook her head. "No. Absolutely not."

"Cloud, you worry too much."

"Nico—"

"It'll be fine, Han," Nico added. "We're not gonna hurt each other." Nico's gaze switched to Erik. "We've both wanted to take a few swings at each other since the day I got into town. Right?"

Hannah stepped closer to Erik. "You're really going to fight him?"

"I won't do any damage." He lowered his mouth and kissed her. "I promise."

She didn't look happy, but she also didn't stop him as he climbed through the ropes.

Nico raised his fists. "Ready?"

"Always." Erik moved his feet, shuffling around Nico.

"I'd like to say you've grown on me since I got to town, but you really haven't," Nico said, voice low so his words only reached Erik.

"You want me to shed a tear?"

Nico threw a punch, but Erik slipped to the side, easily avoiding contact.

"No. I want you to be what my sister needs you to be," Nico said. "She's been through a lot of shit in her life, and she needs a man who's going to protect her...not just physically." He threw another cross punch, and again Erik swung to the side.

"I plan to protect her every day of her life."

"Yeah?" Nico jabbed, and Erik blocked it. "I know about your past. I know about the people you've lost."

Erik continued to dance, not letting Nico's words distract him. "Is there a point to you telling me this?"

"That's a lot of baggage."

"You're right. It is."

"I can see you're trying to do better. But what happens when there's a dark day? When your past sneaks up on you, convincing you that love makes you too vulnerable? What happens when your sanity is put at risk?"

The old Erik would have been scared by Nico's words. Hell, the old Erik would have folded and agreed that there was every chance of that happening. But he wasn't the old Erik anymore.

"I'll make sure I'm okay so that her and our child are okay."

Erik threw his first cross punch. Nico dodged, and Erik followed it up with a jab, catching him in the ribs. There was no way the hit didn't hurt, but Nico barely reacted, just lifted his fists and shuffled back.

"You kill people for a living," Nico growled.

"I put in my notice."

Nico raised a brow, directing another punch Erik's way. "No shit?"

Erik blocked the hit and returned the blow, catching Nico in the side a second time. "I'm gonna be there for her and our baby. I'm gonna be everything they need me to be. And I'm getting the help I need so that I don't let the darkness of my past beat down on us."

"I want to believe you."

"I don't really give a shit if you do or not. Hannah loves you. It's the only reason I tolerate you."

"Similarly, I don't really care what you think of me."

Erik threw two cross punches and a jab. Nico blocked each one before jabbing Erik in the gut.

"What about you?" Erik asked. "You got any enemies outside the trafficking ring who could hurt her?"

"Not one."

Erik threw a cross punch and Nico blocked.

Movement from the side took Erik's attention. Charlie was watching them, moving toward the ring. Erik was only distracted for a second, but that was all Nico needed.

The punch caught Erik in the face.

There was a gasp, and a second later, Hannah was beside the ring. "Nico! You said no one would get hurt!"

"I'm fine." Erik straightened, barely feeling the sting.

There was still a hard look on Nico's face, and something told Erik they wouldn't be friends anytime soon.

CHAPTER 20

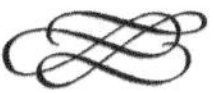

"Come in the water, Angel."

Hannah shook her head. She sat on the edge of the heated pool, her feet dangling over the side while Erik treaded water, hands on her thighs. It was Andi's lap pool, and most of it was so deep she couldn't touch the bottom.

The right side of his mouth lifted. "Why not?"

"I'm unteachable?"

"No one's unteachable."

"*I* am! I'm twenty-four and can't even tread water." Not only that, but after her near-drowning experiences in the last few months, she was pretty sure her fear of water was at an all-time high, which was not good for her stress.

His hands skirted up her bare thighs, gliding over her insulin pump to her hips. "You know I wouldn't let anything happen to you."

"Fear isn't rational."

He inched her forward. "Trust me to keep you safe."

She ran her finger over a muscle in his forearm. Erik had been urging her for a while to let him teach her how to swim, and she'd finally given in and agreed. Although, in this moment, she was kind of regretting that decision.

But then the other part of her, the stronger part, knew she'd gone through and survived so much worse. She could do this.

Come on, Hannah, you've got this.

With a straightened spine, she took a deep breath and slid into the pool. The warm water cascaded over her body as Erik's hands curved around her waist, keeping her above the surface.

"How are you feeling?" he asked gently.

Her breaths tried to shorten, but she focused on the feel of Erik's skin under her fingers. On the way he held her, so strong and firm.

The last time she'd been in this pool was when Owen had shoved her in at Andi's party, and she'd almost drowned. Erik had jumped in to save her. If he'd been a few minutes later…

"Scared." The single, honest word slipped from between her lips.

His mouth touched her ear. "You're safe."

"Safe," she repeated, trying to convince herself.

It was strange…a part of her knew she was safe in Erik's arms. Knew that there was nowhere she was safer, and he would never let harm come to her. But another part of her, the part that was beyond reasoning with, never felt safe in a deep body of water.

She expected Erik to get straight into the lesson. To maybe put some distance between them and get her to kick her legs. Was that what they did in swimming lessons? She had no idea.

He did neither of those things. Instead, he held her against his body as he moved around the pool, sometimes treading water, sometimes walking in the shallow end.

When a kiss touched her shoulder, she shuddered. Then he kissed her again, this time higher, just below her ear.

She tilted her head, giving him better access. His kisses continued, each one causing a wave of awareness to tingle over her skin.

"Erik…" His name came out as a needy whisper.

"Mm?"

"I don't think this is what Andi had in mind when we asked to use her pool."

He found a sensitive spot on her neck and began to nibble. "What my sister doesn't know won't hurt her."

She shuddered, bit by bit, her tense muscles relaxing.

She thought he might trail his mouth up to hers, but he didn't. He just kept kissing and nibbling, working his way across her flesh. Her body relaxed further, until she almost forgot she was in the water.

"Ready?" he finally asked, his voice deep and rumbly.

"Hm, I'm ready for something."

He chuckled, and that sound moved deep into her belly.

His mouth left her skin, and she wanted to groan. Or maybe she actually did, because he laughed again. "Okay, I'm going to hold you up with my hands beneath your stomach while you stretch out."

The heat left her body. "Are you sure?"

"Safe…remember?"

She nodded, her stomach twisting as she reluctantly untangled her legs from his waist. His hands went to her belly and, slowly, she straightened her limbs so she was floating.

Her heart immediately sped up, but she repeated Erik's words in her head.

Safe.

"There you go." His words were soft and gentle. Coaxing. They continued that way for a couple of laps before he paused. "Now I'm going to walk through the water, taking you with me. As I do, kick your legs."

She followed his instructions. At first, the movement made her body feel unstable, speeding up her heart once again and igniting a new wave of fear. With each kick of her legs, her fear lessened, and the action required less effort and conscious thought.

"Good," Erik eventually said after they'd done a few laps. "Now, we're just going to doggy paddle today, so I want you to paddle your arms."

Again, her heart thumped, but she worked to keep the fear at bay. "You're going to keep a hold of me while we're in the deep end, though, right?"

"I won't let you go, Angel. I promise."

She nodded before taking a breath and paddling her arms. It took a few lengths of the pool to feel comfortable, but eventually it became easier, almost like muscle memory.

They did that for a while, until Erik stopped them in the shallow end.

She grinned at him as she set her feet on the bottom of the pool. "I think I'm getting the hang of this!"

"You're doing amazing. Want to try it on your own?"

Some of her confidence slipped.

"You can start in the shallow end," he said, "and swim to me on the other side of the pool. I'll be right there to grab you if you need me. It won't take me long at all."

She nodded, even though what she really wanted to say was a loud *hell no*. But at the same time, she was damn sick of being so vulnerable around water and so ready to conquer this.

She watched Erik move away from her. He didn't go all the way to the end of the pool, instead treading water in the middle.

Okay, now it was up to her.

With a steadying breath, she shoved down her fear and pushed off the edge of the pool. She started kicking, then paddling her arms as she moved. It wasn't easy to keep her head above water, but her head didn't go under.

Holy heck…she was doing it! She was actually swimming! Doggy paddle, but still.

Too soon, the fact she couldn't touch the bottom began to

play on her mind. Taunt her. Tingling in her belly, slowing her kicks and making her paddling clumsy.

Memories of the night Marco threw her into the river came back to her. The way the water had pulled her under, slipping over her head and filling her lungs. The helplessness…

She tried to remind herself that she was fine. That she had a safety net in Erik. But her movements had become rigid.

Suddenly, she was sinking below the surface, first her feet, then her waist. But before her head could dip under, strong fingers wrapped around her arms and tugged her up.

Erik pulled her straight into his arms, his eyes boring into hers. "Are you okay?"

"I started to panic," she said, breathless. "I remembered Marco throwing me into the water and it just messed with my head. I couldn't concentrate."

"It's okay. Sometimes our head convinces us we can't when we really can. Luckily, the mind can be convinced. It just might take a few more practices." His lips curved into a smile. "You swam half the length of a pool by yourself. I'm so damn proud."

"Really?"

"Yeah. You did amazing for a first lesson."

The disappointment shifted into something else. Something better. Lighter. "I did, didn't I?"

"It was damn sexy."

She got no warning. One minute he was looking at her like she was the center of his world, and the next his lips were crashing onto hers.

She gasped, and the second her lips parted, his tongue slipped inside her mouth, tasting her. She groaned, her legs wrapping around his waist and tugging him closer. The hard edge of the pool suddenly pressed to her back.

Erik was everywhere. Against her chest. Her core. His fingers tangled in her hair.

His hand lowered to her chest and slipped into her bikini top.

When his thumb found her nipple and grazed back and forth, she groaned, her skin burning at the touch.

Almost of their own volition, her hips began to grind against him, and his cock hardened against her core.

Her skin tingled when he pulled his hand out of her top and smoothed it down her belly. He slipped it inside her bottoms and swiped her clit.

Her entire body shook so violently, the only thing that kept her in one place was Erik's arm around her.

He continued to stroke and play until his finger moved to her entrance. This time, her breath stopped altogether as he pushed inside. She whimpered, her fingers digging into his shoulders, threatening to break skin.

His mouth tugged from hers and lowered to her breast. When his lips wrapped around her bare pebbled nipple and sucked, her entire body burned. The throbbing was so strong and deep, she was sure she'd fall over the edge any second.

He began to pump his finger faster, his thumb moving in circular motions over her clit. She was barely hanging on when his teeth grazed her nipple, then he sucked.

That's when she broke. Shattered into a million pieces. She opened her mouth to scream, but his head rose and he caught her mouth with his own, swallowing the sound.

Pleasure rippled through her, groans and cries pouring from her chest as Erik's finger continued to move, making sure she felt every last lick of pleasure.

She reached for his waistband, but he caught her wrist, his mouth separating from hers. "That was just for you, Angel."

She opened her mouth to protest, but an engine sounded from the driveway. She gasped and tried to pull away, but Erik didn't let her go. Instead, he straightened her bottoms like he had all the time in the world.

In fact, she barely had time to pull herself together before not only Andi but Henry and Brigid were beside the pool.

Hannah frowned, her breaths barely even. "What are you all doing here?"

Brigid held up a takeout bag. "Andi told us you were here, so—"

"Wedding planning!" Andi finished.

* * *

ERIK HEADED down the hall of Andi's house to the office. After he and Hannah had showered and changed, they'd gone to the living room to find a shit ton of wedding magazines and Chinese takeout on the coffee table. That's when he'd received a call from Chandler.

He waited until the door was closed to answer the call. "Chandler?"

"I have a lead on Moreno."

Erik straightened. "Tell me."

"I found CCTV footage of him in a hotel bar in Leavenworth. I tried to follow him by hacking street cams but lost him when he got to the edge of the city."

Erik cursed.

"But...I managed to identify the guy he met at the bar. A Lowie Chang. He runs a gang out of Seattle."

"What the fuck is Moreno doing with a gang leader?"

"Likely more hired muscle."

He was a dead man. "Can we get a location for the guy?"

"I've got one. But Erik...Chang's dangerous."

The muscles in his forearms bunched. "No, *I'm* dangerous. Especially if this guy is helping Moreno get to my woman."

"Fine. I'll give you his location on one condition."

"What?"

"When you go, you take Rachel with you."

"You know I can't do that. If I'm gone, I need Rachel to watch Hannah."

"Isn't Nico there?"

Erik barely held in the growl. "*No.*"

"Fine. What about Nate? You said your brother was coming home for a few days, right?"

He was. Plus he was a SEAL, capable of protecting her, and more than that, Erik trusted him to protect her. "Fine. If Nate can stay with Hannah, I'll take Rachel."

"Cool. I'll send through the details of his location."

"Thanks." He ran his fingers through his hair. "I've said this a few times, but thank you for helping us on all this. I know technically it's outside of your job description."

Chandler laughed. "There's no technically about it, Hunter. This has nothing to do with our government work. But you should know, *most* of what I do for you has nothing to do with the job. I help because you're a friend. And even when you get out, I'll still help, because you sure as hell better believe that you're staying in my life."

"I'm so fucking grateful for you, man."

"Well...that's just because I haven't told you who helped me get this information."

Erik's fingers tightened on the phone, already knowing. "Nico."

"Yep."

"Helped how?"

"He and I have been connecting daily about our search efforts. He actually found Moreno, and I identified the guy he was with."

"Well, I'm glad he's proving useful and didn't just chase down the lead on his own."

"You're right, he *has* proven useful."

Erik frowned. "You almost sound like you like the guy."

"Like? Nah, I don't know him. But he's good at what he does. Or at least, his company is. He doesn't seem like a bad guy, though."

Fan-fucking-tastic. Everyone liked Nico but Erik. "I've gotta go."

"Come on, Hunter, you have to admit his backstory checks out, and he hasn't done anything wrong since arriving in town."

Yet...he hadn't done anything wrong *yet*. "You're right, he's been *so* great," he replied sarcastically.

Chandler sighed. "Okay, I'm gonna go. But just remember, he's your fiancée's brother. Soon, he'll be family."

"Don't worry, I am all too fucking aware of that. Thanks again, Chandler."

He hung up and took a moment to calm the hell down before moving out of the office. He heard Hannah's laugh before reaching the living room. Damn, the sound was beautiful. A soft, lyrical note that floated through the air and hit him square in the chest.

"I just want a simple dress and a simple wedding," Hannah insisted.

"Simple?" Brigid argued. "Han, you only get married once. Be extravagant! Get all the flowers. Wear all the ruffles."

"Honestly," Hannah said. "I don't need any of that. I'm marrying the man I love. I only need him."

Something warmed in Erik's chest.

"Yeah, you lucked out with her."

Erik turned at the sound of Andi's voice from behind him. Fuck, how had the woman snuck up on him? "What are you doing lurking in the hall?"

"Went to the bathroom. Came back to find you eavesdropping on their conversation like a creep." Andi stepped closer. "She lucked out too, Erik. She's so lucky to have you. You've both truly found your person."

"Thanks, A."

Andi opened her mouth just as her phone beeped. They both looked at the screen to see it was her home security alarm—notifying her the perimeter alarm had been breached.

CHAPTER 21

$\mathcal{E}$rik moved into the living room. Hannah, Brigid, and Henry were fine—still talking, with no idea the alarm had been set off. It was only when Hannah's gaze collided with his that she paused in her conversation.

"Erik…what is it?" she asked.

"An alarm in the driveway was activated."

All three of them straightened, while Andi touched his arm. "It could have been a wild animal."

She was right…it could have. But he wasn't taking the risk. He pulled out his phone and texted Rachel. She wasn't far from Andi's place and wouldn't take long to get there.

Then, quickly and systematically, he moved around the first level, pulling all the blinds closed and checking that all entry points were locked. When he returned to the living room, he pulled his Glock from his holster.

Hannah rose from the sofa. "Erik, we should call the police. If it's Moreno, he could have lots of guys out there."

"I need you guys to do that while I check the perimeter. It doesn't take much to throw a brick through a window and gain access." He met his sister's gaze. "Go into the bedroom. Lock the door. If anyone but me tries to get in, go into the *bathroom* and lock the door."

She nodded quickly.

Instead of going to the front door, Erik headed toward the office and was about to open the window when quick footsteps sounded behind him.

Hannah grabbed his arm. "Erik—I don't want you to go out there by yourself."

He turned, hating the worry that glazed her eyes. The way she clenched his arm a bit too tightly.

Gently, he cupped her cheek. "I'll be okay, Angel. I know how to look after myself."

"How do you know you'll be okay? There could be ten men out there."

"Then I'll take them out, one by one." When her frown deepened, his hand slipped to the back of her neck and he lowered his forehead to hers. "I can do this. Trust me to keep you and the others safe."

"And you. You have to keep *you* safe too."

"I will. I promise." He had no fucking business promising her that. But right now, he'd promise the woman the damn moon if it smoothed the worry line between her brows. She didn't need any more stress.

He kissed her, his lips lingering a moment longer than they should have, but damn it was hard to leave her.

"Lock the window after me, then go to the bedroom," he whispered when they separated.

The second she nodded, he turned and opened the window. His feet were silent as they hit the ground, the only noise around him the whistle of wind in the trees.

The sun was almost fully set, the property around Andi's house cloaked in darkness.

It was fine. He liked the dark. In fact, he preferred it. It felt like an advantage for him.

When the quiet click of the window lock sounded, he pulled out his Glock again and remained close to the house as he moved around the exterior. He studied the tree line, trying to locate anything out of place. Anything that didn't fit.

When he saw nothing, he lowered his body and crept to the trees bordering the driveway. It was quiet. Too quiet?

Maybe Andi was right. Maybe it had been an animal that had activated the alarm. But he didn't stop. He slipped through the trees, his gaze continually shifting around the area. He was just pausing behind a tree when something caught his attention in the distance. It was a small flicker of movement. A shadow slipping through the night…a person.

They saw him at the exact moment he saw them.

Erik shot forward, his feet slamming into the dirt as he gave chase. The person took off.

Fuck, the asshole was quick.

He forced his body to move faster, pumping his arms. Jumping over tree roots. No matter how hard he pushed himself, he never gained on the runner. Not a fucking inch.

When the guy reached the road, he turned left. For a split second, Erik lost sight of him. But he heard a car door slam shut in the distance. The sound of an engine.

He'd just reached the road when the car sped away.

Goddammit! He'd lost him. Not only that, but the guy hadn't turned on his lights, and it was too dark to see the plate numbers.

His hands fisted, every part of him wanting to hit something. To ram his fist into a tree and let the pain dull the frustration.

He turned and jogged back toward the house, keeping his Glock firmly in his grasp in case he met more enemies. He didn't think he would. He'd seen and heard no one else and the asshole who'd run certainly hadn't waited for anyone.

He was halfway back when something sounded behind him. It was subtle—a foot touching the earth. Most would have missed it. He didn't.

Quietly, he slipped behind a tree and remained completely still as he listened. Whoever it was, they were good. So good, most wouldn't have heard the minute sounds of them growing closer.

He waited three more heartbeats before turning, Glock raised.

Rachel stood in front of him, her own pistol up.

He lowered his weapon. "You're here."

"Of course I'm here. You texted that you needed backup." She holstered her pistol. "I parked on the street so they wouldn't see me coming. You find anything?"

"Did you park to the left or right?"

She tilted her head toward the street. "Right. Why?"

Damn. "I chased an asshole down the drive, but he turned left. I didn't get his plates."

"Moreno?"

"No. This guy was too fast. Maybe someone he hired. But I have no fucking idea why he'd just send one." He didn't understand a lot of what Moreno was doing.

"Who's in the house?"

"Andi, Hannah, Brigid, and Henry."

"Is it possible the guy trailed one of her friends, hoping they'd lead him to Hannah?"

"Anything's possible."

Rachel scanned the area. "When he got here, he probably figured there was less security than at your house and considered this a good place to attack."

"Maybe. Or maybe he was waiting for backup."

Anger washed over Rachel's face. "Your sister can stay with me tonight if she needs to."

He ran his fingers through his hair. His sister was damn stubborn, but hopefully she'd listen to him and stay with one of them, for tonight at least.

"Thanks. Let's do a perimeter check before we go back

inside."

* * *

HANNAH FIDDLED WITH HER BRACELET, her fingertips moving over the small angel charm.

Where was he? Why was he taking so long? Had he found an enemy out there? God, she hated that he was alone. Yes, he was confident, and for good reason. He was well trained. But good training didn't even the numbers if he was faced with an army of enemies who were similarly trained.

"Hey."

Hannah blinked and looked at Brigid. The four of them sat on Andi's bed, door locked and curtains pulled shut.

"He's going to be fine," Brigid said softly.

"You don't know that. It's dark, and there are so many unknowns."

Andi touched her thigh. "If there was ever a person you didn't need to worry about looking after himself, it's Erik. I swear it's like he was born with this innate ability to protect himself and others. I think he was training in my mother's womb."

Hannah gave a small smile. "I know how good he is. I should trust that he'll be okay, but it's hard."

"Because you love him," Henry said simply. "When we love people, we worry, regardless of whether it's warranted."

So true.

Her watch vibrated and she looked down, cringing when she saw her Dexcom was warning her about going low. She hadn't yet eaten any of the food in the living room after her swim because, well, she hadn't exactly been expecting this to happen.

Andi peeked over her shoulder, glancing at her watch. "I have something that might help."

She rose from the bed and moved to the dresser drawers.

After opening the second one, she dug to the bottom of her socks and pulled out a bag of sour worms. Hannah grinned.

"Oh my gosh," Brigid gasped. "You are my soul sister, keeping candy in your bedside drawer."

Andi lifted a shoulder. "I've always had a sour worm addiction, and growing up, if I didn't hide them, my brothers would eat them all. It's a habit that's stuck with me into adulthood."

"Erik actually took a bag from your stash the night of your thirtieth birthday party," Hannah said, cringing. "I meant to replace them but forgot, sorry."

"That's okay. He bought me a bag of them after that night. The sneaky bastard never told me he knew where I stashed them." She opened the bag and set them in the middle of the bed.

Brigid scoffed. "If my brother had known about sour worms in my drawer growing up, he'd have stolen them every single time."

Hannah chuckled. Brigid and her brother weren't close, and that was just one of the reasons.

"Erik's very strategic," Andi said. "He'll never give up knowledge if he doesn't have to."

Oh, yeah, that sounded like Erik. Particularly when she'd first started dating him. She glanced over to Henry. "How's Leo?"

"The man is a dreamboat." Henry took a sour worm. "I'm trying to go slow after the shit with Owen, and Leo's been nothing but understanding."

Hannah swallowed the lump in her throat. "I'm sorry about—"

"Don't." Henry held up a hand. "Hannah, I've told you, nothing that happened with Owen is your fault."

"It is though. He targeted you because you're friends with me, as a way to get close to me."

Henry reached out and touched her thigh. "And I gave him an in way too easily. I fell for his act quickly, and that gave him access to you."

She put her hand over his and squeezed. "I'm glad you haven't let that affect your trust in men."

"Leo makes it easy." He bumped Brigid's shoulder. "Meanwhile, this one's been fantasizing about a certain former Marine."

Brigid gasped. "Henry! I told you that in confidence."

He rolled his eyes. "You know you would have shared it with everyone eventually."

"I am *not* fantasizing about Jake," Brigid pushed. "Just considering joining a gym for the first time in my life."

Andi grinned. "He is a bit of a hottie."

"Even if something did happen," Brigid continued, "which I'm not saying it will, I'm not rushing into anything."

Henry slipped an arm around her shoulders. "You take all the time you need."

Brigid leaned into him. "Thanks." She turned to Andi. "What about you? Any great loves in your life?"

She scoffed. "Nope. My life is work, work and, oh, you know, the occasional work in between."

"Where's the fun in that?" Henry asked.

"I get to help people, so I take solace in that."

Hannah bumped her shoulder. "And you're very good at what you do."

"Thank you."

Noises sounded from the hall. Footsteps.

Hannah tensed, her heart jumping in her chest. Was it Erik? Or was it someone else? The others heard it too, because everyone's eyes rose to the door.

Henry stood just as Hannah's phone vibrated. She looked down to see the text.

Erik: It's me. I'm in the hall.

The air rushed from her chest. "It's Erik."

She climbed off the bed and moved to the bedroom door, then unlocked it and pulled it open. She stepped into the hall just as Erik reached the room, Rachel behind him.

Relief skirted through Hannah's belly. But also something else. Something she hated. A familiar jealousy. That Rachel could be something to Erik that *she* couldn't. An ally. A teammate.

It was stupid, especially considering the situation. She should be glad Erik had someone watching his back and helping him.

Erik cupped her cheek. "Are you okay?"

She nodded. "Did you find anyone?"

"Yes. One person. They ran and got away."

One person…not an army of them. Thank God. "But you're safe."

"I'm safe."

CHAPTER 22

*H*annah watched Erik as he pulled on his black sweater, nerves swimming in her belly. Tonight, he and Rachel were going to Leavenworth to find a man by the name of Lowie Chang. A dangerous man. A gang leader.

Every part of her rebelled against the idea. She wished he had more people on his side. Two seemed like such a small number. Hell, it *was* a small number, especially when Chang had God knew how many people.

Erik slotted his weapon into his holster, then looked at her, concern flickering in his hazel eyes. "Angel, I wish you'd stop looking at me like that."

"Like what?"

"Like you're not going to see me again."

God, even putting that into the air hurt. "Chang's dangerous. You told me that yourself. He'll be well protected."

Erik walked toward her. Slow, predatory steps. "*I'm* dangerous, Angel. And so is Rachel. We're also smart. We're going to get him alone and get any information he has on Moreno."

"How are you going to get a man like him alone?"

He lowered his head and hovered his mouth over her ear.

164

"Just trust that we have this handled." He kissed down her neck. "And give my brother hell tonight."

Despite everything, she laughed. "I'm actually really looking forward to it. I haven't spent nearly enough time with him. I'm going to ask him *all* the questions."

Erik groaned as his phone beeped. "He's here."

He slipped his fingers through hers and led her downstairs. The knock came on the door moments before Erik pulled it open. Nate stood on the porch, with Rachel beside him.

Hannah's jaw dropped.

Rachel wore a short, skintight red dress. Her breasts pushed against the thin material, and there was a slit down one side. It went so high it almost reached her hip. Not only that, but her makeup was perfect, her hair down and curled.

Gorgeous. The woman looked *gorgeous*…and Hannah couldn't help but feel just a bit self-conscious about her yoga pants and baggy sweater.

What exactly was the damn plan tonight?

"Hey. Ready to go?" Rachel asked, voice all business and eyes on Erik.

"Yep." He turned toward Hannah, lowering his mouth to hers. "Stay inside. Stay safe."

"*You* stay safe." She rose to her toes and kissed him. She wanted to pause everything and remain in the kiss for endless minutes. To extend the time she got with him. But too soon, he was lifting his head, his lips leaving hers.

His gaze flashed to Nate. "Look after her."

"With my life."

Erik held his brother's gaze for a beat before moving out of the house. Hannah watched the two of them walk to Erik's Corvette, which he'd parked in front of the house. Before sliding behind the wheel, he met her gaze and winked, then disappeared inside the car.

She nibbled her bottom lip, a million emotions running

through her. Concern for his safety. Anxiety that something would go wrong. And something else. Something hard and uncomfortable that came alive inside her every time Rachel could be his protector and partner and she couldn't.

"Are you okay?"

Her gaze finally pulled from the drive to Nate. "Of course."

He studied her for a moment before lifting a bag she'd missed until now. "Ready to make burgers?"

"*Make* burgers? I thought we were ordering in?"

He laughed, closing and locking the door, then alarming the house. "Hannah, it's my first dinner with my future sister-in-law. I plan to wine and dine you, but without the wine, of course."

Her lips tugged up at the corners as she followed Nate into the kitchen. "You don't need to do that."

"Oh, but I do." He set the bag on the counter and started pulling out ingredients.

Hannah peeked over his shoulder, spotting the ground beef and a dozen other things. "You don't need to impress me."

"My hamburgers are the best you'll come across. Wait until you taste my burger sauce. It's a secret recipe that tastes just like Big Mac sauce but better. Trust me, by the end of tonight, you'll be wondering if you chose the wrong brother."

She laughed. "I'm intrigued. Although, you should know, the Big Mac sauce recipe has been shared around on social media for a long time."

"Yeah, but mine is different. Better. More authentic, with a sweet tang to it."

She bit her bottom lip, grateful that Nate was able to put her at ease so quickly.

Her pump beeped at her, letting her know it was time for a change. "Sorry, I just need to change my pump, then I'll help make everything."

"No, you won't. I've got this. *You're* making my first niece or nephew. You get to rest."

She could really get used to this treatment.

Hannah grabbed her PDM from the kitchen counter and deactivated her pump before pulling her old one off her stomach.

Nate glanced at her. "How often do you have to do that?"

"The pump lasts ten days. The monitor only three. It sounds like a lot but trust me, it's better than pricking my finger and injecting a million times a day."

She grabbed a new Omnipod, then some insulin from the fridge. Using the pen, she put a hundred and thirty units of insulin into the pod and waited for the pump to beep to tell her it was ready.

"So you prefer having the pump and monitor?"

She glanced up at Nate. "It's life-changing. I have a lot fewer highs and lows. Don't get me wrong, there are still annoying things about them, especially the pump. It's bulky, and I have to remember my PDM when I go places. But I'm really fortunate to have access to them. *Everyone* should have access to these medical tools."

"And they don't because of cost?"

She held the PDM against the pod so that it could prime the device by circulating the insulin. "Yeah. Insurance doesn't always cover it. Some people take out two sets of insurance to pay for the equipment, which is not an option for a lot of diabetics. Some people don't have any insurance at all, and they go without. It's awful."

She was so incredibly aware of how lucky she was, but she wished everyone was as lucky as her.

She pulled the stickers off the back of the pod and pressed the pump to her left thigh, keeping it on the same side of her body as the monitor.

Then, lifting the PDM, she hit start. Scrunching her eyes, she waited for the five clicks before the pump pierced her body. She flinched.

"I'm sorry it's not easier," Nate said quietly.

Her eyes opened to see real compassion in his gaze. "Thanks. Me too. And I'm sorry you have to babysit me tonight."

He laughed. "Trust me, eating burgers with my gorgeous soon-to-be sister-in-law is no hardship."

God, it was easy to like this man.

Her gaze shifted to the window, her mind returning to Erik and what he was doing tonight.

"He'll be okay." Her attention shifted at Nate's words. He was watching her closely as he chopped an onion. "Erik's smart, and he knows how to protect himself."

"I know. But these are dangerous people."

"Both he and Rachel have come up against deadlier opponents, and they've won…every time."

She nibbled her bottom lip, nodding. "Rachel looked beautiful…" Oh God, why had she let those words slip out? They were like word vomit. She wanted to dig her head into the ground in embarrassment.

Nate paused. "She's playing a role tonight. They're both professionals, and all she and Erik will be thinking about is the target. And more than that, the only person *Erik* ever thinks about in that way is you."

She knew that. Or at least, she should. She'd never been an insecure person, but Rachel was just so many things that Hannah wasn't. "How do you know that?"

"People only need to look at the two of you together to know that. You own that man."

Some of the tightness in her muscles eased. "I'm not usually a jealous person. It must be the pregnancy hormones."

One corner of his mouth lifted. "Nothing my amazing burgers can't fix."

She laughed.

He was just turning back to the onions when his phone vibrated. He frowned, any humor leaving his face. "Erik gave me access to his security system. Someone just pulled up." He fiddled with his phone. "I don't recognize the car."

He moved toward her and slipped his fingers around her upper arm, gently tugging her to her feet. "Stay close."

When he pulled a gun from a concealed holster, her breath caught in her throat. Suddenly, he looked every bit the SEAL she knew he was.

Her heart started to pound, fear trickling through her veins.

Nate reached the door and looked out the peephole—and his muscles visibly relaxed. "Goddammit."

She frowned. "What?"

He tugged it open. Andi climbed the steps, a dish in hand. "Hello, my family!"

"Andi, what the hell are you doing here and whose car are you driving?" Nate growled. "This is a protective detail."

She rolled her eyes. "I'm not going to let my new sister-in-law be subjected to just *you* all night. My car's at the mechanic and he lent me this one. I'm armed with brownies and quick humor. Plus, I heard you're making burgers."

Hannah laughed. Now she really wanted to try these burgers.

When Nate still didn't look happy, Hannah lifted a shoulder. "I mean, *I'm* always ready for brownies."

"See?" Andi patted Nate's shoulder as she stepped past him. "I'm a welcome visitor."

Nate scowled as he closed the door, but there was a hint of a smile on his face.

* * *

THE HOTEL BAR WAS BUSY. The sound of talking and music and glasses clinking echoed around Erik. He ignored all of it, focusing on one man—Chang. The gang leader sat at the bar with another man. To onlookers, it would seem they were alone. But Erik knew better.

"Target's sitting on a stool in the center of the bar, wearing a suit jacket," Erik said quietly through his earpiece to Rachel and Chandler. "He's talking to another man, probably a guard, but also has two more guards at each exit and three at the table behind him."

Erik only knew that because of the way the men held themselves. And their gazes also regularly returned to Chang.

That, and the concealed weapons Erik could just make out.

"He's got five men outside," Chandler said quietly, watching CCTV footage from his end.

"That's fewer than I thought," Rachel replied, a hint of humor in her voice. "This will be a piece of cake. I'm making my way over to him now."

Erik suppressed the smirk as he lifted his beer to his lips and barely sipped it. "Cocky as usual, Rach."

"Confident," she corrected.

He didn't have to wait long. Rachel moved through the bar with ease, people stepping aside to let her through. Other men didn't even try to hide the way they stared at her ass and breasts.

Scumbags.

Rachel squeezed in beside Chang, immediately leaning over the bar so her breasts almost tumbled out of the dress.

"Laying it on a little thick, aren't you, Rach?" Erik asked, beer glass still at his mouth.

Chang glanced toward her, his gaze immediately zeroing in on the full cleavage. Fuck, was the guy gonna start drooling? Maybe this would be easier than he'd thought. Erik almost felt sorry for him…almost.

"Hi. I'm Lowie," Chang said, eyes barely rising to meet hers. "Can I buy you a drink?"

Rachel turned to look at him, her gaze roaming over his face, then his chest. It was a slow inspection, like she was weighing up whether he met her standard. "Sure."

He straightened, a hint of a smirk on his face, like he'd just won something. "What will you have?"

"Chili Martini."

Chang's brows rose, but he didn't say anything, instead turning and flagging down a bartender. Once the drink was ordered, he looked back to Rachel. "So…do I get a name?"

"Tammie."

"Tammie. Been here before?"

"No, I'm from out of town. I don't know many people here." The drink was set in front of her, and she took a sip.

As the two spoke, Erik watched the body language of Chang's men. Some were monitoring the exits. Some the windows. Others had eyes on Chang. None of them were overtly obvious about what they were doing.

"This guy has a shit ton of protection, despite Rachel's confidence," Erik said under his breath as he lifted the beer to his mouth again.

"He's got his finger in a lot of pies," Chandler said. "That makes him a man who needs all the protection he can get."

He turned his gaze back to the bar to see Chang leaning close to Rachel, his hand below the bar, likely on her thigh. She had a smile on her face. It would be easy to assume it was fake, given the circumstances, but Erik knew better. She was genuinely smiling because Chang was falling for her act, hook, line, and sinker. Smiling because she knew the guy was screwed.

"I have a room upstairs if you'd like to join me," Chang said quietly, his voice just reaching the earpiece.

Bingo.

"What's in your room?" Rachel asked flirtatiously.

"Come and see."

"Bit cliché," Erik muttered under his breath.

There was a beat of silence. Erik stared at his beer, but from his peripheral vision he saw Rachel and Chang step away from the bar. Chang's men straightened.

Erik got up from his stool. He was closer to the exit, so he made it out first. Rachel would also stall Chang to make sure Erik made it upstairs first.

"Going to the fourth floor now," Erik said through the earpiece.

Chandler had already accessed the hotel system to find Chang's room, which they had learned had a connecting door to the neighboring room for one of his security personnel.

"Deactivating the fourth-floor security cameras."

Erik stepped into the elevator and pressed the four button.

"Done," Chandler said, moments before the door opened and Erik stepped out. When he reached the security officer's room beside Chang's, he knocked and turned, so anyone looking through the peephole wouldn't see him.

"Who is it?"

"Housekeeping." Erik kept his voice deep and low.

The second the click of the door sounded, Erik turned and grabbed the guy before the door was fully open, one hand going over his mouth, the other spinning him so his back was against Erik's body. He quickly stepped inside and closed the door with his foot, then tightened his hold until the struggling asshole passed out cold. He dropped him to the floor.

"I'm in," Erik said.

He made quick work of zip-tying the guy's wrists and ankles and taping his mouth.

"Rachel's just coming up the elevator," Chandler responded.

Two minutes later, Erik heard Rachel's voice in the earpiece.

"Uh, no one but us in the room," Rachel said firmly.

"He's my security," Chang responded.

"Well, he can still *be* your security in the hall. Unless you want me to leave? I'm not one for an audience."

There was a short pause, and Erik readied himself to go in and help her if she needed backup. But quiet words were spoken between Chang and his guy.

Then there was the soft thud of a door closing before Chang spoke. "Drink?"

"Whiskey on ice."

"I like your style."

"So," Rachel said, voice husky, "you haven't told me nearly enough about you, Lowie. Do you live here or are you in town on business?"

"I move around a lot. Right now, my guys are helping someone with a job."

"You have guys who work for you. I like it. You sound…important."

"You don't need to fill your head with the business of men, honey. Here."

"Actually, that's the thing—I do." There was the sound of movement before a quiet grunt came over the earpiece. Then Rachel's voice again. "Ready for you, Hunter."

Erik opened the connecting door to see Chang on the floor, flat on his stomach, Rachel's knee on his back and a knife at his throat.

Damn, she was good.

"Call for help and I slit your throat," Rachel whispered into Chang's ear.

"Who the fuck are you?" he growled.

"I'm someone who kills for a living, so don't think I'd hesitate in ending your life right here and now."

Erik took out his gun, lowered to his haunches, and pressed it to Chang's temple. "You were with Miles Moreno this week. Why?"

Chang frowned. "What?"

Rachel pressed the knife harder to his throat, blood trickling out of a small wound. "Answer the fucking question."

Chang scowled. "He hired one of my guys to hack a security system a few weeks ago."

Fury tightened Erik's fingers around the Glock. It *had* been Moreno…and Chang had helped.

"He came back to hire more help, this time muscle for a job," Chang continued. "We couldn't agree on a price, so nothing's been arranged yet. We're in the middle of…negotiations."

"Did he say when the job was or what it involved?" Erik asked.

"No. I don't even think *he* fucking knows. Said he hadn't worked out the details yet but needed at least ten of my guys."

Ten? Fucking animal.

Erik lowered his voice to a hard line. "Let this be your one warning, Chang—if you help Moreno, if you give him so much as *one* fucking man to help his cause, I will *destroy* you. I will dismantle everything your little gang has created, then, when you have nothing left, I'll come for your life." He leaned closer. "I'm not a man to fuck with. And I always follow through on my threats. Do you understand?"

Chang sucked in a sharp breath. "What's it to you if I help him?"

Rachel lifted his head by the hair and slammed it to the floor. "Answer the damn question. Do you understand?"

There was another soft growl from Chang. "Yes."

"Good." Erik removed the gun from his temple. "We'll be watching you."

Rachel delivered a blow to the back of his head. When his body went limp, they both moved back to the connecting room.

"It's done, Chandler," Erik said, closing the connecting door and slipping the lock.

"Good. Setting off the alarms now."

The second the blaring noise sounded through the hotel, Erik and Rachel slipped out of the room. The guard was so busy trying to gain access to Chang's suite, throwing his shoulder to the door with his back to the connecting room, he didn't notice Rachel or Erik moving into the hall and in the opposite direction.

CHAPTER 23

*H*annah woke and rolled onto her back as a wave of nausea crawled through her belly. It was always worse in the morning before eating breakfast. Most days she was fine, but every so often she'd be sick as hell. She did whatever she could to avoid it because if Erik caught her throwing up, his eyes always glazed over with concern.

Slowly, she opened her eyes.

"Erik!" His name was a gasp. He was sitting on the edge of the bed right beside her…and in his hand was a box of crackers.

Oh, God, what did she do to deserve this man?

"Morning, Angel." He handed her the box.

"You're my savior," she said, pushing up to a sitting position and slipping the box from his fingers. "Thank you."

She held off adjusting her pump for insulin as she nibbled on a cracker. If she was sick after she dosed the insulin, the insulin would still be in her system, but there would be no sugar to be broken down, which would cause her to go low. She'd take her dose at breakfast.

"Sorry I couldn't wait up last night. By nine p.m., I couldn't keep my eyes open. I think your family thought I was crazy, going to bed so early."

"My family knows you're creating our baby. Listen to your body. If it needs rest, you rest."

Her heart softened, and she continued to munch on the cracker for a few seconds before finally asking the question she needed an answer to. "How did last night go?"

He brushed a lock of hair from her cheek, his expression giving nothing away. "Rachel got herself invited to Chang's room. I entered through the connecting hotel room, and, after a bit of pressure, he told us Moreno wanted to use some of his guys for a *job*."

"The job being…me."

The pad of his thumb swiped over her bottom lip. "Rachel and I let him know what would happen if he did that."

She ran her finger along the edge of the next cracker, worry tightening her chest. "But won't he know who you are now and be angry about what you both did last night? What if he comes after you?"

"He *doesn't* know who we are. But on the off chance he starts digging and finds out, Chandler's keeping a close eye on him. You're safe from him."

"It's not me I'm worried about."

"You don't need to worry about me either."

How many times had he told her that? "I'll always worry."

He leaned in and kissed her. "Don't. How was last night? I heard Andi came by."

Hannah grinned. "I love your siblings. Andi's very good at putting Nate in his place, and Nate just takes it in his stride."

Erik laughed. "The two of them are only a year apart in age, so they're very close, which is sometimes a good thing and sometimes less good."

"They're both amazing. And so are Nate's burgers. I ate two!"

She finished another cracker and smoothed a hand over his leg. "I'm glad you're okay."

"I was always going to be okay."

She cocked her head. "You say that, but there's always going to be risks to the jobs you do."

"Well, I guess it's lucky that I won't be doing government work anymore."

Her head tilted in question. "You mean it's official?"

"Yeah, Angel. I'm all yours and Squid's."

"Squid?"

He lifted a shoulder. "Our baby looked a bit like a squid on the last scan."

She laughed. "You're right, they did."

"So…have you peeked at the gender?"

Her brows rose. The envelope was in her bottom drawer, and as far as she was aware, untouched. "No! Have you?"

"No, I haven't. I told you, I don't mind finding out or waiting."

She nibbled her bottom lip. "The impatient part of me wants to know, but there's this other part of me that wants to wait. That likes not knowing right now."

He nodded slowly. "Waiting sounds like a good option to me."

"You'll just do whatever I want to do?"

"Yeah. Because I love you."

"I love you too." Her hand slid over her belly.

He followed her movement with his gaze. "Have you felt any movement?"

"Not yet. I think it's too early."

Then he did something she wasn't expecting. He lowered his head, lifted her shirt, and kissed her belly. The air stuttered out of her, and she had to remind herself to breathe.

Slowly, his mouth trailed up her chest, then her neck before settling behind her ear and whispering, "You are going to make an amazing mother, Angel."

Tears she couldn't explain gathered in her eyes. Maybe

because a part of her needed someone to tell her that. Maybe because coming from her baby's father, the words hit deeper.

She cupped the back of his head. "And you, Erik Hunter, will make one amazing father."

His head lifted, eyes burning into hers. Then he kissed her, lips sealing to her mouth, tongue slipping inside, weaving with hers. Her breaths started to shorten, heartbeat picking up, when his phone rang.

He growled and tugged it from his pocket, his mother's name flashing across the screen.

"Answer it," she whispered, leaning back and pulling another cracker from the box, even though what she really wanted was more of the soul-ravaging kisses.

He squeezed her arm before rising and answering the call. She lifted her own phone to see a text waiting for her from Brigid.

Brigid: You are required to be at Erik's parents' home tomorrow night at six p.m. Wear white. We're wedding planning.

She frowned, reading the message again before responding.

Hannah: I'm required to wear white for wedding planning?

Brigid: Yes. It's a Hunter tradition to wear white during wedding planning. Don't question it.

She looked up to see Erik stepping back into the room, phone still to his ear, fingers running through his hair. "Okay, we can do that. See you then, Mom." He hung up, eyes falling on Hannah. "Apparently, we're expected at Mom's house tomorrow night."

"I know, Brigid just texted. She said it's a Hunter family tradition to wear white during wedding planning, so that's my dress code."

A slow smile curved his lips, but he said nothing.

"It's *not* a Hunter family tradition, is it?"

He lifted a shoulder. "It might be."

"But isn't." She could read between the lines. "Are they throwing—"

"You a bridal shower? Yeah, I think they are. Mom told me to wear warm clothes in case I go outside."

"In case…meaning boys will be kicked outside and girls kept in." She laughed before a soft smile settled on her lips. "We're so lucky to have the people we have in our lives."

"We are. Although, I'm not sure a party is a good idea right now."

She reached for his hand and slid her fingers through his. "There's a lot of security at your parents' house. Security *you* put in place. I'd argue we're just as safe there as here. Maybe more so if Nate and others are there."

"True. And I want you to have a night off from worrying about everything."

Honestly, a night to just be with all the closest people in her life sounded wonderful. "You're so good to me."

He leaned down and kissed her cheek. "Nope. Not nearly good enough, actually. You deserve the world."

She slipped her fingers into his hair and tugged him close. "Well, let's have the world then…together."

He growled, the crackers disappearing from her fingers as he pushed her to the bed and crushed his lips to hers.

* * *

ERIK SCANNED the street as he climbed out of his Corvette and moved around to Hannah's side. They'd just gotten back to Hannah's work after an appointment with her endocrinologist, followed by her obstetrician. Everything was fine with her sugar levels, and the obstetrician was happy with the progress of the pregnancy.

Every time Erik heard the baby's heartbeat, he felt the same myriad of emotions. The wave of protectiveness. The disbelief that he was having a child. And the love. Yeah, a shitload of love for the little person who hadn't even been born yet.

His hand moved to the small of Hannah's back as he led her into her office.

Taylor stopped when she saw them, her eyes lighting up. "Hey! I got the invite for tomorrow night, and I am *so* excited! I'm thinking of bringing strawberry and goat cheese bruschetta. What do you think? Or is that a pregnancy no-no? I can't remember. It's been so long since I was pregnant."

Hannah's brows rose. "Tomorrow night?"

"Yeah, to your—wait. Was it a surprise? Crap! Brigid didn't mention that part, but maybe it was implied? Was I not supposed to say anything?"

Hannah chuckled. "It's okay. We worked it out. And strawberry and goat cheese bruschetta actually sounds really good."

"Oh, phew. For a moment I thought I'd spilled the beans on a big secret. Great. I'm so excited!" she repeated, squeezing Hannah's arm before entering her office.

Hannah grinned at Erik as she stepped into her own office. "Brigid's never been able to pull off a surprise. When she tried to throw me a surprise twenty-first birthday party, I think half the town said 'see you at the party' the week of."

"Did you still act surprised?"

"Oh yeah. I thought I did a really good job too, until I looked at Brigid and realized she saw right through it."

"I don't think acting's your forte. But maybe that's because I can read you like a book."

She cocked her head. "Really? What am I thinking right now?"

"That I'm the best thing that ever happened to you." Her lips twitched, and he stepped forward. "That you have the best baby daddy around, and we're going to make a pretty damn awesome family." He swept his arms around her waist.

"That's not fair. I'm *always* thinking those things. The only time I'm not is when you're bad."

He lowered his head and nibbled her neck. "With you, it's impossible to be good."

He was about to kiss her when a knock came at the door.

She chuckled and stepped back. "That'll be Jake."

"I'll wait in the lobby."

"Thank you." She stepped back. "Come in."

"Hey," Jake said as he entered the room. His gaze shifted to Erik. "You joining our meeting?"

"Nah, I'll be out here." He clasped Jake's shoulder as he passed him, then he lowered to the couch and texted Chandler.

Erik: Any activity from Chang?

Chandler: Not that I can see. In fact, half his team seem to be flying to Seattle today.

Thank fuck.

Chandler: I just sent you the forms you need to fill out for your resignation.

Over the next half hour, Erik went through the documents and filled them out on his phone. He was just finishing when the door to the building opened and Nico walked in, two coffees in hand.

Erik's muscles involuntarily tensed, and he stood. "What are you doing here?"

The guy almost looked amused. "I'm obviously here to knit a fucking sweater."

Erik's mouth didn't so much as twitch.

The door to Hannah's office opened, and Jake stepped out.

Hannah wore a smile on her face. "Thanks, Jake. I'll get on booking a photographer for the house."

"Great."

The second Hannah saw Nico, her face lit up even more. Her brother brushed past Erik and pulled Hannah into a one-armed hug, mindful of the beverages.

When they separated, she looked over at Erik. "Want to come in?"

He shook his head. "I'll wait here."

There was a flash of disappointment in her expression, then she disappeared into the office.

"Clench that phone any harder and it'll break, Hunter."

He shifted his attention to Jake.

"Her foster brother, right? He's been coming into the gym," Jake said.

Erik shoved his phone into his pocket. "Yeah."

"And you don't like him?"

"Nope."

Jake's gaze felt like it saw everything Erik wasn't saying. "I find it hard to trust too. Wanna talk about it?"

Erik sighed. "The guy used to be involved in some bad shit. I don't like him being around her."

"You think he'd hurt her?"

"My gut says not intentionally. But at the same time, I don't know. I don't know him well enough."

Jake lifted a shoulder. "Only one way to fix that."

Yeah, that wasn't going to happen. Not anytime soon, anyway. "Everything okay with selling your place?"

"Yeah, Hannah's been great. I took her out to have a look at the house the other day, and she thinks a fresh coat of paint and a few changes will make a big difference. So I'm getting on that in the next week. Then she'll price it and get some professional photos taken."

"That's great."

"You coming back to the gym anytime soon?"

He smirked. "You know you won't be able to keep me away."

"Good." He patted Erik's arm. "I'll catch you around."

Erik remained on his feet the entire time Nico was in her office. He couldn't sit. He was too damn tense.

When the door finally opened, Nico's gaze went straight to him. "Don't worry, Hunter, she's in one piece."

The fucker had the balls to knock against Erik's shoulder on the way to the door.

He gritted his teeth as he entered her office. Hannah was on her feet, throwing out the empty coffee cups.

"Hey." She stepped into his arms. "You feel tense."

"I'm fine."

She tilted her head. "No secrets. Tell me what you're thinking."

He was pretty sure his distrust for Nico wasn't a secret. "That you're beautiful."

He was about to dip his head when she set her fingers on his lips, stopping him. "I'm going to ask you another favor, and before you say no, I need you to know how much this would mean to me."

Why did he get a bad fucking feeling about this? "Okay."

"If I am being thrown a bridal shower tomorrow night, and you'll be celebrating with the guys, I'd like you to suggest to whoever is organizing yours that Nico be invited."

The air hissed from his teeth. "Angel—"

"I know. You don't trust him. You don't like him. And I so get it. There's a lot of history there, and you're not going to just wake up tomorrow and be best friends. But he's important to me. And so are you. You're both family, and I really think that if you spend just a bit of time together, some of the ice might thaw."

Every fucking part of him wanted to say no. But then she looked at him with her big blue eyes, pleading, and no part of him felt capable of doing that. "I'll text Nate."

Hope sparkled in her eyes, and she sighed, leaning her head against his chest. "Thank you."

CHAPTER 24

"*R*eady?"

Hannah looked at Erik, nerves fluttering in her belly. "I don't know. Can you be ready for a surprise bridal shower that isn't a surprise?"

He cocked his head, taking his hand from the wheel and closing his fingers around hers. They'd just pulled up in front of his parents' house, but neither of them had made a move to get out.

"I'll be with you."

"Until they kick you outside." She tilted her head. "Thank you for asking Nate to invite Nico."

There was a small tightening of his eyes. That was the only hint that her brother made him uncomfortable. She knew he hadn't wanted Nico here. It killed her that two of the most important men in her life didn't like each other. She kept telling herself that with time, things would get better, but would they? Or was that just a delusional wish of hers?

"You know I would do anything for you." He lifted her hand and kissed the back of it right as a knock came at her window.

She jumped and turned to see Brigid standing there, tapping her watch-less wrist.

"I think that's her telling us to get out," Hannah said under her breath as she opened her door and looked up at her best friend. "Hey."

"Any other day and I'd be mad at you for not coming straight in, but today, I'm too dang excited to give you hell." She beamed. "I have a surprise for you!"

She linked her arm through Hannah's and tugged her toward the house, but before stepping inside, Brigid turned and shook her finger at Erik. "No boys inside. You're out the back."

Erik looked up and down the street before facing Hannah. "I've got a stream to the security system on my phone. I'll know the second anyone breaches it." He stepped closer and kissed her. "Call if you need anything."

"She will." Brigid yanked Hannah inside the house before Erik could continue, locking the door after her and alarming the system.

"Brigid—"

"Surprise!"

Hannah's head shot up at the loud cry to see the living room full of people. Henry and Leo. Andi and her mother. Taylor. Even Rita from the Black Bean. There were balloons and drinks and food. A banner hanging from the ceiling read: *To the future Mrs. Hunter.*

Hannah bit her bottom lip, then smiled widely as she turned to Brigid. "Was this your idea?"

"Yeah. It's been a tough few months for you, so I thought what better way to turn it around than a bridal shower to celebrate your engagement."

Hannah tugged Brigid into her arms, her mouth going to her ear. "Thank you. I don't know what I'd do without you."

Brigid hugged her back. "No. I don't know what I'd do without *you*. You're the best friend I never knew I needed."

She squeezed her friend tighter. The second they separated, others moved in on her, pulling her into sweet hugs, telling her what a beautiful bride she'd make and how happy they were for her.

When something at the back of the room caught her attention, she stopped, jaw dropping.

"Oh my God." Her gaze swung to Henry and Brigid. "You made a *cereal bar?*"

Henry grinned. "Yep. Every cereal you can imagine. But only oat milk."

"We also have a donut and cookie bar," Brigid added, turning to the next table. "Drinks table. And pizza is in the oven."

"You guys are amazing."

"Yes, we are," Andi said, walking toward them. "Ready for the first game?"

Hannah frowned. "Depends on what it is."

"We're starting with an easy one." Brigid grinned at Henry. "Toilet paper brides."

Hannah laughed as the two of them went to grab the toilet paper. She was about to sit down when Erik's mother, Jennifer, approached again. At first, the older woman was quiet, simply pulling Hannah into a second embrace though they'd just hugged a few minutes ago. Then her mouth moved to Hannah's ear.

"Thank you. You have changed my son's life and brought him back to us. It's a debt I will forever owe you."

Tears gathered in Hannah's eyes, but she blinked them back as they pulled out of the embrace. "There is no debt, Jennifer. He's changed my life too."

She brushed a lock of hair from Hannah's face. "Having you in this family has been such a blessing. I can't wait to make that official, my child."

My child… Hannah's pulse took off at a new, faster rhythm. God, Erik's family had been such a gift. "Thank you."

Andi joined them. "Mom's right. And boy did we need another girl to even us out."

Hannah laughed. "Thank you. Both of you."

"All right, everyone, time to start our first game," Brigid called.

A mocktail was pushed into Hannah's hand as she was led to one of the stacks of toilet paper rolls.

* * *

ERIK MOVED around the back of his parents' home, a smile immediately tugging at his mouth at what he saw. A fire pit was burning in the middle of the yard, all of his closest loved ones sitting around it, beers in hand. His father and brother. Norman from Black Bean. Jake and Rachel. And of course, Nico.

But the person who *really* drew his attention was the tall man in glasses, giving him a crooked grin.

Chandler.

Fuck, he hadn't seen his friend in years! He crossed the space between them and pulled the guy who was more of a brother than a friend into a hug.

"It's been too fucking long," Erik growled.

Chandler returned the hug. "You're not wrong."

He pulled back. "When did you get in?"

"This morning. I'm here for just shy of two weeks."

Not nearly long enough, but Erik would take what he could get. "Thank you for coming."

"Anything for you, brother."

Erik went around, shaking hands and hugging his family and friends. When he reached Nico, neither of them smiled, but Nico dipped his head. "Thanks for the invite."

"Hannah wanted you here."

Humor sparked in his eyes. "I figured. Still, you extended the olive branch."

"You're her brother."

"That I am."

That was about as warm and cozy as their relationship got at the moment.

Nate's arm slid around Erik's shoulders. "Now, we have a mobile bar to the right with every drink you could ask for. And beside it, you'll notice the food truck, which does the best damn burritos you'll ever eat."

Erik's gaze shifted to the food truck. Damn, it smelled so good.

"And to the left," Nate continued, "we have the playing field for our backyard ax-throwing league."

Erik's gaze shifted to the target boards. "Ax throwing?"

His father came to stand beside him, arms crossed. "Well, we had to think about what you'd like to do at your bachelor party. You like danger, so naturally our minds went to weapons, and we can't have guns going off and scaring the neighbors. We ended on ax throwing."

Rachel stepped close, bumping his shoulder. "Ready to get your ass kicked?"

"Shouldn't you be inside with the girls, painting nails and talking dresses?" Erik teased.

She lifted a shoulder. "I'll go between parties. There was no way I'd let you win the ax throwing without going through me though."

He chuckled. "Confident as always, Rach."

Nate came toward him, ax in hand. "All right, Mr. Bachelor. You're first."

Erik accepted the ax. "Need me to set the standard?"

"You wish," Nate scoffed. "I've put myself last so no one feels bad when they don't come close to it."

Yeah right. Erik moved toward the target. There were three circles—an outer blue, a middle red, and an inner blue. Wire fencing had been set up on either side of the target, and there was a line he had to stand behind to throw the ax.

Erik had done a bit of ax throwing when he was younger, but that was a long damn time ago.

He stopped behind the line and lifted the ax with both hands. After a deep inhale, he stepped forward and released it.

Inner blue circle.

"Whatever," Jake scoffed from behind him.

Erik laughed.

The next hour was a mix of drinks, food, and ax throwing…not that Erik was drinking much. A couple sips of beer and that was it. He needed a clear head in case anything happened. He also continuously checked the security system. Even though it would alert him if anyone arrived, checking it was more for his peace of mind.

"Hey, buddy."

Erik looked up at Jake as he took a seat beside him. "Jake."

"How are you doing?"

"Tonight, or in general?"

"Both."

"Tonight, I'm good. We've had a bit of…trouble, though. An asshole's been targeting Hannah and I'm struggling to pin him down."

Jake's muscles tensed. "Fuck. That's not good. Anything I can do to help?"

"Not right now, but I'll let you know if that changes."

"I'm here for whatever you need."

"Thanks. How's Charlie?" It took a lot for Erik not to tense just saying his name, but since he'd started therapy, it had gotten a tiny bit easier. Everything had.

Jake lifted a shoulder. "He's okay. Having him here isn't easy for me, either. I still struggle with the memory of what he did at times. But once we sell the family house, I'm sure he'll leave. He's always on the move. I told him he didn't have to come at all. That

I'd sell the house. I think a part of him came here for *you*. To get your forgiveness."

Erik frowned, something hard coiling in his gut. "I think I might be close, just not quite there yet."

"I understand."

At the sound of raised voices, he looked up to see Nico and Rachel arguing. About what, he had no fucking clue, but Nico had a brow raised and he looked thoroughly amused, while Rachel was poking a finger into his chest. It reminded Erik of the start of his relationship with Hannah, when she'd poked her finger into his chest while yelling at him.

Nate lowered into the seat on the other side of Erik. "Enjoying your evening?"

Erik smiled at his brother. "It's great. Thanks for organizing this. I know others would have helped, but I'm sure you were the main player."

Nate lifted his shoulder as he sipped his beer. "You'd do the same for me."

"I would." He gripped his brother's shoulder. "Still, thank you. How are you and your team doing?"

Exhaustion stretched over his brother's features. "We're tired, man."

"Everything okay?"

"Not really. Since losing Jasper, we've tried to keep going, but it's almost like we're playing at being SEALs now and just going through the motions. We can't seem to recover from losing him." He dipped his chin to his chest. "I'm thinking about leaving."

His brother had implied that before but never said it outright. "What would you do?"

Nate laughed. "Well, that's the fucking question, isn't it?"

"You could work at my gym," Jake suggested.

Nate lifted a shoulder. "Maybe. I can't sit behind a desk. I'd need to do something with my hands. I don't know. Nothing's concrete yet. I might stay."

"Whatever decision you make, it will be the right one."

Nate met his gaze, emotions flickering through his hazel eyes before he dipped his head. "Thank you. One good thing to come out of this last year—I'm so fucking glad you're where you are, Erik. You deserve every damn bit of happiness."

"Thank you. Not a day passes where I don't acknowledge how lucky I am that she saw past my mask, crashed through my walls, and decided to love me."

Not a single damn day.

CHAPTER 25

$\mathcal{H}$annah leaned back on the couch as her friends talked around her. Her night had been filled with smiles, laughter, and food. It was everything she'd needed.

She'd of course been named the best toilet paper bride and answered almost every question in the "how well do you know your husband-to-be" game correctly. The activity she'd really failed at was not saying the words "bride" or "wedding" all night. The two words had been labeled forbidden, so of course, everyone was out to trick one another into saying them so they could steal the toy ring every guest had received.

Hannah had lost her ring within the first five minutes of the night, while Brigid's fingers were covered in them.

Brigid dropped beside Hannah on the couch, her head falling on Hannah's shoulder. "Outsmarting people is exhausting."

"But it comes so naturally to you."

She glanced up, a wide grin on her face. "Have I told you how much I love you?"

"At least a dozen times, but feel free to repeat it."

"I fucking love you, Han."

"I love you too." She pressed a kiss to her friend's head.

"Do you think I'll find my tall, dark, and handsome hero too?"

"I do." She tucked some hair behind Brigid's ear. "I think he'll pop up at the perfect time."

Henry lowered to the couch, nudging Brigid's shoulder. "Or maybe he's already shown up in the form of a very good-looking gym owner."

"Who are you calling good-looking?" Leo joked.

"You," Henry said quickly. "Always you."

Hannah laughed as the door to the house opened and the men started filing in. Her gaze went straight to Erik. God, how was it that just a few hours apart felt like a lifetime, and she was all too ready to throw herself into his arms?

He dropped to his haunches in front of her. "Ready to go, Angel?"

She nodded, leaning forward and resting her head against his shoulder as exhaustion pulled at her limbs. His hand smoothed down her back.

She rose to her feet and turned to Brigid, Henry, and Leo. "Need a ride home?"

Leo shook his head. "Nah, I didn't drink much. I can drive."

Hannah nodded and looked at Brigid, but before she could open her mouth, someone else spoke.

"I can take you home if you need, Brigid?"

Everyone's gaze shot to Jake.

Hannah bit the inside of her cheek to suppress the grin.

Brigid's cheeks heated. "Oh…um, okay. Thank you."

A man Hannah had never seen before stepped behind Erik. He was tall, with dark hair and blue eyes behind black-rimmed glasses.

Erik stepped back. "Hannah, this is Chandler. Chandler, Hannah."

Her eyes widened. "Chandler? As in, saves-us-every-time-we're-screwed Chandler?"

His expression tinged with humor. "The one and only."

Without hesitation, she pulled him into a hug. "Thank you… for everything."

Chandler hugged her back. "You're welcome, Hannah. It's nice to finally meet you."

The next twenty minutes were a flurry of goodbyes. She offered to help pack up, but Jennifer wasn't having any of it, instead shooing her away to be with Erik.

When she and Erik were finally in his Corvette driving back to his place, she leaned her head back, closing her eyes. "My heart is so full."

"Mine too, Angel." Erik squeezed her hand. "I take it you had a good night?"

"The best. My belly is full of cereal, donuts, and pizza, I had amazing conversations, and I was awarded prettiest toilet paper bride of the night."

"Toilet paper bride?"

"My team went with a white toilet paper tiara, and a long ball gown with a train. It was a stunner."

He chuckled. "I'll take your word for it."

"What about you? How was your night?"

"It was great. The main event was ax throwing."

"Of course it was. Let me guess, you won?"

"I won…just. Although Rachel and Nico weren't far off."

Her heart gave a little thud at the sound of her brother's name. "Thank you again for inviting him."

"Well, I'm not sure how much fun he had. Rachel was riding his ass the whole night."

The corners of her mouth lifted. "She's good for him. He needs someone to put him in his place."

"Rachel's definitely good at that."

"Jake's a good guy, isn't he?" The words were out of her mouth before she could stop them. "I can trust him with Brigid, can't I?"

He squeezed her fingers again. "He's the best guy."

"Good. Brigid deserves some good in her life after James."

There was a small narrowing of Erik's eyes at the mention of James's name.

For the rest of the drive, Hannah watched the stars twinkle in the sky, her mind forever moving, thinking about the future. About her and Erik's wedding. Their baby. About what their lives would look like when the danger was gone and they could just…live.

"We're home."

She blinked. She'd been so caught up in her own thoughts she hadn't realized he'd already pulled into the garage.

She turned to see him watching her closely.

He swiped a lock of hair from her cheek. "What's going on in that beautiful head of yours?"

"Do you ever wonder what our lives will look like in five or ten years?"

"If you'd asked me that a month ago, I would have said no, because I already knew it would be you and me and that was all that mattered."

"And now?"

"Now I wonder what color our child's eyes will be—as blue as the sky like yours, or hazel like mine. I wonder if they'll be tall or short. If they'll have your big smile or my scowl. Your patience or my short temper."

Emotion welled in her chest. "Maybe both…a bit of you, and a bit of me."

"Yeah, that's what I think too." He cupped her cheek. "I wonder if I'll be a good dad."

"You will be the best father this child could ask for."

"How do you know?"

"Because you already are. You love harder than anyone I've ever met. And you are so easy to love in return."

She lifted his hand and kissed it, but she didn't stop there. She pressed another kiss to the inside of his wrist, then a bit farther up his arm. Without caring about the lack of space in the car, she undid her seat belt and climbed over the middle console onto Erik's lap.

"Angel," he drawled. "What are you doing?"

She straddled his body with her thighs, her dress riding up to her hips before she lowered her head and nibbled on his neck. "I'm showing you just how easy you are to love, Mr. Hunter."

As she kissed up his neck, she reached for the base of his shirt and tugged it over his head. The second his chest was bare, she grazed her fingers over his flesh, feeling every inch of him.

When her lips finally neared his mouth, she nipped at the corner, while her fingers worked the button and zipper of his jeans.

He gripped her hips tightly, his chest moving up and down in quick succession against her.

"I love you so much that sometimes the intensity of it scares me," she whispered, continuing to nip and play at his lips. "When we're apart, it feels like a physical pain deep in my chest. I often wonder if it's normal to love someone so deeply. But then we come back to each other, and it feels like my soul has been returned to me. Like you're my reward for keeping it together while we've been apart."

Her hand slipped into his open jeans and briefs, and the second her fingers wrapped around his already hard cock, he grabbed the back of her head and crashed his mouth to hers with a growl.

She moved her hand over his length while his tongue swept inside her mouth, tasting her. She lost herself in that kiss. Lost her sanity. Her sense of the world around them. She lost everything but him and them and this moment.

When his hand slid inside the top of her dress and he cupped her breast, she moaned. His thumb swiped her nipple back and forth, causing a cry she couldn't stop to tear from her throat.

He did it again and again, setting her on fire. She moved her hand faster, pumping him against her clit, the wetness between her thighs building until she desperately needed more.

She tugged her mouth from his, moved her lips over to his ear again, whispering, "I need you."

A growl reverberated from his chest, and he tore her panties from her body in a violent tug. Immediately, she lifted her hips so his tip was at her entrance.

She kissed him one more time before whispering, "You and me, Erik, forever."

Then she slid down.

* * *

ERIK GROANED deep in his throat as her slick walls surrounded his cock.

Heaven. Absolute fucking heaven. He ground his back teeth to stop from pumping up into her. To give her time to adjust to him.

He reached up and dragged the straps of her dress off her shoulders. Her creamy breasts came into view, and his cock hardened to an almost painful degree.

She cupped his face and lowered her head. The second her lips touched his, she rose up before lowering back onto his cock. He growled. She did it again, her tongue weaving with his.

Every thump of his heart was for her. Every breath. Every whisper of life. Everything he was, all Hannah's. She confirmed that at every touch. He was irrevocably chained to her.

He took his mouth from hers and lowered his head, then captured her nipple between his lips. She cried out as he sucked, her fingers tangling in his hair, pulling the strands.

He swiped her nipple with his tongue, up and down, then in a circular motion, his hand cupping her other bare breast.

Fuck, she felt good around him.

Hannah's head tilted back, the sounds releasing from her filling his chest and burning his skin.

Switching to her other breast, he gripped her hips, lifting them and slamming her back onto him harder. Faster. He was so fucking close, but he needed her to get there with him.

He trailed his mouth back up her chest, pausing on her neck to suck before finding her mouth again. He slipped his tongue inside, tasting her sweetness…like a damn fruit.

When he found her clit, he pressed with his thumb, causing her to jolt. He did it again, this time moving in a circular motion.

The moans from her lips became louder, her breathing faster. He took her in. All of her. Casting every sound and motion to memory. Every gasp of air. Every flicker of movement. It was his.

He thrust up into her, his thumb never slowing. He knew the exact moment she teetered on the edge. Her walls tightened around his cock, her fingers digging into his flesh…

He moved his mouth to her ear, nipping on her lobe before whispering, "Fall for me, Angel. I'll catch you."

And she did…her body broke around him, her scream whipping through the car, cutting through the silent night.

He kept pumping, kept moving his thumb over her core, until the throbbing of her walls became too much and he growled as his own climax took him, destroying him, just like Hannah did, every second of every day. She annihilated him.

CHAPTER 26

Hannah typed out an email quickly. It was almost quitting time, and man she was ready. Pregnancy exhaustion was kicking her butt today. A week had passed since her bachelorette party, but she felt like she needed an entire month to recover, and she hadn't even drunk anything.

It was crazy.

She'd just hit send when a text came through.

Nico: Any chance I can come by for dinner tonight? I miss you.

Her smile softened. She'd been working so much she'd barely seen him this week.

Hannah: Sure. But I should warn you, Rachel will be there too.

Nico: Even more reason to come. That woman loves me.

Hannah laughed out loud. She was pretty sure it was less love and more…well, she wasn't sure. Hate was too strong of a word. Frustration?

"Who has you laughing like that?" Leo asked from the doorway.

She looked up. "Nico."

Leo didn't know the full story behind Nico's return. That he'd been declared dead and was now living under an assumed name.

She was grateful he'd chosen the name of Nixon though. It meant she could keep calling him Nico in public and made things just a bit easier.

"Ah, yes," Leo said. "The infamous brother. Everything going okay with his return?"

"It's great, except…"

He titled his head. "Except what?"

"I just wish he and Erik would get along. They have a history, so I know I'm asking a lot but…they're both just so important to me."

"Sometimes these things take time," he said softly.

"You're right, I'm being impatient." She grinned at him. "How are you and Henry?"

"Damn, I love the guy."

Hannah's eyes widened. "Love?"

He chuckled. "Yeah, love. I know it's fast but—"

"Hey, if I've learned anything over the last several months, it's that the heart doesn't care how much time has passed. I'm so happy for you both."

He dipped his head. "Thank you. I'm staying for a while to catch up on some work. Henry's coming over with takeout. Want us to order you some?"

She shook her head. "No way am I intruding on that. Besides, Rachel's here so I'll go soon, save her from the boredom of watching the office when nothing's happening."

"I saw her out there waiting."

"I feel bad, but Erik wants me protected and he's with his friend Chandler this afternoon."

"Good. You *should* be protected." Leo straightened and tapped the doorframe. "Well, have a good night. And don't stay too long. The work will always be here, and rest is important."

"You too."

When Leo stepped out, Hannah turned back to her computer. She had so much to do and could honestly stay for hours. But

Leo was right. She needed to rest for both herself and her baby. And not only that, but it wasn't fair to Rachel for her to stay all night.

Quickly, she turned off her computer and grabbed her bag. When she moved out of her office, she saw Rachel standing by the lobby window, a hard expression on her face.

Hannah stepped toward her. "Everything okay?"

The other woman turned, the frown immediately shifting into a smile. "Yep. Ready?"

Was she worried? Hannah knew that Erik was concerned about what was potentially coming from Moreno, but he tried to hide it from her. Was Rachel doing the same?

Hannah nodded. "Yes."

Rachel's gaze never stopped moving around the street as they walked out of the office and to her truck. Even when they started driving, her eyes continually shifted to the rearview mirror.

"Are you sure everything's okay?" Hannah asked quietly.

"Yeah, just watching our backs. Erik would never forgive me if I let something happen to you." She dipped her head toward the glove box. "I've got some snacks in there if you're hungry."

Hannah's brows rose and she opened it to find a stash of food —the same treats Erik kept in his Corvette. She poked through candy and chips and snack-sized nut packets. "Wow. Did you do that for me?"

Rachel lifted a shoulder. "I've been meaning to do it for a while, seeing as I've been watching you so much."

Okay, this woman was officially too good to her.

"Thank you." She grabbed a bag of nuts before opening it and nibbling on a few, glancing back at Rachel. "Not just thanks for the snacks, but for looking out for me. I know it's not how you'd choose to spend your days."

"I'd do anything for Erik."

For some reason, even after everything, there was still that jolt of insecurity in Hannah. She hated it, but no matter how hard she tried to stop it, it never went away. Rachel was strong and badass in a way Hannah would never be. She had a bond with Erik so different than Hannah's.

Rachel's gaze shot across to her, her brows flickering. "Because he's like a brother to me. You know that, right?"

God, did every emotion playing in her heart show on her face? "Yeah, Erik's told me you've never dated."

"Never even came close. The very idea makes me want to gag…no offense."

Despite everything, she laughed. "Really?"

"Yeah. He's family. All I care about is his happiness…with someone else."

Rachel said the words with such certainty, and she sounded so genuine, that something lifted off Hannah's chest—a weight that had been pushing her down since she met the woman. "I guess I just feel insecure sometimes because you're so strong and courageous."

"Hannah, I'm the way I am because I've seen so much shit in my life. And I'm angry ninety percent of the time. Trust me, you don't want to be like me. I envy you and your calm. The way you've overcome everything that's been thrown at you with such strength and grace."

Hannah's brows rose. This beautiful, brave woman envied *her*?

"Being here in Redwood, seeing the life Erik has created for himself, has actually made me want new things," Rachel said softly. "It's made me want to slow down. Maybe find some new hobbies. Something for me."

"That's amazing, Rachel."

They were just rounding a bend in the road when something in the middle of the street had Hannah gasping and straightening in her seat. "Oh my God, is that—"

"A body."

It was just lying in the center of the road, so still. "Do you think they're…"

"I don't know," Rachel replied when Hannah couldn't finish. She stopped the car and pulled a gun from her holster. "I'm going to check their pulse. Stay in the car with the doors locked."

Hannah nodded quickly, her heart thumping wildly. Rachel climbed from the car, gun drawn and gaze darting to the trees on either side of the road. Everything in Hannah wanted to call the other woman back, but at the same time, they couldn't just leave this person there. Even if they were okay, the chance of a car speeding around the bend and running them over was too high.

Rachel was just lowering to check the person's pulse when a flash of movement to the side of the road caught Hannah's attention. Her breath stopped when she saw the glimmer of metal in the tree line. A gun?

Without thinking, Hannah undid her seat belt and threw open her door. She opened her mouth to call Rachel's name, but before she could utter a sound, multiple men came toward the other woman from both sides of the road.

Immediately, Rachel rose and fired at two men, but even though they dropped, there were too many coming toward her from all directions.

A big guy grabbed Rachel around the throat from behind. She threw him over her shoulder, but two more men were already on her. She fought hard, and Hannah almost thought she'd win.

Then she saw the syringe in one of the men's hands.

No! Hannah went to run forward, but a body slammed into her from the side, cutting off the air in her lungs as she hit the side of the truck.

She tried to throw an elbow into her attacker. Kicked back at their knee. But before she could do any damage, something slammed into her head, sending her world into darkness.

* * *

"This is the last one?" Erik asked, scanning the document while sitting at the table in Chandler's hotel room.

"Yep. Sign it, and you're officially out."

Erik stared at the resignation contract. The last step in leaving his job. He wasn't sure if he'd expected to feel hesitant or unsure. He felt neither of those things.

He touched the pen to paper and signed his name. "Done."

Chandler whistled as he took the document. "You're out. Any regrets?"

"None. It feels good."

"Great, that means you've made the right decision." Chandler's features softened. "I'm glad you found something more important to you than your job. We should all be working to live and not living to work. I've been waiting for you to get there."

"Me too." He shifted his gaze toward Chandler's computer. "You find anything new on Moreno?"

"I've been working with Nico's company, and actually…"

When Chandler stopped, Erik straightened. "You found something."

"Kind of. We've been keeping an eye on Chang and his group, and while he hasn't made contact with Moreno…his second-in-charge has."

The fuck?

Chandler scrubbed a hand over his face. "We've got some guys keeping tabs on him and some of the other key men in the organization…but I'm almost certain they're going to make a play against you and Hannah."

Erik's muscles strained, his limbs suddenly itching to get back to her. "Keep me updated."

He rose from the desk and moved across the room. He'd just wrapped his fingers around the door handle when Chandler touched his arm. "Hey. You okay?"

"No. And I won't be okay until Moreno and everyone who's

sided with him is locked down. You're staying in town for a few more nights?"

"Yeah. Flight leaves Sunday."

"I'll see you again tomorrow." He walked out of the hotel room, instinct making his feet move faster.

The entire drive back to his place, his skin crawled with the need to see her, touch her, hear her voice, Chandler's words repeating in his head again and again.

I'm almost certain they're going to make a play against you and Hannah.

When he reached the house, he frowned. Where was Rachel's truck? They should be home by now.

He parked in front of the house and climbed out, pulling his phone from his pocket and calling Hannah's number. It rang too many fucking times. Erik stepped into the house and immediately noticed the alarm was on.

They weren't home. Still, he instinctively shouted their names. "Hannah? Rachel?"

He tried Rachel's number as he searched the house for them. Just like Hannah, the woman didn't answer.

Fuck.

He ran outside and across to Hannah's place. She rarely went there, and again, Rachel's vehicle wasn't out front, but by this point, he was desperate.

He stepped inside and searched every room while letting the quiet crawl over his skin and burn his flesh.

Empty.

He lifted his phone again, this time calling her office.

"Reuben's Real Estate, Leo speaking."

"Leo, it's Erik. Is Hannah there?"

There was a short pause. "Uh, no, Hannah and Rachel left about forty-five minutes ago. Why? Is everything okay?"

Shit. "She's not home. If she shows up or contacts you or Henry, let me know."

"Yeah, of course."

He hung up and was heading back to his house when a car pulled into his drive. The second Nico was out of the vehicle, Erik grabbed his shirt and shoved him against the GT. The rational part of his brain knew this wasn't Nico's doing, but searing panic overwhelmed everything else.

"Where the fuck are Hannah and Rachel?"

Nico's eyes narrowed, and he shoved Erik's chest. "What do you mean, where are they? They're not here?"

"No."

"Hannah texted me earlier. She should be home."

Fear spread like wildfire in Erik's chest. He ran back to his Corvette and had just started the engine when Nico slid into the passenger seat.

"What the fuck are you doing?" Erik growled.

"I'm coming with you to find her."

Erik wanted to kick the asshole out, but there was no time to argue. He pressed his foot to the floor and sped out of his driveway.

"Where are we going?" Nico asked.

"I'm driving back to the office on the same route they would have taken, to see if there are any signs of them on the way."

Nico pressed something on his phone before lifting it to his ear. "I need a location on Chang's men."

There was a small pause. "What the fuck do you mean, you lost them?"

Ice slid over Erik's skin, and he pushed his Corvette to move faster, barely clearing the turns.

"Find them—*now!*" Nico yelled.

Erik rounded another corner and slammed his foot on the brake as his heart crashed against his ribs.

Rachel's truck. It sat in the middle in the opposite lane, passenger door wide open.

Erik climbed out of the car and ran toward the truck. He

knew what he'd find, but he needed confirmation that the hell he was living in was really his reality.

He checked the front, then the back of the truck, cursing loudly.

Empty. The truck was empty…and Hannah and Rachel were nowhere to be seen.

CHAPTER 27

Hannah groaned as pain radiated through her skull. God, she felt like she'd been hit by a ten-ton truck.

She tried to lift her hand to massage her forehead, but something against her wrists restricted her movement. What was that?

She gave another tug. Again, she was met with resistance.

Wait, was that…rope?

Suddenly, little flickers of her last memory flashed back into her head. Of the body in the middle of the road. Rachel climbing out. And those men…

Her eyes flashed open, and immediately light caused a new wave of pain to cascade through her head. The room wasn't even that bright—it was just that her head hurt so much.

It took several blinks for the room to come into focus, and another two for her to see the other person across from her.

Oh God…

"Rachel?" There was no reaction to Hannah's call. Not even a flicker of movement or a flutter of eyelids. "Rachel, wake up!"

Rachel sat tied to a chair across the room, her eyes closed and head hanging forward at an odd angle.

Hannah tugged harder at her restraints. She glanced down to see, similar to Rachel's, her feet were tied to the legs of a chair.

How much time had passed? What were her glucose levels? She had no idea. Her head was hurting, and she felt sick from the pain, but who knew if that was her glucose levels or if she'd received a hit to the head. Maybe both.

Anxiety started to crawl up her throat for her baby. She had to get out of here.

She tugged harder, her gaze once again moving across the room. "Rachel. Can you hear me? You need to wake up. Please!" She was so still, Hannah wasn't even sure the other woman was breathing.

She had to stay calm. Had to figure out a way to get both of them out of this.

She scanned the room. The space was big, with a staircase going up on the right. There were a couple of windows, but they were high, almost at the ceiling, long and thin.

Were they in a basement?

When footsteps sounded on the floor above her, she paused in her struggles, gaze shooting to the ceiling. The rattle of a door-knob sounded a second before feet appeared on the stairs.

Fear sickened her belly, and her breath caught at the sight of three men approaching. The guy in front wore a suit, while the two men behind him were in T-shirts and jeans. The men in jeans were big, their muscles stretching the fabric of their shirts.

"Miss Jacobs. You're awake."

She shifted her gaze back to the man in the suit. It was oddly jarring to have a man she'd never met use her name and speak to her as if he knew her.

"Are you Moreno?"

The corners of his mouth lifted. "I am. I don't usually involve myself in the legwork of these…transactions, but you're a special case. You've become somewhat personal for me."

"Why? I'm nothing to you. Why can't you just forget about me and let me live my life?"

He laughed, but the sound was too smooth and practiced. "I am a proud man, and when someone wrongs me, I need retribution." His gaze shifted to Rachel, eyes narrowing. "This government fucking contractor and your boyfriend killed my team, decimating my business. It's only fair I decimate what's theirs, don't you think?"

Anger straightened her spine, and even though she knew she should keep her mouth closed, she couldn't. He'd done too much damage already. "What I *think*, is that anyone who's in the business of selling human beings as if they're possessions doesn't deserve the air they breathe."

"And yet, I do breathe. Quite easily, may I add."

God, what was wrong with this man? Was he really so indifferent to the suffering of others? "What did you give Rachel? Why isn't she waking up?"

"Don't worry about her. Soon, you'll never see her again. I have a very…special buyer lined up for her."

Her chest tightened, a cold dread slipping over her skin. "She won't go down without a fight."

"I know. But my buyer likes to break a strong spirit."

He was sick. "You do know I'm type one, right? I won't survive long without insulin and carbs."

"I've informed your buyer. He'll know what to do to keep you alive…if that's what he chooses." Something beeped from his pocket, and he checked his phone. "Ah, your friend's buyer is here."

Panic swelled in Hannah's chest, making her limbs suddenly numb.

Moreno turned and headed toward the stairs.

"He'll find you, you know," Hannah said, not able to just let him walk away like this. "Erik. And he'll destroy you."

Moreno paused, looking at her over his shoulder. "Let him try."

The door closed behind him and his men, and Hannah began to tug at her hands and feet again, desperate to get free. She had to get out before this buyer arrived. Before *Rachel's* buyer took her. But the rope was too tight, and she had no weapons.

"Rachel! Come on. Hear my voice. Wake up. Please! We don't have a lot of time."

At the small scrunch of Rachel's eyes, hope danced in Hannah's chest.

"Rachel! I need you. *Please wake up.*"

This time, her arm twitched.

"We've been kidnapped," Hannah continued. "We need to get out. *Now.*"

Another twitch, closely followed by a small groan...then finally, Rachel's head lifted.

Yes!

Rachel blinked, her brows tugging together. "Hannah?"

"Moreno got us," Hannah rushed out. "We're in a basement God knows where. He's got a buyer lined up for both of us, and yours just arrived."

Her eyes hardened, some of the fog slipping away. There was a small clicking sound from behind her.

"My ring folds out into a tiny knife," Rachel said quietly. "I'm gonna get us out of here, Hannah."

It didn't take long at all for Rachel to cut through the rope on her wrists. Then she leaned over and sawed at the ones on her ankles. She'd just worked her way through when the click of the door unlocking sounded above them.

Hannah's breath caught, but Rachel didn't look fazed at all. She set the rope back around her ankles to make it look like she was still tied to the chair and slipped her hands behind her back. She'd just hung her head and closed her eyes when a man appeared. It was one of the muscles Moreno had walked in with moments ago.

Nerves tingled up Hannah's spine, and it took everything in her to remain perfectly still as he made his way toward Rachel. She wasn't sure if Rachel heard him or just sensed his closeness, but the second he lowered in front of her, her arm swung out, the tiny dagger in the ring slicing across his neck and slashing his throat.

He dropped to the floor with a wet gasp. Bile churned in Hannah's belly at the sight of the blood, but she shoved it down.

Rachel didn't even blink. She rose, checking the man for weapons, and found both a gun and a knife. Once the weapons were in hand, she took two steps—only to stop and wobble on her feet.

Hannah opened her mouth to ask if she was okay, but Rachel's gaze cut to her and she quickly shook her head. She was right. They had to be quiet. Quick and quiet.

Rachel straightened and made her way to Hannah, using the larger knife to cut through her bonds, freeing her within seconds.

Hannah rose and took a step toward the stairs, but Rachel grabbed her arm and shook her head again. Instead, she lifted the chair Hannah had been sitting on and placed it under one of the windows. She was about to climb up when, again, she wobbled and grabbed the wall.

Hannah touched her arm and pointed to the window, indicating that she would do it. She climbed onto the chair herself, took the knife from the woman's fingers, and shoved it into the lock. Thankfully, the window was old and the lock only took a couple of turns to break.

Footsteps sounded above them again, causing the fine hairs on Hannah's skin to stand on end, but she didn't let that slow her down. She pushed the window open, grabbed the ledge, and with the help of a boost from Rachel, she pulled herself outside.

She turned and slipped one arm down. "Come on," she whispered. "I'll help you up."

The door at the top of the stairs opened.

Instead of climbing out, Rachel shook her head. "Run."

Hannah's heart jumped into her throat. "No, Rachel—"

"*Run, Hannah. Now!*"

Rachel turned and aimed the gun toward the stairs.

With gritted teeth, Hannah ran, the sound of gunfire exploding through the air from the basement.

* * *

"YOU SURE CHANG'S IN LEAVENWORTH?" Erik growled as he sped down the street.

"Yes." Nico typed quickly on his cell. "My guy has eyes on him right now. He's in his hotel bar."

Erik took a hard turn. Jake and Nate were going to the same location. Every second that ticked by had his blood pumping harder and the fear churning inside him faster. Fear that Hannah and Rachel were hurt—or worse. That Moreno had taken them somewhere Erik would never find them. And fuck, he was scared about Hannah's diabetes.

"We'll find them. Rachel knows how to take care of herself, and she'll protect Hannah."

Erik's fingers tightened on the wheel. "Unless they've done something to incapacitate her." Hell, an hour ago he'd have said no one would ever be able to take someone with Rachel's training.

"I believe we'll get them back," Nico said quietly.

Erik wanted to agree, but he'd felt the loss of loved ones before, and right now, he was being thrust straight back into that hell. It would be so easy to fold. To believe that history was repeating itself.

He gritted his teeth and refused to let the fear win.

He pushed his Corvette to move faster, breaking every goddamn road rule there was.

When they finally arrived at the hotel, Erik had barely stopped the car when he was up and out. Jake and Nate climbed out of a car nearby. He'd called them for backup the second Nico had found Chang's location. He needed all the damn backup he could get, and he trusted both men with his life.

He met their gazes before moving inside the hotel foyer. Chang was easy to spot in the bar.

Every muscle in his body locked, itching with the desire to run straight over, grab him, and put bullets into his fucking body until the asshole told him where his woman was. But that would just get him killed.

Instead, he forced his legs to walk purposefully to the bar.

A guard immediately cut him off, stepping in front of him. Erik didn't hesitate—he grabbed the guy and slammed him onto a nearby table. He pulled his Glock and aimed it at the asshole's head. At the same time, he felt guns pointed at him from around the bar.

"Who the fuck are you?"

Erik didn't look up at Chang's voice. From his peripheral vision, he saw Nico, Nate, and Jake all aiming their own weapons.

"Tell your men to lower their weapons," Erik growled. "Unless you want a fucking blood bath."

He knew the chances of that were slim. Chang had no fucking reason to trust Erik.

"You…I remember your voice. You're the asshole from my hotel room." There was a small pause before Chang surprised the shit out of him by complying. "Lower your guns." There was a brief pause where no one moved. "*Now.*"

Finally, Erik saw the muzzles move away.

"Let him go," Chang said quietly. "He'll let you pass."

Slowly, Erik released the guy and turned to Chang, lowering his pistol but not holstering it. "Where are they?"

Chang's eyes narrowed. "Where are who?"

"Two people were taken from me today." He took measured steps forward, all too fucking aware of the weapons that could easily lift and fire on him. "Important people. People I would tear down the fucking world to get back."

"As sad as that is, I don't see what that has to do with me. I did what you said. I cut communication with Moreno. I'm not helping him."

"*You* may have, but some of your men went ahead without you. They helped him take someone from me. And now, *you* will help me get her back."

Chang took a moment to process Erik's words. "You know this to be a fact?"

"Yes." It was Nico who answered. "I've had guys following your men. Your second-in-charge, Tommy Myers, has been in contact with Moreno. Now we can't find him."

If any of the information surprised Chang, he didn't show it. "I will help you on one condition. When we're done, you leave me the fuck alone. I don't want any attention being brought to my…business."

"Done." Erik would agree to give this man the fucking moon if he helped him get Hannah back.

"I have GPS on Myers's phone. Something he isn't currently aware of." He pulled out his cell and opened an app. Just seconds passed before he handed the cell to Erik. "He's here."

Nico stepped forward, putting the location into his phone.

Erik's eyes narrowed on Chang. "You're sure this is where they are? You're not fucking with us?"

"No, I'm not fucking with you. I told my team we weren't taking the job. If some of them went against orders, I want them to know what happens when they don't listen. Make sure they burn."

CHAPTER 28

*H*annah's feet pounded the ground as she ran, her knuckles white as she fiercely clenched the handle of the knife. Everything inside her wanted to go back and do something to help Rachel, but she'd just be a distraction. A burden Rachel needed to protect. She had to trust that Rachel's training and the gun in her hand would be enough to save her.

Air whipped through her lungs, branches cut into her flesh. It was dark, and she could barely see the ground beneath her feet. But every time she stumbled, she righted herself, forcing herself to move forward while praying that she found help. Rachel risking her life for Hannah's freedom would not be for nothing.

When the smell of fire tinged the air, hope sprang to life in her chest. Was it campers? Would they have a phone? Some way of connecting with Erik or the police?

Her head pounded and her body screamed to stop and rest, but she ignored all of it, needing to do her part and call for help. If Rachel could fight an unknown number of enemies, she could remain on her feet and keep moving forward.

God, Erik! He'd be losing his mind. Not only because she was gone, but because she was pregnant, and Rachel had been taken too. Three of the most important people in his life.

The smoke became visible in the air, the voices growing louder. She was nearing the source when something sounded behind her.

The crunching of feet against leaves. The cracking of a branch.

Someone was following her—and they weren't being quiet about it.

Shit!

She lunged behind a tree, where she dropped to the ground and forced her breaths to silence.

The footsteps grew louder. When they passed the tree she hid behind, she covered her mouth, certain if she didn't, a sound would escape and give her away.

When no one stopped, she sagged in relief.

Muffled voices continued from the campsite. They were too far away to make out what was said, but Hannah didn't stick around to try to listen. She rose to her feet and moved quietly into the woods in a different direction. There was the distant sound of running water, but she didn't let that stop or slow her. In fact, there was every chance the water would lead her to more people, or if she followed it, maybe a town.

When a wave of dizziness hit, she had to grab a tree to keep herself upright.

She was low. She didn't need her watch or phone to tell her that.

But it was fine. She'd been low before. She'd find help and get food.

Slow and steady, Hannah.

Carefully, she let go of the tree and kept moving, taking deep breaths as she went. Every step felt sluggish, but better that than no steps at all.

When she reached the water's edge, the usual fear didn't grip her throat. She'd only done one more lesson with Erik since that first time in the pool, but already she was feeling more confident around bodies of water.

She gripped the knife tightly as she walked along the bank.

"Stop, or you're a dead bitch."

Hannah froze at the male voice, her blood running cold. Slowly, she turned, keeping the knife behind her back so he wouldn't see it in her grasp.

A man stood in front of her, gun trained at her chest. It was the other guy who had stood with Moreno in that basement. And he looked just as big and dangerous now as he had then.

"How did you find me?" she asked.

He stepped forward. "I'm good at tracking."

"Is Rachel okay?"

"Fuck if I know. I started following you the second a guard saw the open basement window." He approached her slowly. "I doubt it. There are a dozen of us. The bitch couldn't overpower that many men, not with the drugs we put in her system."

He clearly had no idea who he was dealing with. "Please…just let me go. You can tell them you couldn't find me."

"I don't think so." He grabbed her arm and lowered the gun.

Before he could take another step, she swung the knife, slicing his cheek.

He swore, fingers instantly releasing her.

She stumbled back, her foot catching the steep bank of the river—and suddenly, she was falling backward. She screamed, her arms whipping through the air, but there was nothing to grab. She hit the water, the cold shocking her system, then she was racing down the fast-moving stream.

Her first instinct was to panic. To let fear seize her lungs and choke her. It took all of her effort to fight it. To remember Erik's whispered words during their lesson…*you're safe.*

She forced her arms and legs to move, to keep her body up so her head was out of the water. When she hit something in the water, pain ricocheted through her limbs and her head dipped below the surface, that familiar panic once again pricking at her skin.

Safe...remember.

Safe. She was safe in the water, just as Erik had told her. But she had to swim.

Again, she forced her legs to move. Her arms to glide through the water. When she hit a huge boulder, the air was knocked from her lungs—but she just managed to grab onto it.

For a moment, she did nothing but focus on catching her breath. Then, with a deep breath, she kicked off the rock, propelling herself toward the far bank. She barely reached dry ground before the river tried to take her again.

Using every scrap of energy and strength she had, she tugged herself out of the water. She knew she had to get up and run again. The guy would come looking for her, and he wouldn't be happy. But when she tried to stand, little black dots danced in her vision.

A splash sounded from behind her, and she gasped and turned to see the man had jumped into the water and was swimming toward her...and swimming fast.

Three breaths. She allowed herself three steadying breaths before rising to her feet and locking her knees. She'd just stepped forward when fingers wrapped around her ankle and tugged her to the ground. She screamed as she fell.

* * *

ERIK HAD WANTED TO DRIVE, but all three guys had refused to let him. And okay, he wasn't in the best damn head space to be behind the wheel. This time it was Nate in the car with him while Nico and Jake drove behind. Police had been called, but who the fuck knew how long they'd take to get to the cabin. Every minute was a fraction of time Moreno had to do something to Hannah and Rachel that Erik couldn't undo. To send them somewhere Erik wouldn't find them.

"We'll get there in time," Nate said quietly, obviously feeling his tension. "We won't be too late."

Erik's fingers tightened around his Glock. "We will because we have to. I'm not losing anyone else from my life."

"No. You're not."

When the driveway came into view, Erik's muscles tightened. Every fucking part of him itched with the need to get out and kill the fuckers responsible.

The driveway was a long dirt road with the house out of view. Nate slowed, positioning the Corvette to the side of the driveway, while Jake stopped behind him.

Erik was out before they'd come to a full stop. Nate cursed, but it was Nico who grabbed his arm and spun him around. "*Stop*. You're going to get yourself killed."

"I need to get to them!"

"We all do. We're gonna get Hannah and Rachel, and when we do, they're gonna need you to be okay. So be smart. I will *not* be the one to tell Hannah you died because you were an idiot."

Erik ground his teeth together, but *fuck*, the guy was right. Nate and Jake came to stand with them, weapons in hand.

"Jake and I will approach the house from the left and move in through the back," Nate said, all business. "Nico and Erik approach from the right and enter through the front. Let's keep each other alive and get the women out safely."

Erik was moving the second Nate finished speaking, slipping into the woods and running through the trees toward the house. Nico cursed but followed. At least he was keeping up.

When they reached the tree line surrounding the house, Nico grabbed his arm. "Wait."

Four vehicles sat in front of the house, all with tinted windows. One man stood by a car, while another stood by the front door.

Erik screwed a silencer onto his Glock before lifting the weapon and firing twice. Two kill shots to the head. Both men dropped before they knew what was coming.

Then Erik was moving again, keeping low as he crept toward the house. He could just hear Nico behind him. One brief pause—then he quickly stepped into the house.

All he saw was chaos. Utter, fucking chaos.

And in the middle of it…Rachel.

She held a man against her as a shield. As they entered, she fired at another.

She stood at the top of a set of stairs, with seven men scattered around her, some in suits, some in T-shirts.

Erik immediately lifted his own Glock and started firing. Nico did the same.

Nate and Jake rushed in from the back of the cabin just as the last man fell.

Rachel dropped the guy she'd been holding—and started to fall. Nico ran forward, catching her before she hit the floor. She didn't look good.

Erik was moving toward her when a flicker of movement to the left had his attention shifting. Every fucking limb in his body turned to steel at the sight of Moreno slinking through a door down a short hall.

Erik raced across the room, knowing his team would cover him if there were any more enemies hiding. He reached the room in time to see Moreno trying to climb out the window.

He fired, getting the asshole in the leg. Moreno dropped, and Erik lunged on him, caging him to the floor. "Where is she?"

Moreno growled. "Get the fuck off me!"

"Tell me where she is or get a bullet to the head."

"You and your bitch friend have taken *everything* from me! You think I'd tell you shit? I have nothing left to lose."

"There are things worse than dying." Erik shoved the muzzle of the gun against his shoulder. "I could cause you pain like you've never imagined. I could make you *beg* for death. Last chance. Where. Is. She?"

Nate stepped into the room, gun aimed.

"She ran," Moreno finally said. "To the east. One of Chang's men followed her."

"If you're lying—"

"He's not," Nate interjected. "Rachel confirmed it."

Erik rose and moved to the living room, knowing Nate would keep Moreno subdued. He headed straight for the door, briefly noting that Nico was still looking after Rachel. He was just stepping outside when his phone rang, Chandler's name flashing on the screen.

"Can't talk, Chandler. She's in the fucking woods and I need to find her."

"That's why I'm calling." The tapping of keys sounded. "I've been keeping an eye on the location you sent me. I intercepted local police communication, and there was a call in from some campers about a suspicious guy who approached their site. They sent in their coordinates. I'm sending them to you and the other guys now."

They hit his phone and Erik immediately headed that direction, not caring about how loud he was as he raced through the woods or that he'd left his team behind in the house. He needed to find Hannah and he needed to find her *now*.

He smelled the smoke before he saw it. He was almost at the campsite when he heard a scream. It sliced through the air, cutting straight into his chest.

Hannah.

He changed direction again, sprinting to the right and toward the sound of water. Every step felt too slow. Every second drawn out and multiplied.

When he reached the water's edge, he followed it down, gun never lowering.

They saw each other in the same fraction of a second, the

rushing water between them. The asshole's eyes locked on Erik, his arm tightening around Hannah's neck as they both climbed to their feet. Then the muzzle of the gun was pressed to her skull. Her lips were blue and her body shaking.

"Let her go," Erik shouted, letting the anger drown out his fear.

"Can't do that," he said firmly. "I've been paid to bring her back, and I always deliver."

The fury in Erik's chest heated, spreading through his veins. "Everyone at the cabin is dead except for Moreno. He'll be arrested. If you don't want to die too, put the gun down and I might just let you live."

The guy's brows flickered like he wasn't sure whether he believed Erik. "You're lying."

"I'm not. I'm also not lying when I tell you I'm a good fucking shot. You have three seconds to release her before I shoot."

Three.

The guy's eyes shifted over Erik's head.

Two.

"I don't fucking answer to—"

Erik fired, getting the asshole in the forehead. As Hannah crumpled, Erik dove into the stream of water, pushing his body to make it to the other side as quickly as possible before climbing out and pulling Hannah into his arms.

CHAPTER 29

*H*annah sipped some juice as she leaned heavily into Erik's side. She sat perched in the back of yet another ambulance. Paramedics had placed a blanket over her shoulders, but with her wet clothes, there was no way of chasing off the chill. All she wanted was to go home and get warm.

People moved around her. Police. Paramedics pushing gurneys with bodies. She hadn't seen the two people she needed to see the most—Rachel and Nico. They were in another ambulance while paramedics checked Rachel over.

The woman had to be okay. She'd saved Hannah, and in turn, almost lost her own life.

"How are you doing?" Erik asked, his gravelly voice pulling her out of her thoughts.

"I left Rachel to face an entire house of armed enemies while she could barely stand."

"She needed you gone so she could focus on ending them. She couldn't have done both at the same time." When Hannah didn't respond, Erik shifted closer, cupping her cheek. "Angel, don't feel guilty. Rachel is well trained, and she proved that today. She's alive, and everyone against us is dead or arrested. If you'd stayed, she'd have been distracted."

"I know, I just wouldn't have been able to forgive myself if something happened to her."

"And I wouldn't have survived the loss if something had happened to *you*."

She leaned into his touch. "Moreno's finally been arrested. We don't have to keep looking over our shoulders."

"Thank fuck for that." He tugged her into his chest, and she breathed him in, finding the comfort she so desperately needed.

"Hannah?"

At the sound of Rachel's voice, Hannah straightened to see the other woman walking toward them, Nico close by her side.

Hannah shot straight to her feet, ignoring Erik's growl, and wrapped her arms around the other woman's shoulders. "Are you okay?"

She pulled back to see Rachel had a few cuts and bruises on her face. Her clothes were torn. But other than that, she looked her normal self. "Of course. You thought those assholes were going to get the better of me?"

Despite everything, she laughed. Still, tears pressed at her eyes. "I was so worried."

"Hey. I'm made of some tough stuff. I'm fine. More than fine, because I got to end the fuckers who thought they could kidnap and sell us and get away with it. They underestimated me...and they paid the price for that."

God, she was unbelievable. "You're amazing, Rachel."

"No. I was *pissed*."

Nico nudged her hip. "With good fucking reason."

Hannah swallowed. "Are the drugs out of your system?"

"My head's still a bit foggy, but I'm doing better. No chance of me falling again. This guy insists on being my damn shadow."

"And that's how it'll stay," Nico said softly, no hesitation in his voice. His gaze shifted to Hannah. "You okay?"

"Yeah. A guy chased after me into the woods, but Erik shot him. I should mention that I fell into the river and am proud to report, I did *not* drown." She smiled at Erik. "Thanks to him."

He kissed the side of her head.

"I'm proud of you, Cloud."

She looked back at her brother. "Thank you for coming."

"When you need help, I'm there. Every time."

She stepped forward and slipped her arms around him, finding that familiar comfort. That feeling of family.

"Hannah Jacobs?"

She stepped back to see a couple of police officers joining them. "Yes."

"I'm Officer Paul. Is now a good time to talk? We've already spoken to Miss James."

Nico squeezed her arm before he and Rachel turned to walk away. As Erik's arm slipped around her waist, she took a breath before starting at the beginning. She detailed everything she remembered, from the moment Rachel stopped the car at the body on the road to Erik finding her in the woods and shooting her attacker.

By the time she was done, the exhaustion was well and truly tugging at her limbs. Hell, she could barely keep her eyes open.

"All right, she's done for tonight," Erik said before she could. "You have any more questions, call us tomorrow."

Before she could take a step, Erik slipped his arms around her back and legs and lifted her against his chest. Normally, she'd insist on walking. But right now, his wide chest and his strong arms offered too much warmth. So she leaned into him, letting his pine scent bring her every comfort she so desperately needed.

* * *

ERIK PULLED into his driveway but didn't immediately move to get out. Hannah slept in the passenger seat, her chest rising and falling with her deep breaths.

Today had scared the shit out of him. The events of the evening had been on repeat in his mind. From the moment he found her missing to seeing her held at gunpoint…it would scar him.

He listened to the soft breaths as they eased in and out of her chest. They were everything. *She* was everything. She was here. She was alive, and so was his baby and Rachel. Everyone he loved was safe, and the enemy was finally gone.

His phone lit up with a message.

Chandler: You get home safe?

Erik: Yeah, just pulled in.

Chandler: You okay?

Erik: No. But I will be.

Chandler: Yeah…you will. I'm glad everyone's safe. Get some rest.

Rest? He barely slept most nights. After today, he'd be lucky to get an hour.

Shoving his phone into his pocket, he climbed out of the car and moved around to Hannah's side. Her clothes were still damp, and she still had a blanket around her from the paramedics, but at least her hands weren't cold.

When he lifted her from the car, a small groan slipped from her lips. He kissed her head, moving his mouth to her ear. "I've got you, Angel. You're safe."

She nuzzled into his chest as if, even in her sleep, she heard him. Trusted him.

When he reached the bedroom, he laid her on the bed before carefully undressing her and slipping one of his shirts over her body. Then he pulled the sheets and blankets up and perched on the side of the bed, grabbing her lancet. The assholes had taken her phone and Apple watch so until they were replaced, and the information from her Dexcom linked, they'd have to use this.

Her eyes opened as he pricked her finger and set the drop of blood onto the test strip.

One twenty-six. Good. Her levels were okay. The paramedics had kept a close eye on them, and Nate had grabbed some of the snacks from his car, but the pregnancy in combination with everything that had happened tonight meant her levels could change quickly.

"Can I tell you something?" she asked, voice quiet.

His gaze flashed up to her face, focusing on the specks of navy in her blue eyes. "Anything. You know that."

"Even before you got there tonight, you saved me."

"What do you mean?"

"I started to panic when I hit the water. But your voice was in my head, reassuring me that I was safe. You saved me."

"*You* saved you, Angel. Your strength. Your refusal to give up."

Her smile was soft. "All so that we could return to you."

We…meaning her and the baby. Fuck, his love for them was out of this world.

Slowly, he lifted her shirt and kissed her bare stomach. It was a sweet kiss, and his lips lingered. When he lifted his head, he found her mouth, touching his lips to hers before whispering, "I love you, Angel."

"More than anything else."

CHAPTER 30

Hannah pulled up outside the farmhouse. It was large and the land was beautiful.

Today was her first official day back at work after a few days off. It felt good to be getting back into a routine. Not only that, but it felt *great* to not look over her shoulder. To not have to have Erik or Rachel trailing her all the time. She could finally just…be. Focus on work and her pregnancy and her upcoming wedding.

Wedding…gah! She was getting married soon. Her friends thought she deserved a big, ritzy celebration, but all she wanted was their closest friends and family. All she *needed* was Erik.

She climbed out of the car, noting that Jake, Charlie, and the photographer hadn't arrived yet. The guys had painted their grandmother's house and put in some new flooring. Once the photos were taken, the place would be listed online within a couple days.

When her phone rang, she looked down to see Erik's name. Even after all this time, her heart still kicked when she knew she was about to hear his voice.

"Hey."

"Hey, Angel. How's the first day back going?"

She laughed. "It's only ten in the morning. I've answered a few emails, and now I'm at Jake and Charlie's grandmother's home, waiting for them and the photographer."

"You're by yourself?"

"Yes, but I am absolutely fine. In fact, it actually feels good to be by myself for the first time in months."

There was a small pause, and she could almost picture Erik frowning.

"It doesn't feel good to me," he finally said. "It feels strange not being with you or having Rachel on you."

"I'm okay. We'll get used to the new normal soon. Are you at the gym?"

"Yeah, I am. So…Charlie's going to be there?"

"He is." At Erik's beat of silence, Hannah tilted her head. "How are the two of you doing?"

"I haven't seen the guy much, but I've been talking about him a bit in my sessions."

She straightened, loving it when Erik opened up to her about parts of his therapy. He'd been kicking ass on so many personal goals lately. "Yeah?"

"Yeah. Charlie was young. He made a mistake. A huge fucking mistake. But he paid a price for it by getting taken off active duty and shamed by everyone who knew what he did. He's been trying to make amends…and it's about time I forgave him."

The air rushed from her chest, pride warming her. "Really?"

"Really."

"I'm so proud of you, Erik."

"Proud enough to come home early tonight?"

She laughed. "Uh, no. It's my first day back. I'll probably work late. But I may pop in and see you on my lunch break."

"I'll take what I can get."

At the sound of a car in the driveway, Hannah looked up to see Jake behind the wheel and Charlie in the passenger seat. "I've got to go—they're here."

"Stay safe, Angel."

"Love you."

She hung up as both men climbed out of the car, and she pulled out her iPad. "Hey."

Jake dipped his head. "Hey, Han. You doing okay?"

She'd seen him once since her kidnapping, and on that day, she'd given him the biggest thank you hug ever. The man barely knew her, yet he'd risked his life to help save her and Rachel.

"I am, actually. Thank you. First day back, so be kind to me." She smiled over at Charlie. "Hey, Charlie."

"Hey." He frowned at her, inspecting her from head to toe. "I heard about what happened. I'm sorry."

"Thank you. I'm so grateful for Jake and all the guys for saving me. And so glad that Moreno's been arrested."

Jake reached out and lightly gripped her shoulder. "I'm glad the assholes are gone."

"Me too." She tapped a few things on the iPad. "Do you want to take me through the house before the photographer gets here?"

Jake nodded. "Sure."

She followed them up the stairs, noticing that they'd added a few potted plants and replaced some of the rotting wood.

"How's the wedding planning going?" Jake asked as he slotted the key into the door.

"We've barely thought about it. All I know is that I want something small, just our closest friends and family. I'd actually be happy to just elope."

"You guys are so damn cute," Jake said with a chuckle.

"Just happy." She stepped into the house, her eyes widening at the clean white walls. "Wow, that coat of paint made a huge difference."

"Yeah, it really lightened the place up," Charlie said with a nod.

She followed the guys around the house as they pointed out

the new rugs in the bedrooms and other pops of color they'd added. The house would have sold in its previous condition, but these types of improvements made her job a whole lot easier.

The bottom floor had the primary bedroom and bathroom, kitchen, dining and living rooms, and a half bath, while the upper floor had another three bedrooms and an additional bathroom.

When they reached the front door again, Hannah locked her iPad and tucked it back into her bag. "I already have quite a few clients I can think of who would love this place, but we should still advertise and have an open house. Create a bidding war. I think we can have it sold within the month."

Jake clapped his hands. "Fantastic. Then I can stop stealing you from Erik. Although, with him no longer working, you'll probably get sick of him already."

Charlie frowned. "Why isn't Erik working?"

"He just put in his resignation," Hannah said softly, still in disbelief that he'd do that for her and the baby.

"What will he do?" Charlie asked. "Doesn't he need the money?"

"He's made a good living over the years through his boxing and government contract work. For now, he's just going to spend time with me and our baby, something I'm not complaining about. Although, I heard you offered him a position as a boxing instructor at your gym," she finished, looking at Jake.

Jake opened his mouth, but Charlie spoke first. "Baby?"

Crap. Sometimes she forgot it wasn't public knowledge. But then, it wasn't exactly a secret either. "Yeah, we're expecting, and we're very excited about it."

"*Erik's* excited about having a baby after what he went through with his last?"

The question threw Hannah, and for a moment, she wasn't sure how to respond.

Jake nudged his shoulder. "Charlie, don't."

"No, it's okay," Hannah said quietly, her gaze shifting from

Jake back to Charlie. "He's doing amazing. He's working with a therapist and has done a lot of healing. He's happy. We both are."

"That's good," Charlie said doubtfully, as the photographer's car finally appeared in the driveway.

* * *

ERIK HELD the pads up for Nate, struggling to keep his feet planted. He'd already done a solid workout. Now it was Nate's turn, and the man was hitting the pads like he was possessed.

Erik hadn't asked him about it. Not yet. He'd just let his brother work through whatever was plaguing him until he wanted to talk.

It was Nate's last day in Redwood before he had to return to his team, and he was spending it here, in the gym. He hit the bag again and again, his muscles visibly shaking, his jaw clenched. When his hands finally dropped, his chest was moving quickly with his shallow breaths.

"Wanna talk about it?" Erik finally asked, pulling the pads off his hands.

"Everything's changing."

Erik frowned. "That's what you want, though, right? You want out?"

"Yeah. I just…being a SEAL is all I've ever known. It's who I am."

"No, it's not who you are." Erik dropped the pads into the box. There had once been a time when he'd thought the same. That time had passed. "We join the military because we want to serve and protect. It's what we do, but it's never who we are."

"Then who am I?"

"Only you can answer that question. And part of the answer will always be…whoever the hell you *want* to be." He lifted his water. "What's your team think of you leaving?"

"We've all had enough."

Damn. It *must* be getting tough out there when an entire team of SEALs was feeling the need to get out before their time. But as hard as that decision was, it would be safer for Nate and his team. Their missions were dangerous, and they needed to be in it a hundred percent or bad things happened.

"I'm proud of you."

Nate's eyes shot up, brows tugging together. "Why?"

"You know your head isn't in it, and you're leaving even though you have no idea what life will look like when you do. That takes courage."

"Maybe that's what I lacked before now." Nate met his gaze. "You and Hannah still good?"

He screwed the cap onto his water. "Better than good. She's my entire world. Everything that's happened to her in the last several months is a huge collective nightmare that will live in my head for a long while. And I still feel the urge to keep her close. Watching her go to work without me this morning…damn, it was hard. But I need to trust that she's safe."

"I don't blame you. But you did let her go. And she'll be okay." Nate grasped his shoulder. "I'm glad your family is finally safe."

"Me too." Fuck, he was glad. Despite the memories, relief had been flowing through his veins these last few days. Hannah had been so happy. Every time she'd smiled at him, it was like a piece of his soul was returned.

When the doors to the gym opened and Jake and Charlie walked in, Erik straightened. For the first time since the guy had gotten to town, Erik didn't feel that rising fury when he looked at Charlie. He didn't feel the burn of resentment or hate. He barely felt anything.

"I'll be back," he said quietly to Nate before crossing the room and stopping in front of Jake and Charlie. "Hey. Everything go okay this morning?"

"It was great," Jake said, nodding. "Hannah approved of our changes. The photographer did what he needed to do, and it's gonna be on the market within the week, hopefully sold within the month."

"That's awesome."

Charlie remained silent, dipping his head in agreement.

Jake cocked his head. "So...you thought any more about taking the job of boxing coach here at the gym?"

Erik wet his lips. Jake had mentioned the opportunity a few days ago. It would involve doing both one-on-one and group sessions. A part of him wanted to do it because he loved boxing. Another part of him didn't want to be tied down to anything right now.

"I'm still thinking about it. Is it okay if I get back to you in a few more days?"

Jake grasped his shoulder. "Take all the time you need. Although, I should let you know that I've already written up a contract, so the second you say yes, I'll be bringing it over for you to sign."

He laughed. "Thanks."

"I'm gonna go change for my shift," Charlie said as he moved away from them.

He was halfway across the room when Erik caught up to him and grabbed his arm. "Charlie."

He stopped and turned, wariness on his face. "Yeah?"

"I'm sorry."

The frown between Charlie's brows deepened. "Sorry for what?"

"I haven't exactly been kind to you since you got to Redwood. We all lost a lot on that last mission, and I can't keep living in the past. We need to move on and live our lives. That's what I'm doing." He held out his hand. "To moving on."

Charlie hesitated only for a second before taking Erik's hand. "To moving on."

CHAPTER 31

*H*annah leaned forward and splashed cool water on her face. The second she'd gotten home, she'd changed into yoga pants and a T-shirt. After washing her face, she intended to go downstairs, order takeout, and pass out on the couch with Erik.

She loved her job, but whenever she missed days, the work piled up and today she'd been run off her feet.

She'd gone home and spent her lunch break with Erik. He'd brought up the boxing job again and she'd, of course, told him that she would support him in whatever he wanted to do.

She grabbed a towel and dried her face. Her eyes were still closed when arms slid around her waist. A sigh slipped from her lips and she dropped the towel, her gaze colliding with Erik's in the mirror.

She leaned back into him. "Hey."

He lowered his head and kissed her neck. "I was missing you downstairs."

"I've only been up here for ten minutes."

"Too. Long." He continued to kiss up her neck before nibbling on her ear.

She gripped his forearms. "You are going to be the end of me."

"Let's go down together then." His hands trailed down her arms and he lifted her new Apple watch, tapping the screen. "You need to eat."

"I can eat later." She spun in his arms. "Right now, I'm hungry for something else." She tugged his head down and nipped his lips.

"Angel…I called Jake to tell him I'm taking the job."

Her gaze shot up. "You did?"

"Mm-hmm. He'll be here with the contract soon."

"Wow! You're going to teach people how to box. Erik…you'll be amazing."

"Thank you. It will be very part-time while you need me."

"I'll always need you. But I want you to have your own thing too." A slow smile curved her lips. "I guess because Jake isn't here yet, we can…" She didn't finish her sentence, instead pulling his head down to taste him.

He growled and tugged her hips into his. His hand had just slid under her shirt and was grazing her side when his phone rang.

He growled while she laughed, resting her temple on his chest. "The world is working against us."

"I've got a lifetime to love you, Angel." He kissed the top of her head before stepping back and answering the call. "You get home okay, Chandler?"

Hannah turned and grabbed her phone, grazing Erik's arm as she passed him. She moved into the hall and down the stairs. In the kitchen, she grabbed the juice from the fridge and poured herself half a glass, topping it with some sparkling water and ice. She'd just lifted the glass to her lips when she heard Erik's harsh curse behind her.

"He's lying," Erik said, voice a hard, deadly growl. There was a beat of silence. "Find out."

When he hung up, a frown was etched deeply into his brow.

Her belly did a little roll, and she lowered the glass to the counter. God, what *now*?

"What's wrong?"

"They finished questioning Moreno. He claims he had nothing to do with the incident where you were shot at behind the house and shoved into that hole, the motorcycle attack, *or* the intruder at Andi's house that night."

Her brow furrowed. "He has to be lying."

"He was adamant, even passed a lie detector test. Chandler said the FBI believe him."

A chill swept over her skin. "But if Moreno didn't do those things, then who did?"

Who would go so far as to dig a *grave* in the woods behind her house or shoot at her downtown in broad daylight?

A muscle in his cheek clenched. He opened his mouth, but before he could respond, his phone dinged.

She looked at his cell. "Was that the home security?"

"Yeah, Jake must be here." He lifted his phone, opening the camera app. "Yeah, it's his car."

She nibbled her bottom lip, worry still flickering through her mind. "I'll make coffee."

She'd just turned when Erik slipped his fingers around her arm and tugged her toward him.

"I'll get to the bottom of this," he said quietly. "Even if I have to question Moreno myself."

She nodded quickly. Probably too quickly. "I know. I'll make coffee for us and Jake."

Erik kissed her forehead before moving toward the door.

She was just heating the milk when voices sounded from the other room. She turned toward the living room, expecting to see Jake. Instead, Charlie stood there, papers in his hand.

He dipped his chin in her direction. "Hey. I was just telling Erik that Jake asked me to bring these forms over."

"Oh. Well, it's good to see you. Would you like a coffee?"

"That would be great, thanks." He handed the papers to Erik. "Jake said everything should be here. He just needs you to read over the terms of the contract and sign a few pages."

Erik took the folder and settled on the couch. The second Erik looked away, something Hannah couldn't identify flashed across Charlie's expression.

What the hell was *that*? Anger? Resentment?

Or maybe she hadn't seen anything. She barely knew the man, after all.

She cleared her throat. "Do you take sugar in your coffee?"

He met her eyes, and there it was again, a small hint of something odd in his expression before he was able to conceal it. "No thank you, Hannah."

What was going on? She was about to turn back to the machine, but instead, she angled her body toward Charlie. "Sorry, where did you say Jake is tonight?"

"Staying back at the gym." Charlie scanned the room subtly, almost like he was studying the house. "He's been working a lot lately. When he's not helping *you*, that is." His gaze shifted to Erik. "Nice place you've got here."

"Thanks, it was my grandfather's," Erik said, focused on the documents. "He left it to me after he passed away."

Charlie's muscles visibly tensed, his hands slipping behind his back. "Well…you really do get everything handed to you, don't you?"

Hannah flinched at the venom in the man's voice, while Erik's head shot up. "Excuse me?"

Hannah crept forward, an uncomfortable pit forming in her belly. "Charlie…is everything okay?"

"Not really." When Charlie moved his hand in front of him, she gasped at the gun in his grasp.

Erik shot to his feet, pulling Hannah behind him. "What the fuck are you doing?"

"I was taken off active duty and shamed—because of *you*. I

was right at the start of my career. I had the world at my fucking feet! But you went out of your way to make sure people punished me for my mistake."

"It was a mistake that cost four men their lives," Erik growled.

"I lost *everything*! My career. My respect. Even my goddamn parents could barely look at me after that. I've had *nothing* since that day, and I still have nothing. While you have everything." He stepped forward. "When Jake told me you lost your wife, I thought at least you'd paid a price too. But I come here to see you're fucking *thriving*. Fiancée. Money. And another baby on the way."

* * *

"You," Erik barked, fury pumping through his veins. "You're the person who's been targeting Hannah."

"Of course I've been targeting Hannah. I want you to *suffer* like I suffered! It's not okay that you get everything while I get nothing!"

The guy couldn't take responsibility for what he did all those years ago, so now he was trying to take Erik's life from him?

Shit! Why didn't he have his fucking gun on him?

"I lost everything too," Erik said quietly, anger weaving through his words. "I lost my team. I left my job. I lost my wife and my child. I've had to rebuild *my entire life*. I've felt more pain than you will *ever* feel."

"You don't think it was the most painful fucking experience of my life to be shamed by my peers? I never worked my way back to where I was. All I ever wanted to do was be a hero for my country."

"And that's why you weren't. You don't join the service to be a goddamn *hero*. You join to be part of a team, to get missions done. To help people. You just couldn't be a team player."

"Shut up!" Charlie's voice was shrill, bordering on insane.

240

"You'll suffer like *I* suffered! I went too soft before, assuming Hannah would die in that hole I dug in the woods. I should have just put a fucking bullet in her skull."

Fury tried to blacken Erik's world, but he didn't let it. He needed to focus on keeping Hannah safe.

"Hell, I should have just shot her at the fucking house this morning," Charlie continued. "The anger I felt when she told me you were *happy* and *healing*…it changed things."

"Charlie," Hannah whispered. "You need help."

"*No*. What I need is the revenge I'm so thoroughly owed."

"What's your plan?" Erik asked, creeping forward a step, eliminating some of the distance between them. "Jake knows you're here. You'll just be arrested and put in jail."

"Actually, my dear cousin, who also thinks I'm a fuckup and didn't speak to me for a good four fucking years, is unconscious in the trunk of his car. This is *his* pistol. And the second I wipe your home security and put Jake's prints on this gun, everyone will assume he did it. Maybe he's been angry all these years that his leader couldn't protect his team."

"You're a dead man," Erik warned, inching another step forward.

He cocked his head. "No. That's you." He laughed, but the sound was almost deranged. "You didn't think about what you took from *me* even once, did you? About the career you destroyed. The pain you put me through."

"I was too busy thinking about the lives you cut short because you couldn't listen to a goddamn order."

Erik's phone beeped from his pocket, but he was careful to keep his expression neutral. While Charlie would probably think it was a text, he knew better. Someone had just approached the house. His curtains were closed, and if it was a car, the sound didn't carry inside.

Was it someone connected to Charlie?

"Have you been working alone?" Erik asked casually.

"Of course I have. I've been *alone* since you took my life from me!"

So someone else was here. Who?

The doorbell rang.

The second Charlie glanced away, Erik shoved Hannah to the floor and lunged, grabbing Charlie's wrist and pointing the gun to the floor just as it fired.

CHAPTER 32

$\mathcal{N}$ico climbed out of his car, his gaze moving over the large-ass house in front of him. He'd been here a couple of times but always felt the same thing…that it was over the damn top with a touch of pretentious. But at least the guy had security for Hannah.

He hadn't let Hannah and Erik know that he was stopping by tonight, and part of him knew that would make his brother-in-law-to-be angry. Especially because Jake's car was here, so they already had company.

A small smile tugged at the corners of his lips. Maybe that was why he'd done it.

For some reason, Erik's anger brought Nico just a little bit of pleasure. Not because he didn't like the guy. Hell, he was actually starting to grow on Nico, to the point he could almost put the "you tried to kill me" shit in the past. Almost.

No, the pleasure he got from Erik's anger came because it was way too fucking easy to rile the guy up.

Did that make Nico an asshole? Probably.

He rang the doorbell and hadn't even lowered his hand when he heard a gunshot.

His muscles locked. *What the fuck?* Moreno was in jail, so who the hell was that? It couldn't be Jake, could it?

He took out the Glock from his holster and tried the door handle. Locked.

Shit.

He ran to the side of the house, where small windows sat near the ground...basement windows.

Using his jacket to muffle the sound, he threw an elbow into the glass, shattering it. After kicking the remaining shards out, he dropped inside to find a home gym.

Quickly and silently, he ran to the stairs. In the hall, he poked his head out to look into the living room. Fury burned hot and fast at what he saw—Hannah on the floor behind the couch while Erik and some guy were in hand-to-hand combat on the floor, struggling over a gun.

Erik threw a punch, but the guy moved his head just in time and followed it up with his own hit to Erik's ribs.

Nico kept the Glock drawn as he crouched, moving across the room and lowering to Hannah's side. "Cloud," he whispered.

She jolted, her head shooting up. "Nico! What are you doing here?"

"Came to see you. Catch me up on what's happening."

"That's Charlie. He's the guy who pushed me into the hole in the woods. He also shot at us from the motorbike. He's a former teammate of Erik's as well as Jake's cousin, and he's trying to kill us."

Goddammit. Just when they thought they'd eliminated the last fucking enemy.

"Come on. Stay low and I'll try to cover your body with my own."

"No...Erik needs your help!"

"I need to make sure you're protected first. Erik would want the same." He took Hannah's hand and pulled her toward the office, remaining low the entire time and making sure to cover her from any bullets. Once inside, he turned to her.

"Close and lock the door and call the police."

"Nico—"

"*Now*, Hannah!"

He pulled the door closed and turned just in time to see Charlie roll, lift the gun, and rise to his feet. "How does it feel, Erik? To know that for once, you're not gonna win? For once, *you're* gonna feel the pain of losing!"

Erik stood in front of Charlie, blocking Nico's shot.

"I've felt ten times the losses you have, and I'm still man enough to create a new life after that pain."

"Is it really *you* creating shit when you have the perfect family to fall back on? When you get everything handed to you?"

Erik laughed. "You're a fucking coward, Charlie. Instead of manning up and facing what you did, you choose to blame others for your downfall. You choose to be a *victim*, when you're far from it."

"I'm gonna—"

Erik swung to the side, and Nico fired, a shot to the chest that sent the man to the floor.

* * *

ERIK WATCHED as paramedics carried Charlie out on a stretcher. He was alive, with a faint heartbeat, but who knew if he'd survive the night.

Erik didn't feel one scrap of guilt for that. He was responsible for Hannah almost dying in that hole in the woods. He was the damn shooter of that drive-by and the person who'd had every intention of entering Andi's home.

How was it possible that a grown-ass man took no responsibility for his actions? That almost a decade later, he was still blaming others?

Erik hadn't been lying. The man was a coward, and whatever happened to him next was squarely on him.

"How's the head feel?" Andi asked Jake.

Erik turned back to his porch. Andi had gotten to the house before paramedics. The first thing they'd done was check the car for Jake, not sure what condition they'd find him in. He'd still been unconscious, head bleeding, but fortunately had woken up before the paramedics arrived.

"It's okay," Jake said with barely concealed anger. "I just can't believe Charlie did all this."

"I can't believe he was going to frame you," Hannah said quietly. "You're his family."

Jake shook his head. "He seemed so genuine about wanting forgiveness for the past. I should have seen past the facade. There was obviously something seriously wrong with him."

"You saw what he wanted you to see," Erik said, gripping his friend's shoulder. "We all did."

"Yeah…still, I'm sorry. I encouraged you to let him back in. I told you he was after your forgiveness."

"Nothing to apologize for, Jake."

Pain shone in Jake's eyes, but he nodded.

"Thanks for coming so quickly, Andi," Hannah said.

She lifted a shoulder. "Always happy to help."

Hannah was still talking to Andi when Nico walked out of the house after talking to the police. Erik grabbed his arm, pulling him to a stop. "Hey. I haven't had a chance to talk to you since everything happened. Thank you for what you did tonight. For getting Hannah to safety and shooting that asshole."

Nico crossed his arms over his chest. "I kind of saved your life, didn't I? I guess you owe me."

He knew the guy was joking, trying to get a rise out of him, but he couldn't even smile. "Yeah, I *do* owe you. Call it in anytime."

"Careful, Hunter, don't go promising something you don't want to deliver."

"I always deliver on my promises." Especially when the favor he was repaying was for his and Hannah's lives.

Nico nodded. "Okay. But really, the best thing you can do for me is to look after her. She loves you, which is why I've decided to get on board with you guys. But if you ever hurt her, I'll come for you."

"I'd expect nothing less. But I wouldn't hurt her. Ever."

"Good."

Nico moved away, and immediately Hannah stepped toward Erik. "Hey. What was that about?"

"I just needed to thank him for what he did today."

Her brows rose, her hands slipping behind his neck. "Does this mean you might be friends?"

"I wouldn't go that far. But at least we won't be mortal enemies."

She rolled her eyes, a hint of a smile on her lips, before the expression slipped. "I'm sorry about Charlie."

Anger rolled through his limbs at the mere mention of the asshole's name. "I always had a bad feeling about him. He just confirmed for me that I should always trust my gut."

"I'm glad you're okay. That we're all okay."

"You have no idea, Angel." He tugged her against his chest, not sure when he'd feel comfortable letting her go. Hannah and their baby were his world, and they'd been threatened one more time.

Never again.

CHAPTER 33

*N*erves skittered through Hannah's belly as she ran her fingers over the silky white dress. The gown was simple, with a subtle sweetheart neckline and thin straps, but it wasn't what the dress looked like that made her want to cry...it was what it represented.

Today, she was marrying her best friend. The man she'd fallen in love with over and over again. So many things had tried to keep them from getting here. So many internal and external battles they'd had to fight.

But they'd won. They'd made it. She was here, standing in Erik's family home, wearing the most beautiful dress she'd ever worn, hair falling over her shoulders in soft waves and perfect makeup on her face, about to commit to the man she loved.

A knock sounded at the door a moment before Brigid's voice called, "Can we come in now?"

She laughed. "Yes."

The door flew open, and the three members of her bridal party—Brigid, Henry, and Andi—all entered, closely followed by Erik's mother, Jennifer.

There was a stream of gasps and hums as their gazes fell on her reflection in the mirror.

Brigid covered her mouth. "Han…you look…"

"Perfect," Henry finished for her, voice soft.

She turned, tears still pressing at her eyes. "Thank you. You all look amazing too. Thank you so much for being with me this morning."

Her bridal party had woken with her and spent the entire morning making sure everything was perfect. They'd chosen pale blue dresses for her bridesmaids and a black suit with a pale blue tie for Henry. Everyone was ready and it was almost time to go.

Andi brushed some hair from Hannah's face, a tear slipping down the other woman's cheek. "You are so perfect for him. My brother is so lucky."

"Thank you. I'm so nervous," Hannah said quietly, the last three words falling from her lips almost of their own volition.

"There's no need to be nervous," Jennifer said gently. "You're his world, and today he gets to make that official."

She wet her lips. "I'm more nervous about *my* reaction to *him*. What if I see him at the end of the aisle and my feet just stop working? What if I can't make it to the other end?"

Erik had literally done that before…rendered her completely still. Caused her to lose every thought and the ability to move.

Brigid squeezed her hand. "Then the man will walk down the aisle and carry you the rest of the distance."

She laughed, because yeah, that was exactly what Erik would do.

She touched her bracelet, the nervous habit in full swing today. They'd only invited a handful of people to the backyard wedding, but she knew she wouldn't be focused on anyone but Erik.

Jennifer took her hand and led her to the bedroom dresser. "I have something for you." She opened the top drawer and took out a small hairpiece. "I wore this on my wedding day. As did my mother." She turned, a soft smile on her face. "I would be so honored if you wore it today to keep the family tradition alive."

Her pulse picked up. Family…because that's what they were now. "I would be honored."

Jennifer reached up and slotted it into one side of her hair. "Beautiful."

"And," Andi added, "it will serve as your something old and something borrowed."

"We, of course, are your something blue," Brigid said, bumping Henry's hip.

"What about the something new?" Henry asked.

Hannah glanced down, about to mention that both her dress and shoes were new, when another knock sounded at the door. Henry went to open it, and Hannah's lips immediately parted at the sight of Nico standing there, wearing a black tux and his hair slicked back. It was the fanciest she'd ever seen him.

Brigid squeezed her arm. "We'll wait in the hall."

Everyone filtered out as Nico stepped in, his gaze roaming over her dress and face. "Cloud, you look beautiful." He lowered his head and kissed her cheek.

"Thank you. You look amazing too." She tilted her head. "Have you seen Erik this morning?"

"Yep, he's out there, ready to stand in place with Nate, Chandler, and Rachel while he waits for you to walk down that aisle."

She took his hand in her own. "Thank you for walking me down the aisle. You were my first protector, and my only family for so long."

"I love you, Cloud. And I will always be both your protector and family."

She tugged him into a hug, familiar love welling in her chest, stealing her breath and her words.

"But I told him," Nico said quietly as they separated, "that if he hurts you, I'll come after him."

"He won't," she said, believing those words wholeheartedly. "But thank you for looking out for me."

He extended his hand, handing her a small white box with a black ribbon. "This is a gift from your fiancé. He asked me to deliver it."

Her brows rose. "From Erik? Really?"

"Yeah." Nico kissed her cheek before whispering into her ear. "Have the best day ever, sister. You deserve it. I love you."

When Nico stepped out of the room, it took her a moment to open the box. She wasn't sure why she was nervous. Maybe because this was her first connection with Erik since yesterday? Because this was her last connection with him before they married?

The first thing she saw inside the box was a note. Just the sight of Erik's handwriting caused her heart to flutter.

You, Angel, were the missing piece of my life. Thank you for putting me back together. Erik xox

When she saw what was below the note, her breath caught. The most beautiful gold puzzle piece charm sat inside, covered in tiny diamonds. She turned it over to see words engraved into the charm.

My missing piece.

A single tear fell down her cheek when the door opened and Brigid poked her head in. "Can we come in again?"

"Yes."

Her bridal party rushed in, and they all gushed over the gift.

The next hour was a blur of movement. People hustling around her. Photographers. Videographers. Her bridal party. Her nerves continued to rise, until there was a visible shake in her limbs as she stood behind closed doors at the back of the house, waiting for them to open so she could walk down the aisle.

Nico stood beside her, and she held his elbow so tightly it was like it was the only thing keeping her on her feet.

"Ready?" he asked quietly.

She shook her head. "No."

He lowered his head and whispered into her ear. "You've got this, Cloud."

Suddenly, the doors in front of her opened. For her first few steps, she watched her feet, sure she'd tangle herself in her dress and stumble.

Halfway down the steps, her gaze finally rose—and she saw him.

Her world slowed, the beats of her heart stumbling over each other.

The heat in his eyes…the uninhibited love…it was everything. He looked at her like she was his entire world. Which was fitting, seeing as he was hers.

The last few steps were easier, and much quicker. When she finally reached the end of the makeshift aisle, Nico kissed her cheek before taking a seat. The second Erik touched her, a deep calm slipped into her veins, swirling through her body.

Home. With Erik, she was home. And there was no reason to be nervous or scared. She was exactly where she was meant to be.

* * *

ERIK WATCHED Hannah from across the yard. She moved her body in time with the music, Brigid, Henry, and Leo on the dance floor around her.

Fuck, she was gorgeous. And she was his wife. It still hadn't sunk in.

From the moment Hannah had walked down the aisle, Erik hadn't been able to take his eyes off her. She was beautiful, in every way possible.

A hand clamped on his shoulder, and he turned to see Nate and Andi.

"Congratulations, brother," Nate said, a huge-ass grin on his face.

Andi threw her arms around him. "I am so thrilled for you both! You deserve every bit of happiness." She stepped back, still clenching his arms. "But heads up, when that baby comes, I'm going to drown it in love."

He chuckled. "I'm counting on it."

"You might have to change the locks," Nate said quietly, receiving a thump in the shoulder from Andi.

She sighed, leaning into Erik's side. "I'm so happy. You're home, married and having my niece or nephew. Nate's coming home. All is right in the world."

Erik turned his attention to his brother. "How are you feeling about the move?"

"Good." He sipped his beer. "Better since Rhys told me he's moving to town with me."

Andi tensed. "Rhys is coming to Redwood?"

Rhys had been Nate's best friend since they were placed on the same SEAL team. Erik had met him a couple of times, but that had been almost a decade ago, before his world had imploded. He was sure his sister had seen him more recently.

"You mean visiting, right?" she asked.

Nate shook his head, completely oblivious to Andi's reaction. "Nope. He wants a change, and he said every time he's come to Redwood he's felt calm, so he's coming here to live."

Andi's lips parted, but before she could respond, their parents joined them, his mom wrapping her arms around his shoulders.

"Darling, what a gorgeous day it's been!" When she pulled back, there were tears in her eyes. "I am so proud of you. For the adversity you've overcome and the man you are now."

Erik wiped a fallen tear from his mother's cheek. "I had a good family supporting me."

She gave him another watery smile before stepping back. This time, his father pulled him into his arms. "You, my son, are a fighter. Thank you."

He tightened his arms around his dad, knowing what the man

was thanking him for. A child's battles weighed heavily on the parent, and he was sure his parents had felt the weight of every battle he'd fought.

Erik pulled back. "And thank you for looking after yourself, Dad."

His father wrapped an arm around his mother's shoulders. "This woman doesn't give me much of a choice."

His mother leaned into her husband's side. "Because family looks after one another."

Erik's gaze rose, finding Hannah once again on the dance floor, her head thrown back in laughter as her friends danced around her.

"Excuse me," he said quietly, stepping to the side. "I'm going to go dance with my wife."

He strode across the yard with purpose, a few people congratulating him on the way, but his focus barely strayed from her. She wasn't looking at him, and when he wrapped his arms around her middle, there was a small gasp before he set his lips to her ear.

"May I have this dance, Mrs. Hunter?"

Slowly, she turned, the sweetest damn smile he'd ever seen on her lips. "Mrs. Hunter…I like the sound of that."

"You have no idea." He pushed a lock of hair behind her ear. "How are you feeling?"

"Better than I've felt at any other time in my life. All the hard stuff that we went through feels worth it because it got us here."

And what a beautiful fucking place this was. "But we're done with the hard. No more danger. No more conflict."

"Well, unless you tell me I can't water the flowers outside your house, or something equally absurd."

He groaned, his lips nipping at her ear. "All that is mine is yours, Mrs. Hunter. Water the flowers. Hell, plant an entire garden."

She laughed. "Maybe I'll do just that. You know, we kind of

have your grandfather to thank for this…for leaving you his home and asking me to look after his garden."

"There is no 'kind of' about it. The old man is watching us right now and laughing because he set this up."

"More reason for me to love him." She nibbled her bottom lip. "I have something to tell you…but I'm nervous."

His chest tightened. Fuck, was there yet another threat he had to look out for? Something that would have them both looking over their shoulders again?

"What is it, Angel?"

"I had a moment of weakness the other day and peeked inside the envelope in my nightstand."

He frowned. "You know the gender of our baby?"

She nodded, looking nervous as hell.

"Tell me!" The words were out of his mouth before he could stop them, and her nervous smile softened.

"It's a girl."

For a moment, he stopped moving, his heart beating so hard it was all he felt. "We're having a girl?"

"Yeah."

Without a second thought, he lifted Hannah into his arms and kissed her. It was long and slow, every bit of emotion inside him coming out in that one kiss. "Thank you," he whispered. "Thank you for this life you've given me. You and our daughter are such a gift."

Tears glistened in Hannah's eyes. "You're the gift."

With a sigh, she leaned her head against his chest, and they swayed to the music.

"Thank you for the charm," she eventually whispered.

His hand trailed down her arm before sliding over the new piece. "I meant it. You were the missing piece of my life."

"And you and our daughter will always be the most important pieces of mine."

Finished? Jump into one of Nyssa Kathryn's other series today:

Mercy Ring
Reckless
Blue Halo
Project Arma

Declan

Cole

Ryker

BEAUTIFUL PIECES

Erik's Salvation

Erik's Redemption

Erik's Refuge

SHORT CHRISTMAS STORY

Hidden Shadows

RECKLESS SERIES

(series ongoing)

Reckless Hope

Reckless Trust

JOIN my newsletter and be the first to find out about sales and new releases! CLICK HERE

ABOUT THE AUTHOR

Nyssa Kathryn is a romantic suspense author. She lives in South Australia with her daughter and hubby and takes every chance she can to be plotting and writing. Always an avid reader of romance novels, she considers alpha males and happily-ever-afters to be her jam.

Don't forget to follow Nyssa and never miss another release.

Facebook | Instagram | Amazon | Goodreads